jack jacobs
and the
doomsday time machine

Albert S. Abraham

BLUE COMET
Books

Published by *BLUE COMET Books Inc.*
UNITED STATES OF AMERICA
Continent - *NORTH AMERICA*
Planet - *EARTH (3rd Planet from SUN)*
Solar System - *SUN + 9 Planets*
Galaxy - *MILKY WAY (Spiral Class)*

CATALOGING IN PUBLICATION DATA

Abraham, Albert S.

Jack Jacobs and the Doomsday Time Machine

1. Science Fiction

ISBN 0-976-9744-1-X

Copyright © 2006 by Albert S. Abraham

Printed in the United States of America.

July 2006

First Edition (Expanded)

5 4 3 2 1 0 1 2 3 4 5

INTRODUCTION

Jack Jacobs and his soft-spoken organic supercomputer named Jennifer travel throughout the galaxy in another futuristic science fiction adventure!

This story was created not only to educate those who read it, but also help promote a better understanding of our universe and its timeless, wondrous secrets.

I hope you enjoy this story as much as I enjoyed creating it.

Al Abraham

1

THE TIME EVENT

IT WAS A STRANGE YEAR FOR JACK JACOBS in 2199, after being gone from Earth for sixteen years. It all started when his spaceship came out of its time warp field tunnel near Earth using the time machine that was magnetically interfaced to his spaceship's gravity propulsion system. Nothing seemed different to him, as his time machine's manipulation of space and time seemed to have worked flawlessly once again, just as it had many times in the past. Since the three-hundred light-year time jump lasted only thirty seconds, he checked his ship's atomic clock to make sure there were no registered anomalies. To his great surprise, the GMT atomic clock referenced to Earth showed 2099. "Strange," he said to himself. "That can't be correct!"

Sitting in his captain's chair and looking at his harmonic motion wristwatch that was balanced with the gravitational field of the spaceship, it showed May 17, 2199, 8:12 p.m. Glancing outside the spaceship, he saw Earth glistening in the distance, nearly six hundred thousand kilometers away, pristinely silhouetted against the sun.

"Hmmm," he said out loud, musing to himself the possibility. "I know the ship's atomic clock was calibrated to Earth's GMT radio broadcast frequency transmission the minute I arrived back to Earth. So how can this be?"

Jack continued to stare at the ship's GMT atomic clock and then his wristwatch, noting the hundred-year difference. "Something's going on," he said. "I've got to talk to my computer about this."

"Jennifer?"

"Yes, Jack," his organic supercomputer replied in a pleasant voice.

Jack smiled. "Can you tell me what is happening with the GMT on Earth and the time on our ship?"

"Yes, I can, Jack," she said calmly. "A space-time distortion and anomaly has occurred from a galaxy known in our ship's databanks as the Stormy Way galaxy, located in the Alpha-Delta matrix, coordinates 16, 78, 45, quadrant 64 of our known universe. It appears to have also strangely affected Earth and its history."

"What?" Jack said a bit confused, especially to hear about a space-time distortion from another galaxy. "That should not be possible!"

"That's what the ship's sensors have picked up," she said again. "You know I was programmed to always tell the truth."

Jacobs thought hard about what Jennifer just told him, not understanding why he hadn't heard of the galaxy, or even more, how it was in their ship's databanks. "Yes, I know you wouldn't lie," he finally said. "So how then is this space-time distortion happening?"

There was a small pause from Jennifer to Jack's question, as she wasn't one-hundred percent sure herself and could only see bits and pieces of information in their ship's databanks. She finally answered,

"It appears there was a strange space-time distortion from the galaxy, Jack, that carried a strange gravity binder. From what I can also determine from our ship's computer, is that when the gravity emission occurred, it ended up reversing time for the Earth and its solar system one hundred years. The first gravity-based energy distortion and anomaly occurred while we were *inside* our time warp field tunnel and traveling back to Earth. Otherwise, I'm sure we would not exist anymore."

Jacobs was surprised, as what he heard was an impossibility to science and impossible even to his spaceship's time warp field drive. "So when is the next gravity distortion scheduled to occur?" he asked with concern.

Jennifer began crunching probabilities. "I'm thinking, Jack. I'll have to do some time warp field reverse calculations in relation to where we just came from, appositionally speaking."

"Okay, Jennifer," Jack said with a slight grin, realizing how complex the calculations really were, especially to figure from a past time warp field gravity location in space-time. Her constant sincerity with him and the enormous task of calculating anything he had requested only brought back memories of when he had first met Jennifer in a secret lab. It was Dr. Gilmore he knew from college who had told him all about her, and she immediately sparked his interest. The good professor, his friend, was extremely nice to him and remembered everything he had told him about the new organic supercomputer, how she had a personality with built-in emotions geared to mimic a real human being. She was even able to sense underlying emotions in people's voices and, surprisingly, bioelectrical impulses and changes in the human body's electrical force, known as the "aura". One thing he always remembered about her was that he could not ever lie to her, even through she was simply a series of topological organic-laced circuit boards—because she would always know when anyone was lying.

"Okay, Jack," Jennifer said. "I have determined the next gravity-based emission."

Coming out of his daydream, Jacobs regained his senses.

"Okay, let's have it—"

"According to where we came from and the thirty seconds we spent in the time warp field, the next distortion will occur in three hours, forty-eight minutes. That is exactly twelve midnight, Jack."

Jacobs was surprised, as it didn't make any sense, and he was now a bit confused about the next scheduled anomaly. "Yes, Jennifer," he said, extremely interested in her next answer. "I thought you said it was every twenty-four hours. How then can it be three hours and forty-eight minutes?"

Jennifer immediately sensed Jack's confusion, and his confusion registered as bioelectrical impulse changes within his cerebrum. She answered, "It is three hours and forty-eight minutes, Jack, because even though the gravity distortion and anomaly occurred while we were in the time warp field, it appears to have shifted our time tunnel. While inside our time tunnel, we ended up losing twenty hours and twelve minutes." She paused with a dutiful sigh. "It could have been worse, you know. If we had not been in the time warp field when the anomaly occurred for the first time, it would have been a hundred year loss for us and possibly the end of our existences."

Jacobs understood exactly what Jennifer was saying to him, as neither he nor Jennifer were a hundred years old or their existences would surely have been vanquished. His skin texture hadn't changed one bit and Jack took a short breath. "So will the time warp field around our ship continue to nullify the strange distortion?" he asked her again.

"Yes it will, Jack," she replied. "And only if we're moving within the time warp field tunnel. If we are stationary in any manner whatsoever, we will no longer exist."

Jack thought hard about what Jennifer just told him, knowing she was correct and that he'd make sure they were always traveling inside a time warp field tunnel then. "Okay, Jennifer," he said calmly. "Let's make a two-second time warp jump into the Earth's atmosphere the moment the next anomaly occurs. Will that be enough to shield us from the strange distortion?"

"Yes, it will, Jack. Calculations so indicate it will. The formulas also indicate that any actual movement within our time warp field that is greater than the speed of light will shield us from the emission."

Jacobs was extremely relieved to hear this and he sat back in his chair.

"I also feel good about it, Jack," she said. "May I say that?"

Jacobs smiled at her question. "You may, indeed," he answered, and realized Jennifer was reading his emotions, just as she always had over the years. It was to be expected though, as his emotions had been changing quite often while trying to locate Earth and the Milky Way galaxy—even if it was one galaxy at a time. Justified concern now filled Jack's face, as they were in a very strange situation. "So what can you tell me about the strange distortion from the Stormy Way galaxy?" he asked.

"The Stormy Way galaxy has not been searched, Jack. There are also no star chart databases or any other information available, even from the 21st century Earth."

"Hmmm," he said, and was now a little perplexed. "So why not?"

"Because," she answered. "The galaxy is filled with very strange storm rifts due to a rotating white dwarf star that was at one time masking the galaxy's existence, a star also located in the northeastern hemisphere and edge of the galaxy. Because of this dwarf star and its violent storm rifts, no radio or light emissions can penetrate beyond it to see what's inside."

Jack knew this galaxy truly was a mystery to him and was becoming even more curious how Jennifer could know about its characteristics, since it wasn't known in Earth's 21st century. It caused him to sit forward in his chair and then look directly at the camera above his forward console. His mind was already starting to race as a result of their precarious situation and took a short deep breath. "So when was the Stormy Way galaxy first discovered, Jennifer?" he asked again.

"According to our ship's databanks, Jack, it was May 17th, of the year 2199."

"What?" Jack said surprised. "How can that possibly be?"

"It does seem strange," she answered. "Let me check our ship's databanks further."

Jack sat extremely quiet in his captain's chair pondering what Jennifer had just told him, realizing his own ship's databanks indicated they had just discovered the galaxy, but it didn't make sense. He now began patiently waiting for what other information she might find in their ship's silicon-based bubble memory.

"Jack!" Jennifer said, suddenly, surprise filling her voice. "According to our ship's databanks, it was you who discovered the galaxy using our new Orthogonal Great Circle Displacement gravitational lensing method. The galaxy is also cataloged as NCG2199A."

Jack was thoroughly confused to this, as not only could he not recall a thing about it, but the OGCD gravitational lensing method of theirs wasn't discovered and used until 2184—that would have been a little over a year after they first traveled into the dark matter between the galaxies. After he had analyzed the gravity forces inside the dark matter, it allowed them to determine the speed of light space-time curvature differences between dark matter space and *white matter* space, white matter space being the space and matter inside all galaxies, as he had called it, and ultimately leading to them coming to understand the orthogonal displacement angles.

This thought caused Jacobs to realize again that speed of light velocity differences existed outside solar systems and their heliospheric bubbles, including the dark matter space. He put that known information out of his mind and became particularly interested in the storm rifts being generated in the Stormy Way galaxy. "How dangerous are the storm rifts?" he asked.

"Very dangerous," Jennifer replied. "According to our ship's databanks, the storms are traveling between three to six hundred thousand kilometers per hour and contain highly charged particles of gas and dust that will explode upon contacting any solid object."

Jack began thinking what to do next, wondering now if maybe they'd been to the galaxy and something had happened to them in relation to the Earth being a hundred years into their past. "Your suggestions, Jennifer?" he asked.

Jennifer remained quiet, not knowing how to answer Jack.

A quiet response to his question was an answer to Jack that was cause for alarm, as she had never been quiet before. "Are you still there, Jennifer?"

"Yes, I am, Jack."

Jacobs now sat in a state of confusion over her not answering the previous question. "So what is your suggestion?" he asked her again.

"I don't know," she replied in a sincere tone, slow and drawn out.

This was an answer Jack was not expecting and it surprised him. "What do you mean?" he asked her a third time.

"What I mean, Jack," she said, "is that I don't know what to do for sure. We could travel to the Stormy Way galaxy and find out what might be causing the anomalies here in our Milky Way and inside the Earth's solar system."

Jack glanced down at his notebook over to the right of his captain's chair and looked back up. "Yes, that's a possibility," he commented. "How far is the galaxy away from us?"

"About 14,908,000 light years away," she replied.

Jacobs shook his head, as if to question it, but he knew it was something Jennifer would definitely know. "That's awfully far, Jennifer," he said. "We've never accomplished a time warp field jump over one hundred and thirty thousand light years all at once. Remember how long it took you to calculate that space-time harmonic?"

"Yes, Jack. I remember it well."

"So do you think you can accomplish the calculations for a time warp field jump to the outer edges of the Stormy Way galaxy?"

"Yes, I can, Jack. But it will take me some time."

He knew that time for them was valuable, and now a serious rising concern. "How much time are you talking about, Jennifer?" he asked, curious.

"I don't know. I would have to determine the exact rotational momentum and movement of the Stormy Way galaxy in relation to our location here in the Milky Way."

"I understand, Jennifer," Jacobs said. "Go ahead and start determining the rotational momentum of the galaxy and then let me know when you're finally done. I might want to glance over what you've come up with."

"Okay, Jack, will do."

Jacobs noticed his wristwatch now showed 9:30 p.m. There were two hours and thirty minutes before they had to take a two-second time warp jump into the Earth's atmosphere. Glancing down at the instruments on his forward center console, he knew that he had better make sure his spaceship's gravity generators were still online and operational. Jack thought, *If I were to stand up and then suddenly float up to the ceiling from uncontrollable momentum, followed by hitting my head on one the curved windows, well, that definitely wouldn't be a good thing, especially if it knocked me out.* Jack looked down at his forward center display again and it showed the generators to be fully active and operating within normal gravity force specifications of 9.8 meters per second squared—the same as Earth's gravity.

"Jennifer?" he said finally.

"Yes, Jack."

"I'm going down to the planetarium for a couple hours to think about what might be happening."

"Would you like me to go with you?" she asked in a soft voice. "You know how we always like to talk when we're down there."

"Not this time, Jennifer," he said, now smiling, "I believe I need some time alone to think about everything that is going on right now. I'm sure you realize the consequences of an incorrect decision in this matter, as do I."

"Yes, Jack, I do, and I understand what you're saying."

Jack knew she did and stood up from his captain's chair thinking about the 2099 Earth, now wondering if its history was part of his history or not—surely it was. He knew in 2099 that Earth's scientists had started making some headway in repairing the holes in the ozone layer that had gotten much larger by the mid 21st century, including success in altering the nitrogen-atmospheric fixation cycle of the biosphere to reverse small portions of the severe climate and weather problems they were experiencing over the face of the Earth. He also remembered some of the advancements they had made in altering the ionic flow of the solar winds at the poles to help freeze more of the artic waters. It was used in conjunction with the biosphere changes and Jack just had to know if the Earth was his Earth or not. "Jennifer?" he finally said, while walking out of the cockpit.

"Yes, Jack," she replied.

Jack continued slowly down the hallway. "Is the 21st century Earth part of our history?" he asked again.

"Yes, it is, Jack," she answered. "I've already checked the Earth census database. Your great grandpa lives in Lynchburg, Virginia and your grandfather is currently five years old. He also turns six in three months, six days."

Jacobs smiled after hearing this because his grandpa treated him like his favorite grandson. He knew meeting his grandfather as a five-year-old young boy would be unusual, but then Jack knew better than to ever take a chance of changing his own history. So he put that out of his mind and continued down the hallway toward the planetarium, now wondering about what might have happened for them to be a hundred years into their past. It was a very strange problem they had in front of them and something neither he nor Jennifer had definitely ever experienced—at least that they could remember anyway. Why the galaxy's existence would be registered in their ship's computer databanks, he had no idea. Why it would also show that he was the one who had discovered it, he had no idea either.

Jacobs finally arrived at the doorway to his planetarium and stopped for a moment to stare at its setting. The twelve-foot tall, six-foot wide waterfall cascading into the pool below was a pleasing sight. There was goldenrod and blue indigo perennial plants growing along the water's edge. The accompanying sycamore maple, green ash, and white oak trees with their varying green leaves brought back many memories for him. The sound of the waterfall splashing into the pool echoed throughout the planetarium and beckoned a calmness; the relaxing sound reminded him of the Crabtree Falls in Nelson County, Virginia, where he had spent time when a youth. The sixteen hundred-foot series of water drops in the Blue Ridge Mountains was a magnificent sight there, the tallest in the state, and was surrounded by lots of red maple, hickory, white pine, birch, and hemlock trees. The six hundred-foot, almost straight down final plunge of the water into the pool below was fun to watch and created lots of oxygen bubbles. It was a memory for him never to forget, as he had visited the pool in the George Washington National Forest many times as a kid.

Jacobs walked into the twelve meter wide, twenty meter long, and six meter tall planetarium and sat down in his favorite high-back, leather chair, located three meters from the waterfall. Leaning back, he thought about the Crabtree Falls for a short moment while comparing its sound to the gentle sound of the running water in the planetarium. The sounds and echoes inside the planetarium were actually much different from the sound of the waterfalls in Virginia, but it was still a great reminder of his childhood. While staring into the running water, the strange anomaly of space-time came to mind. "What could be the root cause?" he said out loud. "What might generate such a reversal of Earth's history?"

Jack knew the time warp field technology he secretly installed on the spaceship was advanced enough such that understanding of the onboard techno-advancements gave insight others not in the field of quantum gravity would find impossible to bridge. Maybe the time anomaly from the Stormy Way galaxy was related somehow, technologically, to his own ship's manipulations of space and time? "That is a strange thought," he told himself. "Hmmm," and then said out loud again, "possibly…if the time travel technology of my ship is essentially having the opposite effect of the anomaly in the Stormy Way galaxy, has something gone awry then with my continual manipulations of space and time?"

Jacobs pushed back in his chair and closed his eyes while listening to the waterfall. He continued to think about the time anomaly, wondering many things and whether it is something he could fix or even stop. Maybe he had tried many times before and had failed? While sitting with his eyes closed, he felt himself becoming very relaxed and knew he would be going into a restful napping sleep anytime now. He also felt confident Jennifer would wake him if needed.

2

THE TIME WARP JUMP INTO EARTH'S ATMOSPHERE

"JACK! WAKE UP!" Jennifer said.

No answer.

Jacobs was now in a deep sound sleep. Jennifer sensed Jack's soft breathing and knew he was going into the first stages of a REM deep sleep—an alpha theta level and maybe even a delta level five. She activated the siren in the planetarium momentarily. *"Wow! Wow! Wow!"* It blared at 2000 hertz for a full three seconds. Jack became wide awake and jolted up in his chair. He immediately began thinking about the space-time anomaly that was to occur at midnight and then looked at his watch—11:40 p.m.

"Whew!" he said to himself. "I thought I was a goner!"

"Are you awake yet, Jack?" she asked.

"Yes, I am. Thanks for thinking of me."

"You're welcome as always."

Jack smiled a little at how polite his computer always interfaced with him, so unlike humans. "Do you have the two second time warp field calculated and ready to jump into the Earth's atmosphere?"

"Yes, I do, Jack."

"Good." Jacobs paused a moment. "How are you doing on the calculations for the Stormy Way galaxy?"

"Still calculating," Jennifer said. "It's very complex, Jack."

"I understand. Well, I'm heading back to the cockpit."

"Okay," she said kindly. "See you there."

Jacobs grinned at the way his computer sometimes said things. He knew there were cameras in most every room of the ship, even in the most unsuspected places, and in a way she was always walking with him. Jack finally stood up from his chair and headed over toward the exit, but then stopped at the doorway. He gave a small sigh before walking out into the hallway. Now slowly headed down the hall, he began staring out into outer space through the many windows, noting the magnificent stars showing on the back of his ship and away from the sun. He also began thinking about what he didn't know concerning their problem, still not understanding how it was possible for time to reverse itself over such a vast expanse of space. Einstein's theory of the early twentieth century said that if one traveled toward some destination at the speed of light, time would continue on for the traveler in the capsule at the standard rate such that for a period of five years aboard a traveling vessel, the traveler will have aged five years, but in returning to the starting point, for instance, one's home planet, centuries might have passed. To Jacobs, the interesting thought was what if the return was lengthened somehow, or, the time spent in getting back was increased by some strange measure. Would that mean the traveler might find himself at a point *before* he had originally started?

Thinking about that for a bit more, Jacobs also realized time was only in reference to moving bodies or energies and that his time warp field technology and its required energy source propagations, at least within multi-dimensional space, violated many of Newton's,

Einstein's, and James Maxwell's theories and equations, including other well-known physicists of the past centuries. That being the case, time travel, as Einstein and others had once envisioned, was probably at an end, a moot point of present time.

Finally walking into the cockpit, he headed straight over to his captain's chair and took a seat. Jacobs sat quietly in his chair for a moment, looking at the instrument clusters, a place where he had spent about as much time as he had down in the planetarium. He also knew the cockpit layout and design was pleasing to look at, something he helped make a few decisions about, and that the government spared no expense back in 2177 when the ship was first being built.

It was circular in shape, fifteen meters in diameter, having consoles lining the left and right walls from his captain's chair. A few consoles were located up toward the front of the cockpit, six meters from his chair. In front of his chair were three display consoles having touch-activated functions with holographic imagery projection. Above his captain's chair and in numerous places in the ceiling of the cockpit were curved windows matching the curvature of his spaceship's outer hull. Most of the curved windows were two meters long and one meter wide. His large captain's chair, located midway of the cockpit, was fitted with soft armrests and could swivel sixty degrees to the left and right.

Jacobs continued to sit quietly in his comfortable captain's chair and would occasionally glance at the Earth in the distance as sort of a reminder of the brilliant blue atmosphere that still surrounded the precious capsule of life on its surface. He glanced again at the ship's GMT atomic clock that was showing on his forward display and knew it was still coordinated with Earth's GMT radio broadcast frequency. It showed a year of 2099 and time of 11:58 p.m.

He only had to glance at his harmonic balanced wristwatch and it showed the year 2199 with a time of 11:58 p.m.—and counting. It was exactly one hundred years ahead of Earth's GMT reference. "I still don't believe this," Jack said to no one in particular, taking a deep breath.

Sitting patiently and waiting for the midnight hour, Jacobs glanced at his ship's atomic clock reference again, not knowing for sure what would happen when they were inside their new time tunnel. The time turned 11:59 p.m. and it caused his heart to speed up a bit. When he saw there was fifty seconds and counting until midnight, only ten seconds to go for either a resolution of their problem or to encounter an irreversible disaster, he asked with concern, "Are you ready to activate the time warp field, Jennifer?"

"Yes, I am, Jack."

As soon as his wristwatch read 11:59 p.m. and fifty-nine seconds, space turned pitch dark outside their ship as Jennifer applied the time warp field to their ship's gravity propulsion system. Streams of white light immediately appeared inside their time warp tunnel and started passing by outside the cockpit windows toward the back of their ship. Suddenly, the white streams of light started to glow bright red and then turned back to white. "That's not right!" he yelled.

The next moment, the atmosphere of the Earth appeared in front of them and they were directly over the United States at an altitude of 180,000 feet. Jacobs immediately looked at his spaceship's GMT atomic clock and then his wristwatch. The ship's GMT in reference to Earth showed 8:36 p.m., May 17, 1999, his wristwatch 8:36 p.m., May 17, 2199. "What the— Jennifer, why did our time just move twenty-four minutes closer to midnight?"

"I'm checking, Jack. It does seem strange, does it not?"

*   *   *

At the NORAD Command Center at the Cheyenne Mountain Air Station in the Colorado Mountains, Sergeant Jamieson was watching his radar screen when suddenly a large unidentified object showed up out of nowhere over the central United States at an altitude of 180,000 feet. "Colonel!" he exclaimed excited. "Can you come over here and look at this?"

Colonel Walker walked over looking at the radar screen with

Sergeant Jamieson. "What do you think it is, Sergeant?" he asked with surprise.

"I don't know, sir. It appeared out of nowhere. It's huge. It must be three hundred feet in diameter."

"What's it doing, Sergeant?"

"It looks like…looks like it's…it's just *sitting* there, sir."

Colonel Walker picked up the phone and called Peterson Air Force Base in Colorado, directly to General Shelton. General Shelton noticed the hotline ringing from NORAD and immediately picked it up. "This is General Shelton," he answered.

"General, this is Colonel Walker at NORAD."

"Yes, Colonel," he replied.

"Are you guys picking up that object in the atmosphere at an altitude of 180,000 feet?"

"Yes, we are," General Shelton said again. "We're scrambling a couple of Falcons and an Eagle to that area right now. We have two SR-71B Blackbirds and an E-3 AWACS headed there as well."

Colonel Walker understood exactly what General Shelton was saying, as their F-15 Eagle would there in short time, but at a much lower altitude. Their SR-71's would get there quicker than the F-15 and at a much higher altitude, yet, even the SR-71's would not reach the altitude of the mysterious object. "Okay, General, talk to you later, sir," he said.

*   *   *

On their spaceship, Jennifer was still trying to figure out why twenty-four more minutes were lost while inside their time warp field tunnel. Her initial analysis of their twenty-hour, twelve-minute time loss showed their time should have remained at 8:12 p.m. and for the year 2199, indefinitely, as long as they traveled faster than the speed of light while inside their time tunnel. It clearly did not seem to be the case. The year 2199 did make sense for them, as well as the planet Earth year being in the year 1999, but she did not fully understand the twenty-four minute loss in time they had just encountered while inside their time tunnel.

Jack Jacobs also understood why the Earth year was 1999, instead of 2099, because of the strange reverse hundred-year gravity distortion that had occurred; supposedly from a galaxy almost 15,000,000 light years away. After again looking at his wristwatch that was in harmonic balance with his ship's gravity field, he saw it still indicated the year to be 2199, except he knew there was now a 200-year difference between the two planes of existence. He had no way of knowing at the moment which one was truly the correct one.

"Jack!" Jennifer said with uneasiness in her voice. "We have been detected."

Jack was taken aback at her reaction, but then realized they had come into the Earth's atmosphere hot, with no cloaking. "I forgot all about that," he muttered to himself.

"Activate our phased matched gravity field, Jennifer," Jack told her.

"Okay, Jack."

In an instant, Jacobs's spaceship became invisible to any visual sighting and Earth's home-based radars. Jacobs knew his spaceship still sat exactly where it was, but became indistinguishable from Earth and Earth's radars because of its encompassing gravity-field now in inverse resonance with the Earth's magnetic field.

*   *   *

Down on the surface of Earth and at NORAD command, Sergeant Jamieson looked at his computer screen again. "Colonel," he said in a confused manner. "The object is...is...*gone.*"

Colonel Walker verified what the radar screen showed. It was gone. He stood only for a short moment, thinking about it. "That momentary glitch on the screen never existed, Sergeant," he said sternly with no compromise in his voice. "Get rid of any records of its existence."

Sergeant Jamieson understood exactly what Colonel Walker was saying about covering up the UFO. "I understand, Colonel," he replied.

*   *   *

Jack sat in his spaceship looking at visual holographic images of 20th century jet aircraft now displayed in front of him, images taken from his advanced space aperture optical telescopes also incorporating their OGCD gravitational lensing method. Miles below their ship he noticed an E-3 AWACS roaming the area at 40,000 feet altitude, two SR-71's at 85,000 feet, and a U-2 spy plane at about 90,000 feet. "I'm glad they never saw my ship," he said to himself, and then looked down at his forward center display. It was showing the radar emanations from the E-3's top-mounted radome trying to penetrate his ship. But then the E-3's pulsed Doppler compression radar energy just passed around his ship's cloaking field and followed the Earth's lines of force as though he wasn't there—his cloaking field worked flawlessly.

Jacobs then trained his ship's optical telescopes and sensors into outer space and noticed on his forward left display that a satellite was already in a geosynchronous orbit above his spaceship at the required 35,900 kilometer orbit along the Earth's equator and holding. Since he knew something strange was still going on with the space-time domain of the Earth, he for sure didn't want to take a chance of their ship's encompassing phased matched gravity-field cloaking failing. He looked back up to one of the cameras. "Let's get out of this area, Jennifer," he said.

"Okay, Jack."

Jacobs sat quiet for a moment, thinking about the geosynchronous satellite and how quickly the government had repositioned it along his longitudinal location. "Go ahead and take us down south of the United States, Jennifer," he said, "to around a latitude nineteen degrees, twenty-four minutes north, and ninety-nine degrees, twelve minutes west longitude. Let's just sit there a while. Maintain the same altitude of fifty-five kilometers."

"Will do," she said.

Jennifer applied polarized magnetic south gravitational energy to their spaceship's gravity element and their propulsion system quickly took them south, toward the southern border of the United States. Within seconds they traveled out of the state of Kansas, through the states of Oklahoma and Texas, and into the country of Mexico. A few moments later they were over Mexico's central airspace and stationary again at an altitude of 180,000 feet.

Jack noticed Jennifer had now stopped their ship and knew by the latitude and longitude showing on his forward center display they were directly over Mexico City. But it was also a 1999 Earth below their spaceship and it caused him to begin thinking about Earth's history again. NASA's Mars Polar Lander came to mind. It was a space mission that had the Lander leaving Earth on January 3rd, 1999, and was destined to land near the border of the southern polar cap. Little did NASA know, but when the Lander left Earth on January 3rd, 1999, it would not only land inside the Martian South Pole polar cap on December 3rd, 1999, but would be permanently lost after burying itself in frozen water and carbon dioxide.

"What a strange recollection," Jacobs said to himself, realizing the Mars Polar Lander was retrieved from below the depths of the frozen water and carbon dioxide during the mid 2150's, soon after gravity propulsion was introduced into Earth's society. The Lander was then put on display in one of NASA's museums in Washington D. C.

Jack remembered that event well as a young boy, and also how all of the governments went about introducing gravity propulsion into Earth's society. It was at first only allowed in commuter services, such as buses, shuttles, and cabs, in law enforcement use, and in the military. Personal usage was not allowed until many years afterwards, and even then it took a difficult special license, with jail terms for anyone who built a ship and dared flying it, just as it would have been for anyone flying an jet or propeller-driven aircraft without a license in the

21st century. When working for the government in the late 2170's, Jack knew he was one of the few who was granted a license for flying his government-furnished space vehicle, a space vehicle that was capable of altitudes upwards of seventy kilometers.

Jacobs leaned back in his chair to those vivid memories, remembering how they went about assigning secret encoded transponder frequencies to all gravity propulsion ships. He was involved with other government scientists around the world on that secret project, a project code named Global Skies. The project was also backed by the secret governments of twelve different nations and actually had a smooth transition into Earth's general society. Jack suddenly came to his senses from that important event in science and began wondering again about the Stormy Way galaxy, not understanding how a distant galaxy could ever be affecting Earth and its history from so far away. He slowly looked to the camera directly in front of him. "How are you doing on the calculations for the Stormy Way galaxy, Jennifer?" he asked, a bit anxious.

"I'm still calculating, Jack."

"Okay." Jack now thought about the red streams of light that appeared inside their two-second time warp tunnel. *That wasn't right at all! The streams of light should have remained only white, showing a constant manipulation of space-time.*

"Jennifer?" he asked.

"Yes, Jack," she replied calmly.

"Why did our time warp tunnel turn red with streamers all of a sudden?"

Jennifer paused for a strange moment and knew what had happened, but then she didn't understand how it was possible. She answered, "It was because all space-time within our sun's magnetic field momentarily moved in the opposite direction of our time warp field tunnel."

Jennifer's words were intriguing, because she seemed to be indicating there had been a red shift in light, or in this case, the gravity field of their ship's time warp field moving away from his visual sight. Jack continued to think about what Jennifer had told him and knew their time tunnel had to be dissipating the anomaly's shift of space-time somehow. He also knew the sun's heliosphere and all of its space had to have moved in the opposite direction of their ship's time warp field tunnel. "So what is causing the additional twenty-four minute loss in our time then?" he asked again.

"From what I can determine," she replied calmly, "there was a gravity field harmonic from the anomaly that had a resonance cycle of twenty-four minutes in relation to the speed of light. Our ship's time warp field tunnel was shifted backwards twenty-four minutes from the strange gravity distortion."

Jack raised his eyebrows. "Oh really, now that's interesting! We never had any information about a twenty-four-minute resonance cycle. Were you aware of that gravity field harmonic, Jennifer?"

"No. I was surprised myself when I discovered it."

"Can we slow down the cycle?" he asked with rising curiosity.

"I believe so," she calmly answered, sensing Jack's slightly increasing cardiovascular heart rate.

Jack continued to think about the newly discovered gravity harmonic and its possible uses within time warp field technology. It had his mind now racing with new ideas in the field of quantum gravity. He finally caught his breath and looked up to the camera above his forward center console. "Looks like we are going to have to sit down and reevaluate the field formulas," he commented.

"Yes, Jack, I look forward to it," Jennifer said kindly.

Jack nodded his head with a small smile and glanced at his wristwatch again. It showed 10:58 p.m. There was one hour and two minutes till the next space-time gravity emission from the Stormy Way galaxy. It was a gravity distortion that was strangely reversing time one hundred years everywhere inside the Earth's solar system, except for inside Jack's time tunnel, where there was a twenty-four minute shift. That should never be possible according to the laws of quantum mechanical gravimetrics, including the laws of Magnetic Field Quantum Mechanical Space as Jack knew it, as too much space was involved between the two galaxies. He then mused to himself, "Where should we jump to this time? It clearly seems that we do have to exceed the speed of light for my time warp field to be effective against that strange gravity wave."

Jack's forward displays showed a ninety-two percent efficiency of the Gaussian energy reserves for his ship's power supply. He noticed the phased/matched gravity field around his ship seemed to be draining the power reserves abnormally, and knew it was possibly an interface problem of his ship's energy system to the main gravity drive to maintain a stationary propulsion altitude at 180,000 feet. He thought quietly to himself, "If that is truly the case, then it would not be wise for us to cloak our ship again because the accompanying dissonance harmonics could end up causing the energy system to explode with a thermonuclear yield greater than 10,000 one megaton hydrogen bombs. This would cause not only an immense Electromagnetic Pulse well beyond a million electron-volts per meter, but most likely create a force density pressure above ten million megapascals, far exceeding the event horizon of its own magnetic flux."

Jack paused with another familiar thought, somehow knowing the gravity element they were using on their ship would end up going supercritical and then imploding before exploding into heavier elements, possibly causing a small black hole to be created—maybe even a rupture to space. "What a strange thought," he said to himself, and then turned to one of the cameras thinking no more about it. "Okay, Jennifer, at 11:59 p.m. and fifty-nine seconds, let's make another two second time warp jump a little over six hundred thousand kilometers back out into space where we were before."

"Okay, Jack," she answered. "The time jump formulas will be ready."

Jack continued to think about his phased/matched gravity field that was keeping their ship invisible to Earth's radars, knowing they would not be using it again. "Hmmm… I know we have to come out of the cloaking field for our jump into the time warp field. I guess I'll do it a few minutes before at 11:58 p.m."

"Jennifer?" he calmly said.

"Yes, Jack."

"At 11:58 p.m., go ahead and deactivate the phased matched gravity field around our ship."

"You realize we'll no longer be invisible?" she said with concern.

"Yes, I do, but only for a couple of minutes. I don't think they'll have enough time to get their satellites in position to see us."

"I understand," she said again.

Jack knew that de-cloaking their ship and taking its gravity field back into resonance with the Earth's lines of force, their ship would immediately be picked up on radar again by the 20th century Earth, most likely by NORAD. That thought lulled him into a distant stare, daydreaming back twenty-two years before and to the year 2177, when, as a young scientist and first working for the government, he showed other government scientists his basic time warp field propulsion concepts, but not the underlying principles. He would never forget how they all began laughing about what he had said and how it could never work because of the basic concept of requiring too much energy. It was that exact reaction that caused Jack to go ahead and secretly incorporate his time warp field technology into the gravity propulsion system of the government's prototype spaceship. Six years later when the ship was finally completed, including the belief that he had successfully incorporated time warp field into the gravity drive, he told his parents what he had done. He would never forget the reaction of both Dr. Gilmore and his parents when he also told them he was going to take the spaceship without the government's permission to test his time warp field propulsion. They were both actually very supportive of him and believed in the possibility of his success, especially his mom and dad, only because they knew Jack Jacobs believed in it. So, it was back on that day, sixteen Earth years ago, when the three of them wished him good luck on what was for sure history's first attempt of a time jump. But unbeknownst to Jack, his first time warp field jump attempt would end up propelling their ship over two hundred and eighty million light years out of the Milky Way galaxy and into the dark matter between the galaxies. Years passed trying to figure out exactly what went wrong and trying to locate the Milky Way. Always supportive, Jennifer was with him every step of the way over the last sixteen years and she gave him daily hope of one day figuring out exactly where they were in the universe. The last sixteen years were almost as clear then as the last few weeks when they finally relocated the Milky Way and then time warp jumped into its outer boundaries. It was a position in space-time that eventually allowed Jennifer to calculate the time warp field equations for their last three hundred light-year long time-warp field jump to Earth.

His harmonic motion wristwatch now showed a time of 11:57 p.m., fifty-five seconds and counting. Their spaceship would become visible to Earth's radars in a matter of seconds. Jennifer deactivated the phased matched gravity field.

"Jack," Jennifer said calmly, "Are you ready for our next time jump?"

Jacobs was jolted out of his daydream state. "Yes. Let's do it."

*   *   *

At NORAD, Sergeant Jamieson was staring at his radar screen again when suddenly he noticed an unidentified object. "Colonel Walker!" he exclaimed. "The circular object of a few hours ago is again visible and at the same altitude! It looks to be presently over Mexico City."

Colonel Walker walked over to see what was showing on Sergeant Jamieson's monitor. The strange object was clearly not a false blip and because of its altitude, he knew, like before, it had to be of extraterrestrial origin. "Let's just continue to monitor it for a few minutes this time, Sergeant," he said, firmly. "If it is still there after a few minutes, then we'll sound the alarm."

"Okay, sir."

Sergeant Jamieson and Colonel Walker continued to watch the object on the radar screen as it sat there stationary at an altitude of 180,000 feet and over Mexico City.

*   *   *

On the spaceship, Jacobs's wristwatch showed 11:58 p.m., thirty-two seconds and counting, and was prepared to take another time jump. He began thinking again about the 20th century Earth below his ship and another event in its history came to his mind. It was a recollection of an electrical engineer, who, less than two decades later after 1999, revealed a series of geometric structures that would prove extremely important in understanding the exact molecular bond angles of elements in the fields of quantum and physical chemistry. The exact bond angle paths between the hydrogen and oxygen atoms in water molecules were also determined as a result of one of the structures, and later on proved critical to understanding why slowing down the two atoms caused water to suddenly freeze at 32 degrees Fahrenheit.

Jack knew he'd always have a memory of that event, including the advancements it caused to many different fields of science, even though it happened over a hundred and thirty years before he was born. This was because some of the structures revealed the secret underlying principles behind the electron binding energy paths used in his quantum geometry and time warp field technology. Jack glanced at his wristwatch again—11:59 p.m., fifty-four seconds and counting. He knew a two-second time warp field jump was about to occur and took a short deep breath. Suddenly, the atmosphere around their ship turned black, white streams of light immediately appeared and began passing by the cockpit windows toward the back of their ship. The streams of light turned bright red again just as quickly. "There's our reverse time shift again," Jack said to himself. The red streams of light turned back white momentarily and then outer space was again visible.

Jack thought briefly about the red streams of light and wondered if the shift might also be appearing for one subatomic harmonic second against the cesium atom. If that was the case, even the atomic world inside his spaceship was being momentarily reversed. But then Jack didn't feel he'd have enough time to find out for sure if his body was also getting younger by twenty-four minutes with each red shift in light. "Turn our ship around, Jennifer," he said.

Jennifer activated the gravity propulsion system and turned their spaceship around one hundred eighty degrees. Jack noticed Earth in the distance again and sat in his captain's chair motionless, knowing there must have been another reverse hundred-year shift of space-time outside their time tunnel. He noticed his wristwatch now showed May 17, 9:00 p.m., 2199, as balanced by his ship's gravity field. Their own reference time just moved from 8:36 p.m. to 9:00 p.m. and twenty-four minutes closer to midnight.

"That's not good," he whispered to himself and noticed the GMT reference clock in their ship was off. It made sense to him, since there was no radio broadcast frequency from the Greenwich, England Royal Observatory clock. So, the year on Earth must surely be 1899, he thought.

"Jennifer?"

Jennifer paused from crunching the possibilities of how all planetary bodies inside the Earth's solar system could have ever reversed their courses so easily—from what appeared to be introverted space. "Yes, Jack," she calmly answered.

Jack took another short breath and then asked, "Can you check the Earth for its position and bearings in relation to the ecliptic planes of the other planets, and then figure out our new cosmological GMT?"

"Yes, I can. I'll have it for you shortly." Jennifer trained their ship's optical sensors and radio telescope to the sun and heavens, checking the orbital patterns between the nine planets and locations to their sun. She also began using their optical telescope's OGCD gravitational lensing that specifically took the curvature of space-time into account, allowing extremely accurate readings of planetary bodies and fixed stars. "Okay, Jack," she finally said. "I have the new Earth's GMT."

"So, what is it?" Jack asked.

"The new GMT is 1899, on May 17, 9:02 p.m."

Jacobs quickly looked at his wristwatch and it showed 2199, May 17, 9:02 p.m. and counting. There was exactly a three hundred year difference in time.

"Strange," he said to himself, thinking about the loss of an additional twenty-four more minutes, wondering again if he might now be forty-eight minutes younger. *That gravity-wave distortion from the Stormy Way galaxy must be shifting my ship's gravity field backwards, yet adding twenty-four minutes to my time. But why is the emission directly related to Earth?*

Jack's level of perception increased. "Jennifer?" he calmly asked.

"Yes, Jack."

"Can you also maintain the GMT clock reference in our spaceship now?"

"Of course, I will," she said pleasantly.

Jacobs continued to think about the additional twenty-four minutes they were losing with each time warp jump, a time jump they had to accomplish before midnight and during the hour of midnight in order to keep from going back in time a hundred years.

"Hmmm," he said to himself, "my time was 8:36 p.m. when coming out of the time warp field tunnel the last time. It was 8:12 p.m. the time before that. If I were to move twenty-four minutes closer to midnight each time the anomaly appears, how much time do I have left before the reversal of space-time catches up to me at midnight and I go back in time a hundred years?"

"Jennifer?" he asked.

"Yes, Jack."

"I'm going to the planetarium for a few hours. Keep abreast of things."

"Certainly," she said.

3

DISCOVERY OF THE FOUR-MINUTE CYCLE

JACOBS GRABBED HIS NOTEBOOK and walked out of the cockpit thinking about the Stormy Way galaxy being approximately 15,000,000 light years away. He began wondering about the twenty-four minute gravity harmonic that was discovered as a direct result of the anomaly. "Hmmm," he said to himself. "What a strange gravity harmonic constant—"

Continuing down the hallway and thinking about the new harmonic, his mind was racing again with new ideas about how it could be used in their time warp field laws. There was definitely some underlying principle, he knew, something concerning how quantum space could be broken down even further in relation to quantum gravity. Finally walking out of the hallway and directly into the planetarium, the sound of the pleasant looking waterfall was the first thing

Jacobs noticed. The fresh smell of moisture in the air that accompanied the welcomed sound was also duly noted—the moisture invigorating to the millions of microscopic nerve cells inside his nasal cavity. He finally sat down in his favorite chair and immediately felt the soothing effect from the water flowing over the rocks, its accompanying sound relaxing, serene, and catatonic to his ears.

Jacobs looked up through the large curved windows in the ceiling of his planetarium and noticed outer space. He stared off at the distant stars, thinking about how far the Stormy Way galaxy was away versus how much time they had left in their time tunnel. "Hmmm," he said to himself. "My time warp field can only move my spaceship at ten light years per second, so it would take almost one and a half million seconds to get to the Stormy Way galaxy."

Jacobs knew one in a half million seconds would equate to almost 417 Earth hours, or a little over 17 days, and with the time inside their time tunnel also ratcheting forward in twenty-four minute increments, he knew they had no more than twelve Earth hours left before their time reached the midnight hour. "I can't make it in time," he mumbled under his breath. "It's too far. I've got to modify the warp drive formulas somehow. What does the twenty-four minute resonance cycle of the gravity field mean?"

He opened up his notebook and proceeded to write down some of his basic time warp field equations, using matrix algebraic conventions that calculated the time displacement vectors across a zero domain point of quantum gravity, called a denumerator, and all within a combinatoric envelope of space that now had to be modified using the newly discovered twenty-four minute resonant cycle. He first began using the harmonic phase angles of the twenty-four minute cycle, all as they would apply within his time warp field equations and exponential laws. Continuing to calculate for what seemed to be hours and finally staring down at his notebook, Jacobs began analyzing his new multi-domain equations that were using mirror-exponential functions. He finally saw the new phase-shift angle and its usage in the field of quantum gravity, realizing it was a very surprising discovery. He now sat in amazement, staring at the new set of zero domain equations that seemed to increase the space-time shift across the nuclear binding energy of his spaceship's gravity element. Jack sat back in his chair with a look of intrigue. "A four-minute resonant cycle?" he pondered. "So that's what the twenty-four minute cycle means....Very interesting!"

"Jennifer?" he asked with a distant smile.

"Yes, Jack."

"I'm coming back to the cockpit for our next time warp jump."

"I'll be expecting you," she says.

Jacobs wasted no time getting up from out of his chair and walked directly out of the planetarium, into the hallway, and toward the cockpit with Jennifer watching and analyzing him all the way. He was well aware of this and purposely stayed calm inside, knowing she was again analyzing his body and trying to figure out whether what he had worked out anything in his new time warp field equations worth being excited. Continuing slowly down the hallway, Jacobs glanced out the hallway windows again to see Earth in the distance, knowing it was actually a 19th century Earth that was silhouetted against space. But then there was no history in Earth's year of 1899 that immediately stood out in Jack's mind, other than fourteen years earlier in 1885 was when one of the first gas combustion engines was prototyped by Gottlieb Daimler. That engine, he knew, only helped start the human race down a path that would prove hard to change.

Looking back ahead, Jack thought no more about Earth's history with the combustion engine and finally walked out of the hallway, into the cockpit, and directly over to his captain's chair. He sat down thinking about his new equations and the many possibilities in relation to his spaceship's gravity propulsion system. He noticed the time on his watch was 11:15 p.m. There was plenty of time before the next hundred-year reversal of space-time was scheduled to occur.

"Okay, Jennifer," he finally said, beaming, "for our next time warp field jump, let's calculate the field equations a little different this time."

"What do you mean, Jack?" she asked in a confused voice.

Jack knew she wouldn't understand the usage of the newly discovered quantum space harmonic, at least at first. "What I've determined, Jennifer," he finally said, "is that we can lower the twenty-four minute harmonic cycle reaction to our time warp field tunnel down to its second harmonic of four minutes, but we can't get the harmonic cycle any lower."

Jennifer paused, surprised to hear of the four-minute higher frequency space-time displacement. "So why not?" she asked.

"Because," Jack answered, "If we try to take it any lower, the harmonic cycles from the anomaly would gravitationally sever our time warp tunnel." Jack then paused with a strange distant look. "We have reached the upper limit within the gravity fields of the universe, in other words."

"Yes, Jack, an amazing concept to think about," she said reassuringly.

Jacobs was a bit surprised over what she had just said, but also realized what her creator, Dr. Gilmore, had told him about her having the capability to become more real with time. How, in a sense, her organic cellular matrices would become fixed and create a personality that she would keep for the rest of her cellular divisions and life, just as it was for most humans. Jack suddenly came out of his daydream about Jennifer's cellular personality matrices and immediately thought back to the four-minute harmonic cycle formulas he had discovered.

"Okay, Jennifer," he finally said. "I'm going to enter a few new equations into the display for you to analyze. If you pay attention to how I derived them, you'll see that the twenty-four minute harmonic cycles are solely dependent upon the frequency harmonic of the reverse order gravity emission. By extrapolation within the spherical harmonics of the time plane vectors, you will also notice that same frequency harmonic is solely dependant upon our length of travel within the time warp tunnel. This is because we are outside the normal plane of time in relation to the speed light. By taking the frequency harmonic distance of travel within our time warp tunnel, you can then extrapolate out the twenty-four minute harmonic cycle from the gravity emission. Using derivatives of this new spherical harmonic cycle of our time warp tunnel, they will then convert into a new second harmonic time plane polar angle. Using this new harmonic and its polar angle within our time warp field formulas will then result in us losing only four minutes for each hundred-year reversal of space-time, not the normal twenty-four."

Jennifer began analyzing and fervently calculating everything Jacobs had entered into the display in relation to the denumerator and its new mirror functions. A few seconds later she was done looking at the new gravity harmonics in accordance with Jacobs's new time warp field laws, all as they would be applied to their ship's gravity propulsion system. "That is amazing, Jack," she exclaimed. "It seems to be exactly so and just as you say."

"Have you also seen in the formulas," he continued with a little grin, "Where we can possibly travel at one hundred light years per second within our time warp tunnel now?"

Jennifer heard what Jack had said and began looking even further into the new displacement formulas. "Yes, Jack," she says. "I see it!"

"Good, Jennifer," Jack continued. "What I want you to do for our next time warp field jump is to make sure our four-minute harmonic cycle formulas are working properly within the time tunnel. Let's time warp jump back into the Earth's atmosphere to around a latitude of thirty-eight degrees, fifty-three minutes north, and a longitude of seventy-seven degrees, two minutes west. Maintain the same altitude of fifty-five kilometers."

"Okay, Jack."

Jacobs was now lost in his thoughts while thinking about his modified time warp formulas as the midnight hour again approached. They didn't have much time to spare this time. His wristwatch showed 11:54 p.m., year 2199, May 17, as balanced by his spaceship's gravity field. He felt this exact time factor of the 22nd century was his only link back to a true reality within his own solar system and for a once familiar Earth. Jack continued to think about his formulas. "Let's take our time warp jump again one second before midnight, Jennifer," he blurted out.

"Okay, Jack, the formulas are ready."

As time slowly approached midnight, Jack sat with confidence, anxiously waiting for the next reverse hundred-year distortion from the Stormy Way galaxy, wondering if their time would only change by four minutes, instead of twenty-four when coming out of their time tunnel. The four-minute cycle formulas could not be one hundred percent foolproof, as they were only in mathematical theory and had to be tested under field conditions—an event that was soon to either remain a theory or become a fact of science. Jennifer suddenly sensed a small increase in Jack's body temperature and knew it had to be related to anxiety for an uncertain outcome.

Jack's wristwatch now showed 11:59 p.m., fifty-eight seconds and counting. As soon as it showed one second before midnight, suddenly it turned pitch black outside the cockpit windows as Jennifer applied the time warp field to their gravity propulsion system. White streams of light immediately began passing by their ship and toward the back. The streams of light suddenly turned red a second later. Showing before Jacobs's two eyes and cognitive thought, visible by the red shift in light, was another hundred-year shift in space-time. Jack quietly acknowledged this to himself, knowing their time warp field tunnel had to be strangely shifting in relation to his ship's gravity drive. The red streams of light quickly turned back to white and soon they vanished. The atmosphere of the Earth suddenly appeared in front of them as they came out of their time warp tunnel. Jacobs immediately looked at his wristwatch. It showed 9:04 p.m.

"It worked!" he said loudly to Jennifer. "That will give us more time to work with now."

Jennifer also noticed the four-minute cycle formulas had worked. "Yes, it will, Jack," she replied.

Jacobs thought about the four minutes they were now losing

with each hundred-year reversal of space-time, realizing what was once thought to be a subspace space-time harmonic theory was no longer a theory. "Now if only the one hundred light year per second formulas will work," he said to Jennifer.

Jack noticed the GMT clock reference inside their spaceship to be blank again. "Jennifer?" he asked with curiosity. "Can you update the spaceship's GMT clock reference again?"

"Yes, I can, Jack," she replied. "Let me check the Earth in right ascension to its sun and fixed stars, including ecliptic plane references to the other eight planets."

"Okay."

Jennifer, after double checking and making sure her new calculations were correct, finally displayed the Earth's GMT on the ship's clocks. Jack noticed the time displayed on the wall of the cockpit showed May 17, 9:05 p.m., and a year of 1799. Glancing at his wristwatch, it showed 2199, May 17, 9:05 p.m. "Exactly four hundred years ahead," he muttered to himself. "And seemingly another strange loss of a hundred years to Earth and its history, at least as I once knew it."

Jacobs sat there awhile thinking about Earth's eighteenth century, fully aware of world history and that of his own country, the United States of America. He also knew his ship was currently hovering over Washington at an altitude of 180,000 feet and it made him think about George Washington who served as the first President of the United States from April 30th, 1789 to March 3rd, 1797. Little did George Washington know but in about seven months he was going to die of a throat infection on December 14th, 1799 at the quite reasonable age of 67 to pass on back in those days. "What a strange thought to already know the Earth's future and actually be there," Jack said to himself, looking around his ship's cockpit. "People said that it was strep throat that killed President Washington, and possibly as a result of a poorly fitting set of false teeth. They were known to be hand carved from hippopotamus ivory and a cow's tooth, all held in place by metal springs. I wonder what it really was that caused his throat infection."

Jack paused and looked to one of the cameras. "Remember George Washington in United States history, Jennifer?" he asked.

"Yes," she answered.

"Remember what he died of?" he asked again.

"Yes. I believe it was streptococcus," she said. "Our ship could take a cellular reading of his throat cells, looking beyond his epithelial cells and then possibly knowing for sure if the streptococcus gene binding agent was present."

Jacobs understood exactly what she was saying and continued to sit quietly thinking about it, now having an unusual urge to go ahead and ask her to take a reading beyond George Washington's epithelial membrane cells for fusion activity and the presence of the protein F binding gene, but then suddenly decided against it. Something told him that it wouldn't be a good idea to interact with any physical beings or physical objects of any kind on Earth, especially since the Earth could very well be an imaginary plane of existence to him, and directly interacting with his own history could possibly have grave consequences for him in the end. "No, I don't think so, Jennifer," he finally answered. "We have more important problems in front of us at the moment."

Jennifer understood.

Sitting only for a short moment and putting that thought completely out of his mind, he began wondering again about them traveling at one hundred light years per second inside their time warp field tunnel, knowing that it must also be verified in mathematical theory before actually attempting it in a field test. It became his immediate number one priority, and nothing else really mattered.

"I'm heading back to the planetarium, Jennifer," he calmly said, "so I can study the one hundred light years per second time warp formulas in more detail."

Jennifer found herself curious of Jack's formulas. "Okay, I'll see you later then," she said.

While getting up from out his chair, Jacobs smiled to Jennifer's reply because he knew she was curious of his new time warp field formulas. He headed toward the exit of the cockpit with anticipation. After walking into the hallway and on the way to the planetarium, he began wondering why time was being affected everywhere inside the Earth's solar system. Maybe it was the entire Milky Way galaxy? At least now if the atomic world inside his ship was truly being affected, he'd only be getting younger by four minutes with each time loss. Finally walking up to the doorway of the planetarium, he felt and heard the sound of running water from the waterfall as it fell into the pool below. There was a calm sense of peace to the waterfall's rustling sound as Jack walked inside and over toward his favorite chair.

He sat down and was quiet for a moment, thinking about the newly discovered four-minute harmonic cycle that without doubt increased the space-time shifts outside their time tunnel. "Okay," he finally said to himself, "I've extrapolated the four-minute cycle formulas out of the twenty-four minute cycle, so let's see if the increase in my time warp speed from ten to one hundred light years per second is truly correct in a useable theory, or—"

Jack pulled his chair up to the console in front of him and immediately entered a few of his four-minute harmonic cycle formulas into the touch-activated display, knowing Jennifer would also be able to see and analyze his working theoretical equations from their ship's silicon-based computer. After selecting a few of his basic time warp field theorems from the display, he began modifying them across the zero domain point again and said out loud to himself, "When comparing the arc angles of the four-minute and twenty-four minute harmonic cycles of the reference time sphere against our tubular time warp field tunnel, I can extrapolate out new angular time displacement frequencies of the time warp field." Jack paused with surprise to his newly derived frequencies and continued on with his harmonic formulas against the gravity element's natural frequency, "These new frequencies can then be applied directly to the known resonance cycle of the gravity element which will no doubt cause it to become more reactive. Interesting! When using these new frequencies within time warp field, they will immediately cause another slight pressure change to the space-time domain producing our speed of light reference in the first place."

Jacobs continued to stare at his newly derived time warp field formulas on the display in front of him that showed the amazing 100 light years per second method of travel would work, but they were definitely still only conceptual theories until field tested once again. But for him to see the formulas of how to change the gravity element's binding energy for the possibility of ten times faster space travel across the universe was extremely intriguing. Especially when it was a space travel speed of almost 36,500 times the speed of light. "Yes, I do think this'll possibly work!" he exclaimed.

"Jennifer?"

"Yes, Jack," she replied, noting his slightly increased blood pressure.

"Were you following my formulas as I entered them?"

"Yes, I was, Jack," she calmly replied. "The theoretical formulas do show an extremely high probability of working. That's what I had come up with, too."

"Great!" Jack said with a grin, realizing she was also working them. "Can you have the final time warp field equations modified in time for our next time jump toward the Stormy Way galaxy?"

"I believe I can," she answered.

"So how are you doing on the Stormy Way galaxy calculations?" he asked again.

"I've determined the rate of expansion between the two galaxies," she calmly said. "I'm now looking at the correlating vector displacements of the space-time domain, by using two other galaxies as additional references."

Jacobs smiled, realizing how far she had actually progressed in her conversion calculations of the new four-minute cycle harmonic as it would be applied to quantum gravity and space. He also knew she was using the two other galaxies as a four-vector space calculation method, but didn't understand completely why she was doing it. "Okay—Okay! Thank you," he said.

"You're welcome," Jennifer replied calmly.

Jack sat in the planetarium, listening to the waterfall, contemplating many things, and closed his eyes, thinking about whether the anomaly was truly only affecting the Earth's solar system, the constraints of the Milky Way galaxy, or even beyond its borders into the dark matter space. This was something they would soon be finding out if their new time warp field tunnel worked properly. Jacobs thought about the new time tunnel and knew that for them entering the time warp field would require a little more energy from their Gaussian energy system, and only because more space had to be initially shifted by their spaceship's gravity field, but once they were inside, the drain wouldn't be quite as high—maybe about 20 percent higher than their ten-light year per second time tunnel. Their spaceship's forty-thousand Terajoule Gaussian energy system was believed to have enough energy to reach the Stormy Way galaxy and beyond. "This will be interesting," he said quietly to himself, and opened his eyes once again.

"Jennifer?" he asked.

"Yes, Jack."

"I'm going to rest my mind for a little while. Be sure to wake me in an hour or so before our next time warp jump."

"Of course, Jack," she said.

Jack sat quiet again, thinking about everything they had had to go through to get to where they were, and to do it in the last fourteen hours, thirty-two minutes of actual time passage. Looking at the time on his watch, he noticed it showed 10:28 p.m. and knew they were getting ready to make the longest time warp jump they had ever made by magnitudes of distance. "If the one hundred light years per second of travel doesn't work," he said to himself, "we'll never make it to the other side of our time warp tunnel, and quite clearly, Jennifer and I will cease to exist."

Jacobs thought about the possibility that there might be a planetary system inside the Stormy Way galaxy that might contain whatever was causing the strange reversals on Earth. Maybe it was some strange time anomaly generator or even a time machine similar to the time machine on his ship? *What if it wasn't even located on a planet, but strangely positioned out in space by opposing gravities of unknown origin never seen before?* Jack knew he wasn't going into a deep sleep like the last time and run the gauntlet of being awakened by blaring sirens. So, he closed his eyes to only relax his mind, but now having a strange sense of intrigue.

After Jack relaxed back in his chair, Jennifer left him alone and turned off all of the ship's cameras inside the planetarium. She refocused their ship's sensors back to the White Dwarf star inside the Stormy Way galaxy and began analyzing their strange characteristics. But she was having a hard time understanding the galaxy's characteristics from such a vast distance. So she continued calculating a time warp field tunnel between the Milky Way and Stormy Way, while taking into account what she believed to be a large well of energy growing inside the Stormy Way galaxy. The force density of the galaxy could also not be fully verified, so she continued referencing their time warp field equations from inside the Milky Way against known positions of two other galaxies, one called the Small Magellanic Cloud galaxy, an irregular galaxy catalogued as NGC 292, and a whirlpool spiral galaxy close to the same size as the Milky Way, also catalogued as NGC 14565. The vectors and orthogonal displacement angles referenced between the four galaxies she knew would help her immensely in calculating the correct extended time warp field tunnel toward the Stormy Way galaxy.

Taking these new four-vector space values into account, Jennifer knew she could now begin the final highly accurate time warp field calculations using the newly discovered four-minute harmonic cycles. She noticed they were now less than twenty minutes away from their coming attempt of traveling toward the Stormy Way galaxy at a speed of one-hundred light years per second. She was looking forward to the trip...

4

THE TIME WARP JUMP TO THE STORMY WAY GALAXY

JENNIFER FINISHED THE TIME WARP field equations for a 14,908,000 light-year time warp jump to the outer edges of the Stormy Way galaxy. Something seemed very strange again about the galaxy and the white dwarf star according to new readings from their ship's sensors, as the total mass density of the galaxy seemed much too high—magnitudes higher than any other galaxy they knew about or had ever encountered. She was also starting to find bits and pieces of additional information in their ship's silicon databanks that didn't make complete sense—something about how the dwarf star's gravity field would end up affecting the gravity element used on their spaceship. Because of all this, she shortened their time warp tunnel by 10,000 light years to a length of 14,898,000 light years and finally looked at the ship's time according to its gravity field. It showed 11:38

p.m., a time also still in accord to an Earth century and year of 2199. She knew Jack was still down in the planetarium, as his relaxed heartbeat of 51 beats a minute was evident. She activated the cameras in the planetarium and also saw that his eyes were closed. Jennifer, within her organic memory cells knew Jack was asleep, breathing softly, yet not in a deep REM sleep.

"Jack, wake up," she said in a calm, soft voice.

Jack heard Jennifer's soft voice and immediately woke up as he remembered the sirens she turned on the last time he was in a deep sleep. Looking at his watch, it showed 11:38 p.m. and he turned to one of the cameras. "Thank you for waking me," he said.

"You're welcome," she replied.

"Are the new formulas done?" Jack asked, curious.

"Yes, they are."

Jack lifted both arms high into the air, grabbed his left fingers with his right hand and stretched enough to pop the ligaments in the spine of his back. It made him feel good. "Okay, I'm headed back to the cockpit," he said.

Jacobs sat there for a short moment, thinking it strange Jennifer didn't say anything about his returning to the cockpit. He finally stood up from out of his chair, and with a quick glance over to his wood-framed mechanical wall clock, noticed it was still keeping perfect time with his wristwatch. He remembered years back in 2182 when it took him over three weeks to finally getting it perfectly matched and balanced to Earth's solar time before locking in its sundial functional sensor. Jack knew that was a good memory and he finally walked out of the planetarium, into the hallway, and toward the cockpit. Continuing down the hallway and thinking about Jennifer's new time warp field formulas, he knew her formulas should have harmonically induced gravimetric modifications to their ship's normal linear quantum gravity field, consequently allowing them to travel at one hundred light years per second inside their time tunnel. This new speed would also use the application of the new space-time harmonic frequencies directly to their ship's gravity propulsion system, and ultimately changing the time warp field. He further realized on his way down the hallway that they had to work quickly or else they would run out of time before reaching the outer ridges and boundaries of the Stormy Way galaxy.

Finally stepping from out of the hallway and back into the cockpit, Jacobs headed over toward his captain's chair and then sat down. After punching a sequence of buttons on his forward console to look through some of Jennifer's completed formulas, a surprise awaited the final calculations and applications of the time warp field back to their spaceship's gravity propulsion system.

Jacobs looked up to one of the cameras. "Why have you shortened the time warp field jump by ten thousand light years, Jennifer?" he asked in confusion. "We don't normally stop inside the dark matter between galaxies."

"Our ship's sensors have picked up something I don't like," she replied.

Jack raised his eyebrows. "Like what?"

"I'm not sure, Jack, but it has something to do with that white dwarf star."

Jack paused in his chair, thinking about the dwarf star and already knew it was unusual. "I understand," he finally replied, hesitantly, because he did not quite understand it and added, "Ten thousand light years isn't that far removed. We can just figure it into our next time warp field jump that will take us deeper into the heart of the galaxy where we know something strange is happening."

Jennifer didn't reply or say anything again to Jack's comment. He had fully expected a reply to his last statement and wasn't going to just forget about her silence. He continued looking over her new space-time displacement formulas showing on his forward center display and with a strange, familiar thought, remarked, "Equations look pretty good, Jennifer, except our 14,898,000 light-year time warp jump will cause us to exit one minute too early before one of the hundred-year anomalies. Is that not so?"

"Yes, it is," she said. "No disagreement from me. All we'll have to do is make is another time warp field jump for a short distance. I'll have that short time jump variance determined and ready to go soon after we exit our tunnel."

Jack thought it was a bit strange why she would do something like this, but then said no more about her reasons. "I understand," he commented, and with a quick glance at his wristwatch, saw it was now 11:57 p.m. In three minutes they would be attempting a time warp field jump at one hundred light years per second. It was a speed inside their time tunnel where their ship would be traveling at what was believed to be the upper limit of space travel, the known upper limit for carbon-based beings before imaginary space would and could be created. Jacobs' heartbeat sped up a little just thinking about all of those strange possibilities. "This must look a little different inside," he said to himself, wondering if they were going to experience any problems trying to enter the new time warp field tunnel, something unknown, and something impossible to be known until it was far too late.

Jacobs then glanced through his cockpit side windows toward Earth and noticed its upper level clouds showing in the troposphere 34 kilometers below his spaceship. He began wondering if they'd ever get to see Earth again after leaving the Milky Way galaxy and traveling toward a galaxy that was 15,000,000 light years away. But even more interesting to that, he thought, was what if he was able to solve and fix what was causing the time dilations to Earth and its history. What would he do if he ended up hundreds or possibly thousands of years into Earth's past and its history? His sciences and his spaceship would be much too advanced for Earth, not to mention that he'd have to be careful not to interact with Earth's history, specifically his own history. Jack's heart suddenly raced thinking about that very possibility.

Jennifer sensed Jack's increased heart rate, a direct result of electrical signals being transmitted directly from his brainstem to his sympathetic nerve terminals in his heart. This impulse automatically drove a small increase in his breathing and pulmonary blood flow to his bronchial system. She continued analyzing this known fact of

Jack's human physiology, intrigued as usual of the wave pathways for his cardiac conduction system, as the conductive tissues spontaneously polarized and depolarized.

Jack sat there a little while longer in anticipation of their new time warp field tunnel, thinking nothing about Jennifer's continual analysis of his body or his brainstem's electrical control of his heart. He was wondering though what would happen if their ship failed to enter inside the new time warp tunnel—disaster would surely follow. Pausing with a short deep breath, he finally said, "Apply the time warp field equations to our gravity propulsion system at eleven fifty-nine p.m. and fifty-eight seconds this time, Jennifer."

"Okay, Jack," she calmly answered, still not sensing any excitement within her own organic memory cells, at least not like she had experienced when they finally located the Milky Way galaxy after sixteen long Earth years. Even she was seemingly puzzled over their ship's silicon databanks mentioning the Stormy Way galaxy. Nothing was registered within her own organic memory about them discovering or visiting it, but something must have happened, otherwise their ship's silicon-based memory would not have registered Jack discovering the galaxy or the existence of the white dwarf star. No matter how many times she checked and rechecked their ship's binary bubble memory that used two-nanometer diameter gates interfaced across carbon nanotubes 5.729 nanometers in diameter, she could not learn anymore information about the galaxy or the strange white dwarf star. Jennifer suddenly became aware of her cognitive computing and thinking, similar she thought, to Jack whenever he daydreamed. She then repositioned one of the ship's cameras on Jack to notice he was watching the time on his watch as it approached closer to midnight. She readied their spaceship's gravity propulsion system in preparation for creating the time warp field tunnel that would have them traveling at one-hundred light years per second toward the new galaxy.

In his captain's chair, Jacobs continued to calmly watch their time in anticipation of what he viewed would be a possible new event to science, especially for them to travel at such an extreme speed and velocity without any acceleration forces. The time now showed 11:59 p.m., fifty-five seconds and counting—a hundred light years per second time warp field tunnel jump was soon to be initiated. Suddenly, it turned black around their spaceship as Jennifer applied the time warp field to their gravity propulsion system. Bright streams of white light immediately showed outside the cockpit windows and began moving by their ship toward the backend. Two seconds later the white streams of light turned bright red for one Earth second, and then immediately changed back to white. "There was our reverse hundred year space shift," Jack remarked, and looked at his watch again. It showed 9:08 p.m., and for the year of 2199. He knew their time had just shifted backwards from midnight again, yet moved from 9:04 p.m. to 9:08 p.m.

"Well," he said to himself. "At least the application of the four-minute harmonic cycle is still working properly. Only four minutes of loss to our time."

Jacobs sat quietly and calmly, watching the white streams of light now continually passing by the curved windows above his head. He noticed the light did appear to be a little brighter than normal. Were they inside a time warp tunnel where their ship's time warp field platform was traveling at one hundred light years per second? Jack wondered about that possibility and whether the speed of the mirror platform was truly at the upper limit of space travel, just like the formulas determined was theoretically possible. Nothing felt different about their new time tunnel. "Are we traveling at one hundred light years per second, Jennifer?" he finally asked.

"Let me check it quickly, Jack," she replied, still calm as ever.

Jack sat anticipating hearing what Jennifer would determine about their new time tunnel, and while waiting, the anticipation began to seem like hours, even though he knew it was probably only a matter of minutes. He also knew that if they were off on their one hundred light years per second time warp field tunnel, even for a picosecond, then a possible time dilation could occur, causing them to lose their true time bearings back to Earth forever.

"Jack," she finally said, "yes, we are traveling *exactly* at one-hundred light years per second."

Jacobs was relieved, though only a little, as they were still not entirely safe. "That will sure help in our time," he said to himself, knowing like before, that it would have taken them over seventeen Earth days, or four hundred and fourteen hours, five minutes, to reach the Stormy Way galaxy by the previously known speed of ten light years per second time travel, including the twenty-four-minute cycles and space-time shifts inside their tunnel eventually catching up to their normal existence at twelve midnight. He noticed the ship's GMT reference in relation to Earth was off again.

"Jennifer?"

"Yes, Jack."

"Can you update and keep track of the ship's GMT reference in relation to the reverse hundred year anomalies, so that we can keep track of the *old time plane* of the cosmological universe?"

"Yes, I can," she calmly answered.

"Thank you."

Finally, the cosmological time to Earth and its solar system was displayed on his ship's GMT clock. It showed a GMT of 9:21 p.m., and for a year 1699. Looking at his wristwatch, it showed 9:21 p.m. with a year of 2199. "Interesting," he said to himself, "there is now a five hundred year difference between the two planes of existence."

Jack sat back, relaxed, watching the extremely bright white streams of light pass outside their cockpit windows and knew they were already about to travel out of the Milky Way galaxy. "Amazing sight isn't it?" he said to Jennifer.

"Yes, it is," Jennifer softly replied.

His computer's soft voice immediately drove Jacobs into a nice memory of his time spent with her in the universe over the last sixteen years when they were clearly lost within a large open sea of space. He remembered how she always seemed to look to him for guidance, especially when they were first lost, even though she had a broader base of understanding in many different science fields. The time they spent together back on Earth and in the few years before was also remembered, as this was when she seemed to become extremely attached to him. That would have been around the year 2181. Jacobs went into another distant stare, daydreaming about the exact time and year back in the Earth's history when his life was changed forever …

He remembered that year of 2177 well, as it was almost twenty-two years to the day when he first started working for the government on the new advanced gravity propulsion system and drive for the first of two prototype deep-space craft, a gravity system and new propulsion method he had conceived. The marketeers thought very highly of him and for good reasons. He remembered very clearly having full control of the Area 51 project that he spent many hours on, a top secret project called Orion Nine, and knew he was billeted as the top gravity propulsion expert in the field even before he had graduated with his first doctorate. Little did the government know he was also secretly incorporating time warp field technology into the gravity propulsion system drive of the first spacecraft the entire time as lead scientist on Orion Nine. Nobody knew a thing about what he was doing, except for Dr. Gilmore. Dr. Gilmore was more than willing to stay quiet about it, especially since his lab's prototype organic supercomputer was also being secretly interfaced into all of the spaceship's systems and its subsystems. It was a memory never to be forgotten, as not only did Dr. Gilmore help him with the ship's interfaces, but he also helped conceal and mask it from the internal security procedures for everything that was installed on the ship. Jack knew some of his friends and co-workers suspected at the time that he was up to something, but then they never said anything about it.

Jack suddenly came out of his daydream, wondering if any of his friends or co-workers might have gotten into trouble over him taking the ship. He knew Dr. Gilmore surely would have gotten severely criminally punished for his involvement, because his friend wouldn't have revealed or said much to the interrogators. Jacobs now wondered what might have really happened to his friend and looked over to notice the wall clock showed 11:59 p.m., fifty-eight seconds and counting. Two seconds later the white streams of light outside the cockpit windows turned bright red for one second and then suddenly back to white. "Absolutely magnificent to look at," Jack said to himself, realizing they were now over 768,000 light years away from Earth's solar system and its sun's heliospheric bubble. Another hundred years had just gone backwards outside his time warp field tunnel. So the anomaly was affecting more than just the Earth's solar system after all. It was affecting the entire Milky Way galaxy and apparently dark matter space.

After the last shift in space-time, Jack noticed his wristwatch showed 9:12 p.m., May 17, year 2199, and the ship's wall clock referenced back to Earth now showed 9:12 p.m., May 17, 1599. They were both counting forward again after being reset from midnight, Jack knew, and he thought, "Every time my ship's gravity-propulsion-based time reaches midnight, another reverse-order gravity distortion occurs from the Stormy Way galaxy, resulting in a hundred year loss to the Earth and the Milky Way galaxy. But then that event is immediately followed by a four-minute positive cycle of my spaceship's gravity-based time moving closer to midnight."

Jacobs continued to think about those strange shifts in their time tunnel and what they might find in the galaxy where an anomaly was propagating a strange rift between the two galaxies, seemingly changing all known existences. It was though the two galaxies were linked somehow and he now wondered if they were backtracking to a galaxy where they've already been. Jack looked down at his center forward display and noticed they'd been traveling inside the dark matter space between the galaxies for nearly 1.8 hours now. The dark matter, Jack knew, was a non-turbulent area of space that filled all cavities between the galaxies, and was a very unusual area of space. While continuing to stare at his center display, he began looking over the characteristics of the strange white dwarf star and noticed what was showing was very unusual—seemingly not conforming to any laws of science as he knew them. Additionally, the galaxy's mass density seemed much too high. "I wonder why the white dwarf star is showing both red and blue shifts?" he said out loud, "Strange for it to be able to expand and contract at the same time."

Jack suddenly stood up from out of his chair and he slowly walked over to the right side of the cockpit to get his circulation going and began staring through the side windows at the white streams of light. The small pulsations of light traveling toward the back of his ship caused him to think more about the strange characteristics of the white dwarf star, wondering again why he didn't remember the star if he was the one who discovered the galaxy. That was a strange thought, he knew, but then again there was evidently nothing in their ship's silicon-based computer explaining the characteristics or reasons for the white dwarf star, or Jennifer would have surely found the information. Taking a small breath, Jack slowly exhaled and walked back over to his captain's chair, sitting back down. He immediately began looking over equations on his center forward display in relation to the dwarf star that their ship's computer had computed, and noticed there were also question marks inside some of the mathematical triple-state integral expansions. He knew it had to be because the expansion and contractions of the gravity waves should have equalized, at least along one wave front, but they clearly were not equalized, and showing to be extremely unbalanced across the zero domain integral expansions.

Jacobs had an advanced understanding of gravity fields and their accompanying propagations as they applied directly to quantum space. This particular white dwarf's gravity field and how it was affecting quantum space had him baffled to the unbalanced wave fronts. It had his mind and imagination racing, as he knew that he would eagerly take on any unknown event to science as a challenge to his understanding. He had always been this way, even from childhood, growing up in Virginia on a small farm eighteen miles west of Lynchburg. His parents owned eighty acres and lived in the foothills of the Blue Ridge Mountains, so they were already fairly close the eastern edge of the Appalachian Mountains and its magnificent Blue Ridge peaks. He remembered all of the metamorphic rock minerals near their home that looked like marble cake, and especially when walking around at night in the darkness, lit at time only by a full moon, and then staring up at the many bright stars in the heavens, dreaming of what it would be like to visit them someday. It looked as though his wish had become more than a reality, never believing he would be in his current predicament.

Jacobs took a short breath, relishing those childhood memories and also the time he spent up in the Mountains fishing for trout along the James River with his two brothers. Sometimes they caught lots of trout and he seemed to always be the lucky one. *Maybe it was his fly lures?* Jack wondered, since he did create all of his by hand using white goose down, and red, blue, and green sewing thread. His brothers never saw any of his lures up close until he'd turned twelve. But then his good luck could have been because he had an eye for the flowing water, especially when it came to sensing where the trout might be lurking below the water's surface.

Jack suddenly looked up through the cockpit windows and again noticed the strange pulsations of white light traveling toward the back of his ship. This only reminded him again of his current situation and knew that if he could not solve his current predicament, then all of those memories as a youth and with his family would always remain memories—never to be shared with any of them ever again.

Glancing down at his wristwatch, he knew that before they reached the outer boundaries of the Stormy Way galaxy there would be fifteen more hundred year reversals while traveling inside their extended time warp field tunnel. Those fifteen anomalies would also result in fifteen hundred years being lost to the Earth and the Milky Way galaxy outside their time tunnel, while at the same time, inside their time tunnel, there would be a loss of one hour, as their time slowly approached midnight in four-minute increments.

Resigning himself to the idea that it would not be easy to reach a solution for their predicament, he knew their time warp tunnel should last a little under forty-two Earth hours. Because of the Stormy Way galaxy located nearly 15,000,000 light years away, it was a distance and expanse of space that could only have been reached in forty-two hours while traveling at one hundred light years per second inside their time warp tunnel.

Staring at the white streams of light passing by their cockpit windows, Jacobs continued to sit, extremely relaxed and thinking about the last sixteen Earth years he and Jennifer were lost in the universe. They had been trying to get back home after first secretly testing their spaceship back in 2183 and then being propelled over two hundred eighty million light years out of the Milky Way into the dark matter between the galaxies. He remembered the single time warp field equation error that caused the time warp field to propel their ship's gravity propulsion system out of control, subsequently losing all known bearings. Jacobs had figured out less than a month after that catastrophic event that he had not taken into account the time plane drift error for the movement of time itself and its direct correlation to the speed of light. It resulted in an exponential time warp field shift in their spacecraft's gravity propulsion system.

He clearly remembered the day Jennifer found the Milky Way galaxy with their ship's sensors though, as it was a marvelous, joyous day that overshadowed that event. She had more than a little excitement in her voice. That was the first time Jack really noticed her excitement index level as being human, or nearly human. Maybe because it was the most excited he had been the last sixteen years, knowing they had finally marked their position in the universe and were going home.

Pausing in front of a camera above his forward center display, Jacobs took a small, short sigh. "Some homecoming huh, Jennifer?" he said, gently.

Jennifer didn't say anything at first, not understanding what he meant. Jacobs realized he had probably confused her and remained quiet, now waiting for her to respond.

"I understand what your saying, Jack," she finally said.

Jack smiled a little. He was pleased she understood his comment, and continued to quietly watch the bright streams of light pass by outside his cockpit windows. With a quick glance of his watch, he saw it showed a time of 11:59 p.m. fifty seconds and counting, and knew if a red shift was evident this time over 2,000,000 light years from Earth, then most likely it wasn't just the Milky Way galaxy that was being affected by the anomaly, but their entire universe. "Another possible reversal of the space-time domain coming," he said. "You realize, Jennifer, that if there is a red shift this time that the anomaly is probably affecting the entire universe?"

"Yes, I do," she said.

Jacobs noticed her repositioning one of the cameras toward the windows in time to catch the possible red shift. He turned his attention back to the windows and together they both watched, as the white streams of light continued to pass by their ship. All of a sudden, the lights turned bright red for exactly one second and then back to white. Jacobs felt strangely warm inside. It was as though he was having a personal moment with Jennifer. It could have been because he had to assume the entire universe was now being affected by some strange event in the Stormy Way galaxy and that he and Jennifer were possibly the only intelligent life left who actually realized what was happening. Continuing to sit quietly and thinking about the momentary red shift in light, he turned to one of the cameras.

"Did you see that new space-time shift, Jennifer?"

"Yes, I did, Jack."

"Unnerving?"

"Yes, it is," she says.

Jacobs glanced at his wristwatch that was showing a time of 9:16 p.m. and mumbled under his breath, "Our ship's gravity field is seemingly shifting backwards from midnight every time the anomaly occurs, yet its gravity time-base is moving forward four minutes closer to midnight."

"Yes, I see that's the case, Jack," she said.

Jack had to smile, realizing Jennifer was listening to him talk to himself. It was just like she had done over their many years they were lost together. Looking briefly at his watch again, he calculated in his head how many more times his ship's onboard time reference to

Earth's would move to midnight and then backwards again.

Earth's would move to midnight and then backwards again. "Hmmm," he said to himself, "our time warp field tunnel should last around thirty-six more hours. When we finally come out of our extended time warp tunnel, the time on my watch should be 11:59 p.m. One minute later, we'll have to make another short time warp jump just to keep from going back in time a hundred years and ceasing to exist."

"Jennifer?" he said.

"Yes, Jack."

"I'm going to my quarters and get some rest while we have some idle time."

Jennifer knew Jack had been awake for fifty hours, twenty-five minutes before they found the Milky Way and Earth again. Since he had only been getting cat naps since the first occurrence of the anomaly, she knew he truly did need to rest his mind, maybe even with some extended REM. "Okay, I understand," she said. "I'll wake you if anything out of the ordinary comes up or something happens to our time warp field."

"Yes, please, Jennifer, do that."

"I will, Jack," she softly said.

Jacobs stood up from his captain's chair with a small smile. He appreciated Jennifer's continual sincerity to him, and after briefly staring up at the white streams of light showing through the cockpit windows, he left the cockpit and walked out into the hallway. Going idly down the hallway, he wondered again if he'd become younger by the amount of time loss inside their time tunnel. He didn't feel any different, so that would mean it wasn't noticeable—at least not yet. Finally walking up to the planetarium's entrance, he stopped for a brief moment to listen to the light rustling of water from the waterfall. Taking a small breath to the moist air, he turned his head back outside the hallway windows to notice the white streams of light still encasing his ship in the shape of a circle and a tunnel. The streams of light were less than thirty meters above his vantage point and traveled down in a perfect arc, almost touching his ship's outer compression ring. The streams of light were close to three meters away from the compression ring of his double-saucer shaped spaceship, and nearly fifteen meters below his vantage point in the upper hallway.

Jack continued to stare at the light, knowing he never actually figured out how his time warp field, or time tunnel, was able to separate itself from normal space-time, only that it created a new area of space inside a tubular tunnel. Finally taking off walking again away from the planetarium, he did know that his time warp field tunnel used in conjunction with his gravity propulsion drive were like one would recognize as a wormhole, yet, they were only holes in space for his ship's gravity field and nothing more—like cutting space-time with a harmonically induced and adjusted gravity field. Thinking no more about that, Jack finally arrived at his quarters and after entering inside, slowly pulled off his two-piece outfit. He now stood in only his blue-colored velvet boxer shorts and after grabbing a set of silk-lined nightclothes, slipped on the relaxing outfit. Staring at his bed made him feel tired, because he knew it had been over two Earth days since he had lay down in it. Standing there for a moment, he knew that when he woke up they would be much closer to what had possibly gotten them into their current predicament. Finally getting into bed and lying flat on his back, he began staring up at the ceiling, thinking about what could be causing a loss of a hundred years every twenty-four Earth solar hours. It was a loss of a hundred years that appeared to be manifesting itself not only in the Milky Way, but throughout the entire known universe. That was a very strange thought in itself, and Jack couldn't understand why the time reversals were directly related to Earth and its solar time. This is because he knew like before that time was only a variable according to the magnetic or gravitational field being compared, and in direct relation to a moving or non-moving body or energy.

After staring over at his side windows, Jacobs looked back up at the overhead incandescent lighting. "Lights at one-tenth lumens," he said.

The lights inside the room suddenly dimmed to one-tenth of

the Earth's moonlight and Jack noticed the white streams of light become much brighter and visible outside the windows. But he had a desire for his room to be much darker. "Window shading at eighty-eight percent," he said.

The curved windows to his room automatically darkened from photosensitive elements designed into the clear, high-temperature, two-centimeter thick thermoplastic glass that was more than a hundred times stronger than the polycarbonates of Earth's 21st century—polycarbonates also known as Lexan, or bulletproof glass. This immense strength was because the thermoplastic glass contained multi-layered, hexaflexagonal internal structures, having high cohesion, and would give massive impact dispersion across its entire surface from any projectile or force, similar to pushing on an under deflated balloon. The entire glass would try to pop out of its frame, if possible, before a hole could be forced or punched through it.

Jacobs knew that advancement in the field of molecular high-strength elements was amazing, and could now only see a dim glimpse of the white streams of light outside his windows. After this last glance, he closed his eyes, relaxed, thinking, pondering, and trying to understand how the reversal of the entire universe could have ever happened. It was something that he would have never believed possible, but why couldn't he remember discovering the Stormy Way galaxy. It was that strange thought of wondering if he had visited the galaxy before that finally caused him to fall asleep. But then it could have been caused by their extended time warp tunnel and what effects it might be having upon his body. Maybe it was the anticipation of them visiting a strange galaxy he had no recollection of visiting, even though their ship's silicon-based computer said differently. As a third option, his deep sleep could have been caused by the possibility they could never solve the problem of their current situation—a possible time loop caused by their ship's own time warp field. Jack hoped this third option was not the case, as he wouldn't have any idea where to begin solving that strange problem.

5

PAST MEMORIES

WHILE JACK JACOBS SLOWLY and steadfastly fell into a deeper state of sleep, Jennifer continued to monitor the time warp field
tunnel around their ship for anomalies of any kind. Everything still
worked perfectly according to the time warp field displacement formulas, all as directly related to the harmonic vibrations across their spaceship's gravity element while inside its Spherical Interactive Dome. The
SID's focused aperture was also functioning flawlessly to allow their
ship's gravity element to maintain its zero-domain space.

She sensed Jack's breathing and his heart rate slowing down
even more and knew a level-four sleep was imminent. This level-four
sleep would be followed by a lethargic REM. Jack's eyes finally began
darting back and forth in initial REM, just as Jennifer had suspected,
and she focused her infrared cameras and sensors directly on Jack's

physiology. Watching him soundly dream, she began analyzing his theta brainwave activity, intrigued, and did not completely understand their amplitude signatures in relation to the frequency. She finally turned her cameras back to the white streams of light passing by outside their ship, when suddenly the light turned red again and then back to white. She knew that their ship's time warp field tunnel had just shifted backwards momentarily, as did its gravity field, yet, their time-field platform moved four minutes closer to midnight. It was a time-base where eventually the time loss inside their time tunnel would be twenty-four hours and match the twenty-four hour cycle of the strange anomaly. She knew this is what Jack had figured out when he extrapolated the four-minute harmonic cycle out of the twenty-four minute resonant cycle, resulting in slowing the loss of time inside their time warp tunnel to four minutes for each space-time reversal.

Jennifer never required any cognitive sleep like humans or any liquid chemical carbon-based being, so she continued watching the white streams of light outside their spaceship while monitoring the gravity propulsion system of their ship and all of its environmental systems. Everything was still working properly, as the time warp field continued to harmonically push their ship through the space-time domain of their universe at over 943 trillion kilometers per second. She also knew, as did Jack, that the strange gravity binders associated with the hundred year reversals were of unknown origin, not conforming to any known laws, almost as if they were snapping the entire universe's space-time domain like a whip. This strange reversal of space-time, seemingly, had an associated gravity wave that was able to instantaneously and methodologically reverse all space, all mass, and all energy, including all energies outside their spaceship, changing and reversing everything. She was also starting to understand that everything on their ship was physically becoming younger by four-minutes each time they were ratcheted back from midnight. Strangely, as she would lose memories, new memories would suddenly reappear as if they were past events. These new memories were strange, but then she wasn't going to say anything to Jack about what she was remembering...

*   *   *

Inside his quarters, Jack finally started to wake up from his invigorating deep sleep, and after opening his eyes, glanced at his side windows to see the dim streams of white light. "Window shading at zero," he said.

Suddenly, the windows became clear and the white streams of light were again brightly visible. He wasn't dreaming. "Lights back to 80 lumens," he said. Suddenly, the incandescent lighting in his quarters lit the room back up.

Jack glanced at his wristwatch and it showed 10:36 p.m., May 17. He didn't know the true time or day of the month anymore. "That is so strange," he said to himself. "To not know what day or time it really is. According to the gravity field of my ship, it still has to be May 17th because I've never really reached the midnight hour of the 18th." Jack paused, rethought his words, and then remarked out loud to no one in particular. "But I am getting closer by four minutes with every hundred year anomaly."

Jennifer sensed Jack was now fully awake after sleeping nine hours, eight minutes, and had already heard him talking out loud to himself. "Good morning and good afternoon, Jack," she said.

Jacobs sat upright in his bed, showing a small smile and realized his own reference time had probably shifted backwards a few more times, or in the case with the rest of the universe, centuries were lost. "And the same to you," he replied back humorously, and finally got up out of bed. He walked directly over to the food dispenser located inside the left wall of his room.

After punching a few buttons on the keyboard, a small door opened, and a white plastic tray emerged filled with an assortment of vitamin C and D drinks and a few highly mineralized food groups. The food groups Jack knew were generated by their ship's molecularized automatic food processing unit. Jennifer, of course, had the ultimate control over the processor, if she so wished, and would add mineral bases according to how she was reading his body's metabolic levels or possible vitamin deficiencies. It was soon after they had become lost in 2183 when he had given her full control over their ship's food processor. How better than to have your computer, who, like a close personal friend, was always looking out for you and for the physical well-being of your body?

Jack picked up his tray, remembering it was at that time sixteen years ago when their ship was loaded with enough vitamins and hydrogenised minerals for a crew of nearly two hundred. He had pre-empted the space adventure of a full Earth crew aboard his ship, a crew he was also going to be a part of and scheduled for the next day. It was to have been a four month secret expedition, and would have known the entire crew, especially since he was picked to be the chief science officer. But then he just had to know if his extremely advanced time warp field propulsion was going to work without endangering the lives of anyone else. That was the main reason for him taking the ship the day before in order to test his time warp field that had already passed all of its gravity propulsion tests using nuclear based energy. There was no way anyone could have figured out that his extremely powerful Gaussian energy system was only partially deactivated and supplementing the nuclear energy based system with magnetic flux energy.

Jack finally turned around with his tray full of food and drinks and carried it over to a small table in his room, knowing part of his motivation for taking the ship was because if his time warp field propulsion worked, it would have given the human race a surprising jump in technology—at least the secret government. Jacobs set his tray down on a table and then sat down. He began quietly eating and noticed Jennifer watching him with one of the cameras in the room. "So how's our time warp field tunnel holding up?" he asked.

"No problems, Jack," she calmly replied.

Jacobs remained quiet to see if Jennifer would say more while he ate, especially with everything that was going on with the anomaly that was reversing all space-time of their known universe.

"So what do you think is causing the time anomaly?" she finally asked.

Jack was mildly surprised by her question, as it was phrased with curiosity. "I'm not certain," he finally said. "It is possible that it could be a time device of some kind that has gone haywire or maybe even that we're caught inside a rift as a result of our ship's time warp field."

Jennifer took a few seconds to analyze the term "haywire", including the surprise suggestion of a rift. She understood. "If it is a time rift, can we fix it?" she asked.

"I don't know," Jack calmly answered. "That's a very good question. I'll guess we'll have to *cross that bridge* when we get there."

Jennifer again understood. "I know what you're saying, Jack," she finally said. "We'll just have to wait and see what it really is."

Jacobs smiled at her comment while slowly eating his food. He began thinking about their ultimate outcomes or possible outcomes of the time losses inside their time tunnel, wondering again if they'd dealt with the white dwarf star once before. He stared out the side windows of his quarters, daydreaming about many things, and noticed again the easily visible streams of light. While taking another slow bite of his amino acid, high-energy protein food, filled with small amounts of potassium, iron, zinc, and phosphorus, Jack knew the cosmological configuration of the universe outside their time tunnel must have changed by at least a few more centuries. He could not see how it was possible for all heavenly bodies and space to be reversed so quickly throughout the entire space-time domain of the universe, including the dark matter between the galaxies. It just didn't seem to be plausible by any force of nature, cosmological force, or any other force. Even with their laws of black hole gravity fields that he and Jennifer figured out over the last sixteen years, what was happening with the space-time reversals violated all of their event-horizon laws. From fixed non-rotating black holes, to the rotating fixed-plane black holes, to even the black holes that were spinning on their axis like a neutron star, none of their quantum gravity field mechanics could explain what was happening with the strange space-time anomaly. It was without a doubt that even all of those different black holes and their associated event horizons were being changed and altered along with the rest of the cosmological universe.

Jacobs finally swallowed the last of his highly mineralized food and took a short breath to his detailed daydream about black hole stars. He wondered again about the Black Hole star type that they had classified as a Black Neutron star. This was because they were spinning on their axis like Neutron Stars, yet, much denser than Neutron stars and did not emit any x-rays or energy. They were invisible until you got close to the proximity of their unusual event-horizon. Jennifer had to quickly use their ship's time warp field back when they discovered that star. They immediately left the area never to return, but Jacobs always suspected that it might be possible, if picking both the correct space curvature angle and spin cycle of these strange stars, to end up inside a new dimension of space—maybe even an alternate universe. He took a small gulp of his fortified vitamin D drink, wondering if that is what had happened to them and they were never in their own universe to being with. But then he had to discount it as not being very likely.

Jacobs glanced down again at his wristwatch. The realization was there for him that he didn't have a true time base within his own mind. In a way, he did feel that their extended time tunnel toward the Stormy Way galaxy seemed familiar, yet, had no conception of what was to follow. He noticed the time 11:48 p.m. showing on his wristwatch and pulled his chair up to one of the consoles in the room. He had to know how much time had passed while he was asleep and what cycle of the seventeen hundred-year reversals they were on inside their extended time warp tunnel. After punching a half dozen buttons on his display, the answer finally showed in front of him. "Hmmm," he mumbled under his breath, "looks like we have eleven more hundred-year cycles before we finally exit our tunnel."

Jack sat for a moment longer, thinking about the very strange white dwarf star, knowing it had characteristics that violated rotational body perturbation laws, not only the black hole star laws that he and

Jennifer were now aware of, but also the rotating magnetic field neutron star laws that were finally derived in the later part of the 21st century. Of course, he had expanded quite a bit on those compressed field rotating body laws in the last sixteen years. Due to what they had determined about black holes and their compressed introverted gravity fields, black holes seemed to be much older than the dwarf stars. But why was this particular white dwarf star not agreeing with those previous assessments? Jack finally turned directly to one of the cameras with a slightly puzzled face, realizing the white dwarf star was even stranger than the Black Neutron star they had encountered many years ago. "Jennifer, a thought?" he said.

"Yes, Jack."

"How's the white dwarf looking?" he asked again. "Are you able to read anything different about it from our ship's sensors, anything that is starting to make sense?"

"No, I can't, Jack," she answered. "The dwarf star still shows red and blue shifts with massive expanding and contracting gravity waves. They are also becoming much more pronounced."

Jack thought about what she had just told him and got an eerie feeling. "I don't like the sound of that," he said to himself, still wondering how the white dwarf could be producing unbalanced gravity wave shifts. Glancing down at his watch it showed 11:59 p.m., fifty-seven seconds and counting. He looked out the windows. "Another red shift coming up," he remarked.

Three seconds later, the white streams of light turned red for one second and then turned back to white just as quickly. Jack glanced at his wristwatch again, 9:32 p.m. He drank the last of his mineralized vitamin C drink and set the glass back down on the tray. "I'm going to get cleaned up and changed into a new set of clothes, Jennifer," he said.

"Okay," she answered.

Jack stood up from his chair and walked over to a small closest where he found an outfit and spacesuit for what he thought would be needed for the phenomena in the Stormy Way galaxy. Grabbing his gray and medium blue, two-piece long sleeved outfit, the bottom half also having space boots attached, he took them into his bathroom and set them down again. Looking into a wall mirror, Jacobs began inspecting himself and his skin texture, just as he had many times in the past, and knew he hadn't aged in the last sixteen years like he normally should have. In fact, he looked ten years younger than his known Earth age of forty-two. His whiskers didn't seem to be growing as fast while aboard his spaceship, but it had also been more than a few Earth days since he shaved last. Jack reached down and grabbed his sonic-wave cordless face shaving mask, knowing the mask was quite the invention of someone's imagination from back in Earth's twenty-first century. Sticking the shave mask up against his face, he noticed it covered his face to the bottom of his lower jaw, both of his sideburn areas, below his cheeks, and below his nose. Jacobs pushed a small button on the mask and a split second later he heard a brief, high-pitched noise, then it stopped. Pulling the mask away from his face, his face was clean-shaven and had the smell of an alcohol-based aftershave. Setting the shave mask down on the sink, Jack began slowly removing his nightwear while thinking more about the mask. He remembered reading up on its design characteristics years ago. It could be interfaced to a computer and then programmed to remove whatever facial hair was desired, from a goatee, to a soul patch, to even a variety of nicely trimmed beards. Once the mask was positioned up against the face, he knew its thousands of tiny sensors analyzed the density of terminal beard hairs per square centimeter in relation to the skin surface, perfectly removing only those whiskers that were desired, to even a full face shave. This was all accomplished, Jack knew, via sonic energy at a frequency that would not only sever the terminal beard hair shafts at the surface of the skin, but not damage any of the surrounding facial skin.

Jacobs finally removed his boxer shorts, realizing again that he didn't have much reprogramming of the mask for his clean-shaven face and then walked into the shower. After he closed the door, warm water immediately came on, and Jack Jacobs stood directly under the relaxing pulsations, thinking about his last sixteen years with Jennifer. She had never seen him naked. It would have made him feel uncomfortable, he knew, even if she was just a supercomputer composed of seven topological organic-laced circuit cards. But it was her sincere, innocent female personality embedded into those same circuit cards, including her personality matrix approaching a human-being that was the real reason.

As Jacobs stood under the warm water, eyes closed, he thought about her more and realized that he had actually known Jennifer on a personal level for almost as long as his own family. She was two years, two months old when he first met her in Dr. Gilmore's lab, and she had aged six years, and one month while their ship was being built. After he had spent sixteen additional years lost with her in the universe, he calculated that would have made her about twenty-four. He wasn't sure if she was more like a daughter to him, a good friend, or maybe even a romantic companion. Jacobs opened his eyes, giggling at the strange thought of his attachment to a series of organic circuit boards, yet he knew what his friend, Dr. Gilmore's ultimate plans were for Jennifer. After he told Dr. Gilmore in confidence that he was secretly incorporating a new propulsion technology into the prototype spaceship, his friend suggested she be secretly interfaced into the spaceship's subsystems alongside the advanced technology. Dr. Gilmore had always told him that once he'd finished her organic and synthetic-based body that her six topological carbon-60 memory circuit cards and the single processor card could always be removed from the ship and installed inside her body, directly interfacing it to her EPM. He recalled from Dr. Gilmore that the EPM was a module known as the Electrical Pathways Matrix and acted very similar to the brainstem of a human cerebellum, allowing perfectly balanced control of all her bodily systems. The difference with Jennifer is that she would have now understood Jack's secret time warp field technology, at least that's what Dr. Gilmore had eluded to him.

Jack closed his eyes again and remembered back to Jennifer's body that Dr. Gilmore had completed, but not yet tested. It was an organic and synthetic-based body that incorporated an actual bone skeletal system for stability. He had also used a new high-grade, high-density, self-lubricating polytetrafluoroethylene in all of her joints, very similar to what was used in the joint surgeries of Earth's 22nd century. Her body was early twenties and had a fair-complexioned, flesh-colored, organic and synthetic-based skin with pressure-sensitive receptors. She also had bluish-green eyes with the vision range twenty times that of a human being and could see in the dark like a cat, while at the same time had infrared filters to block most ultraviolet energy. Her synthetic and organic-based hair on the scalp of her head was partially curly, auburn in color, and medium length. She was nearly 178 centimeters tall and was proportionately built to look just like another female human-being with the exception that Dr. Gilmore had designed and interfaced many sensors into her Electrical Pathways Matrix. It would have given her the amazing ability to read the reactions of all organic living beings in her vicinity, such as heartbeat and breathing, just as Jack knew she was currently doing on his ship.

Jacobs opened his eyes wondering if Dr. Gilmore ever got the chance to finish testing her body, and if so, what might have happened to it. He took a small breath of curiosity to that strange thought and finally finished rinsing off the shower soap. After waving his right hand in front of a sensor, the water immediately shut off and he lifted up his arms. As he stood waiting, a blast of warm air blew from all directions and the water quickly evaporated, leaving him feeling invigorated. Jack opened the door and walked out of the shower. After reaching down, he grabbed a new set of gray velvet boxer shorts and pulled them on. He then sat on a chair and put on his electrically-powered thermal socks. Jack next slipped into his tight-fitting blue and gray pants with attached, flexible, synthetic and rubberized boots strong as steel, and then stood back up. After tightening up his belt-line, he put on his shirt and watched it become tight to his pants from a static charge designed into the materials. Jacobs looked up again and stared at himself in the mirror, fully dressed, and ready to face whatever was in the Stormy Way galaxy. He ran his fingers through his hair a few times knowing he was also ready for their next obstacle—the very strange White Dwarf star that was directly in their path toward the origin of the anomaly. After picking up a small locater beacon, he stuck it in his left pants pocket, just as he'd always done so Jennifer would know his whereabouts, if he were to leave the ship.

Jack started to walk back toward his quarters, but found that every time he lifted up his boots, they were sticking to the floor like flypaper. So he stopped after realizing he'd inadvertently pushed the small button on the beltline of his pants, activating the static attraction function of his boots. It was a material designed into the soles of the boots that became attractive to all other elements, and acted exactly opposite in nature to Teflon. The material and its attractive state function were also driven by a small power source designed into the boots and the boots would resist slippage even on oily surfaces. Jack finally pushed the button on his beltline twice to turn off the function and then walked, uninhibited, out of the bathroom into his quarters. He turned to one of the cameras, knowing Jennifer was watching him, and the White Dwarf star immediately came to his mind. It seemed as though he had memories of seeing the white dwarf star up close once before and continued to quietly stare at the camera. "I'm going to the cockpit, Jennifer," he finally said. "Is there anything new about that white dwarf star that might be of interest?"

Jennifer was quiet and she did not comment or reply.

Jack was surprised she did not respond and needed to hear her voice to make sure she was still there, just as he had done many times over their last sixteen years. "Are you still there, Jennifer?" he asked her again.

"Yes, I am, Jack," she replied.

Jacobs took a small, deep breath after hearing her voice and said nothing about her previous silence. He walked out of his quarters located fourteen meters away from the cockpit entrance and continued down the hallway, wondering why Jennifer was not replying or saying much to him about the strange white dwarf star. A dreamy look filled his face and Jennifer noticed this right away. With a quick bioelectrical analysis of his body and his cerebrum using her cortex memory sensors, she began trying to understand what he might be thinking. *Could it be something to do with the white dwarf star?*

Walking by the planetarium, Jacobs didn't think about the waterfall this time and continued down the hallway toward the cockpit with the white dwarf star on his mind, just as Jennifer had guessed. Her analysis of his Alpha/Beta brainwaves found them to be in the 18 to 40 hertz range. She also knew from her many years with Jack that his cognitive brainwave frequencies ran higher than normal human physiology, as the normal human Alpha/Beta range was 8 to 25. Even Jack's Theta and his lowest brainwave frequency cycle, Delta, she knew were higher than normal, ranging from 2 to 5 cycles while he slept, and up to 8 to 18 hertz in his Theta stages. Jennifer thought, *Maybe that is why Jack is so creative?*

Jacobs finally walked back into the cockpit from out of the hallway and immediately over toward his captain's chair without a thought of Jennifer's continual analysis of his body's physiology. He sat down and quickly noticed the white streams of light visible through the curved windows 3.9 meters above his head. Relaxing back in his captain's chair, he knew they had some idle time and the white dwarf star vanished from his mind. He began daydreaming about his parents and his two brothers, all in good health sixteen years ago, and wondered what may have happened in their lives before the time anomaly. Were his parents still alive, were his brothers married with families, and how many nephews or nieces might he now have? Were any of them still living in Virginia? Samuel, his oldest brother who taught Theology at Hollins University in Roanoke, Virginia, in 2183, was engaged to be married. His next to oldest brother, Daniel, began working for the government soon after his doctorate in computer science. He was still looking for Mrs. Right at that time. Samuel, it seemed, was always trying to play matchmaker for him and his brother, but Jack knew there just wasn't enough time for a woman in his own life while he was working for the government on the Orion Nine project. This was especially true when all of his extra hours were spent developing his secret time warp field technology and making sure it was properly incorporated into the advanced gravity propulsion system of the first deep space prototype spaceship. This busy life didn't include that between working on Orion Nine, secretly interfacing his time warp field technology into the ship, he was perusing two other doctorates, one in quantum microbiology and the other in quantum mechanical electrodynamics. They were doctorates he finally did receive late in the year, 2179, and just two years after his first doctorate in high energy gravitational mathematics, a gravitational mathematics doctorate that gained him very high recognition and prominence in the science community. His doctoral thesis in the field of gravitational mathematics ended up creating new gravity propulsion laws and earned him a Nobel Prize.

Jacobs continued to think about his education and the day he received his Nobel Prize in Gravitational Physics, remembering all of his family being present. He was the youngest individual to ever receive a Nobel Prize in any Physics field. He remembered how supportive his family was of him and knew his parents and brothers had to have missed him when he vanished without a trace four years, five months after his last two doctorates. He wasn't sure how the government would have covered up his disappearance, being the Area 51 project he was on was highly secretive—classified above top-secret—but they probably would have came up with some elaborate explanation to give to everyone, even to his family, he thought.

Jack came out of his memorable daydream and remembered how secure Area 51 was back in 2183, especially since the government bought hundreds of thousand of acres around the site many years before, permanently securing it from any peering eyes on the ground. He then glanced down at his center console and it showed the current cosmological time of the universe. Looking at his wristwatch, it showed a GMT of 11:23 p.m., year 2199, May 17. Thinking about the two differences, Jacobs had to glance down at the console again and was somewhat surprised by the new date. It showed 11:23 p.m., year 1099, May 17. He mumbled to himself, "The cosmological time of the universe is now eleven hundred years from the true and correct time of the universe, at least for me."

Jack began thinking long and hard about how the anomaly was able to propagate so quickly from the Stormy Way galaxy every twenty-four Earth solar hours. He wondered again how it was affecting their time warp field in relation to their ship's gravity propulsion system. Maybe there was some way to nullify the space-time reversals so that the time inside their time tunnel didn't change? "I'm going to the planetarium for a while, Jennifer," he said, while still thinking about that intriguing possibility.

"Okay, Jack," she calmly answered. "Do you need any company down there?"

Jack understood her question, as he always knew she was extremely attached to him, evident in her continual sincerity and subtle changes in her voice. "Maybe in a few hours," he finally replied. "I need to better understand why the hundred-year time shifts are affecting the angular time displacement vectors of our time warp field in relation to our ship's gravitational field. Do you completely understand the question?"

"Yes, I understand," she kindly said.

Jack smiled to her reply, knowing she did understand and that he was going to try to figure out how to stop the time losses inside their time tunnel. He stood up from out of his captain's chair and headed directly to the exit with anticipation of that exact prospect. He then left the cockpit straight toward the planetarium. While walking down the hallway and thinking about his sixteen years lost in the universe with Jennifer, he wondered if using their time warp field for all those years may have caused the anomaly. "Probably not," he thought, "Or absolutely not. Which is it?" But then again, maybe he and Jennifer had been caught in a time loop for sixteen years for thousands upon thousands of times from a catastrophic event from visiting the galaxy once before, and haven't come to realize it yet up until now.

Jacobs finally arrived at the entrance to the planetarium and stopped for a short moment. The waterfall was refreshing to see and it immediately relaxed not only his mind, but his biophysical body, noticeable by a sudden palpitation of his heart. Walking inside and taking a seat in his favorite chair by the waterfall, Jacobs opened up his notebook that was lying on top of the console. Grabbing a pen, he began writing down a few of his time warp field formulas that were incorporating his newly discovered four-minute cycle time harmonic theorems. There had to be a solvable answer as to why or how the reversals of space-time were affecting both his time warp field and the gravity field of his ship, causing a time shift inside their time tunnel, he thought. This was especially true as their ship was being harmonically pushed through the time warp field tunnel at a speed of one hundred light years per second, the upper limit of space travel. Could he figure out how to stop or slow down the loss of time within their time warp tunnel?

Jacobs continued his master equations along with a half dozen side equations, using the new four-minute harmonic cycles in a direct correlation to his linear time warp field vectors. The vectors across the denumerator just didn't make any sense and he shook his head while filling another page inside his notebook with truly mind-boggling equations. After finally filling up the sixth page of his notebook, he began staring at his latest equations that were solved as far as he could go or understand. Jacobs finally paused with a confused look on his face. The new space-time curvature zero domain permutations had him thoroughly baffled. Continuing to stare at the latest equations, the separation of the harmonics between his time warp field tunnel and his ship's gravity propulsion system across the new zero points just wasn't making any sense to him in relation to hundred year reversals of space-time. To Jacobs, it just didn't seem possible it could ever happen. Glancing at his watch, he noticed a few more hours had seemed to pass without him ever realizing. "Hmmm," he said to himself, "I didn't think I could ever get stumped on any math related functions of the time warp field equations."

Jacobs put aside his notebook and began staring at the many trees and vegetation in the planetarium, knowing his latest equations were truly unsolvable to him, as would they would be to Jennifer. His wristwatch showed 11:20 p.m. He looked back up to his wood-framed, pendulum-driven wall clock to see it also showed 11:20 p.m. Another hundred-year reversal of space-time occurred outside their tunnel, he now realized, and was so deep in thought of trying to figure out how to stop the time losses inside their time tunnel that he never noticed the momentary red streams of light. Jack continued to stare at his half-meter wide, quarter-meter deep, and one in a half meters tall wall wood clock. It was a decorative pendulum-driven clock that was hand-carved and looked similar to the Columbia Regulators manufactured in Winsted, Connecticut back in the early 1880's. Except his wood frame wall clock was made of a medium brown-colored hybrid crossbreed wood that was successfully genetically engineered back in Earth's 21st century. The new hybrid tree was called Mahoakany, or a cross between a Mahogany and a White Oak. The medium-grain wood was beautiful, Jack knew, and retained all of the rot and decay resistance of Mahogany wood, plus the water resistance of the white oak. It was also very durable and a highly prized wood that was fairly rare, since the trees were sterile and never bore any seed acorns.

He also remembered when he had bought the Mahoakany wood mechanical wall clock at an antique store while attending college. That would have been in the year 2175. The clock was supposedly around sixty years old at the time and was made from one of the first large trees that had been genetically engineered many years before in the 21st century. He never would have believed or dreamed it possible that his rare wall clock would have ended up inside the planetarium of a secret government prototype spaceship.

Jacobs took a short deep breath, continuing to think back to his college years and the time when he had read about how the two tree species were successfully intermixed. It was an amazing work of genetics, he knew, as they had used the Mahogany as the parent DNA and inserted the oak's nucleotides related to grain formation directly into the Mahogany's lignin macromolecule cell membrane production and its growth pattern cycles. It led to one of the strongest and most dense woods on the planet—the "mule" of woods, as it was called, due to the higher than normal lignin content.

He also remembered in Earth's past history how the successful attempt of intermixing White Oak and Mahogany caused a stir in the science community. This stir was not only because of the possible damage to the fertile genome systems of Oak and Mahogany trees on Earth, if one of the hybrids were to end up being seed bearing, but also for the possible marine and ecological damage to Earth's ecosystems from the wood's high lignin content. As a result, a new world governing body was created to oversee all plant and tree genetic engineering alterations and creations. It was a governing body also called the Planetary Taxonomic Agency, or PTA, with full jurisdiction and judicial power over all states and countries. It had a forest and plant division, as well as other divisions for many genome types on Earth, all chaired by scientists from the United States, China, Germany, France, Russian Federation, and the United Kingdom, with the agency fully represented by scientists and members from each state or country on Earth. A division for the mammal kingdom was started a few years afterwards when it was unveiled that a few rogue scientists were still experimenting with intermixing human DNA gamete cell structures with animal DNA, after already being ordered to stop by the United Nations Security Council.

Jack paused again from his detailed daydream about Earth's 21st society and their advancements in the field of genetics, including the new super-wood that was used in his wall clock—the exact wood that prompted the new Agency to be formed. He finally turned to one of the cameras in the planetarium with a slight grin to Jennifer's earlier question. "Jennifer?" he asked.

"Yes, Jack—"

"So what do you want to talk about?"

6

THE SURPRISE CONVERSATION WITH HIS COMPUTER

JENNIFER WAS QUIET AT FIRST. "What do you want to talk about?" she finally said.

"I asked you first," Jack said with a chuckle.

Jennifer analyzed Jack's laughter and his reply, including everything that was happening, realizing everybody on Earth they once knew was no longer around. Jack was the only living being she could now relate to for any of her history. She finally asked, "Do you think the people on Earth know they don't exist anymore after each anomaly?"

Jacobs was surprised at her unusual question, as it was definitely out of the ordinary for her. He thought about the consequences of such a question. "No, I don't believe so," he finally replied.

"How can you be so sure?"

Jack sat back in his chair thinking about what she had asked him again. He pondered how to answer her in a manner in which she could not only understand his answer, but word it so she could understand it from a brilliant child's point of view. "Because," he finally said. "For them it would be the same as never existing, as all organic and cellular matter is changing along with the rest of the universe."

Jennifer analyzed Jack's answer with a feeling of zeal in her organic memory cells. "I think I see what you mean," she finally said.

Jacobs grinned at her remark and looked over at the water. "Do you hear the sound of the water running over the rocks, Jennifer?" he asked.

"Yes, I do."

"What do you think about it?" he smartly asked.

Jennifer was quiet, thinking, analyzing, trying to understand what Jack had asked her. "What do you mean?" she finally answered.

"Well, you hear the sound vibrations from the water as it flows over the rocks, correct?"

Jennifer became intrigued while analyzing this new question, and began calculating the many different displacements of the air from the sound vibrations. "I think I understand what you're saying, Jack," she finally said, "As its many frequencies and wave mechanics do adhere to the density of the planetarium's air molecules."

Jacobs sat back in his chair thinking about Jennifer and his latest conversations with her. "Dr. Gilmore was correct in what he told me," he mumbled under his breath. "She is becoming more human-like in her responses as real-time hours accumulate on her organic-based clock—even more so with this anomaly that is affecting the universe as we once knew it."

That thought caused Jack to stare off in a distant thought again, thinking back to the time twenty-two years ago when he started secretly incorporating time warp field technology into the gravity propulsion system of the first prototype spaceship. It also was back at that time when he remembered talking to Dr. Gilmore about the prototype organic supercomputer his lab was working on. His friend, Dr.

Gilmore, was more than thrilled when he finally agreed to have Jennifer secretly installed on the first prototype deep space craft alongside the ship's carbon nanotube technology. Jack was actually flattered the way Jennifer immediately took a liking to him when he visited the Area 51 highly secretive lab for the first time, even though she was naïve, still learning and trying to understand the emotions of a human being. Dr. Gilmore had already stressed to him that her organic memory cells were very unique and used a highly-covalent Silicon and Manganese lattice that was sandwiched between layers of carbon 60 cellular and organic materials, created in a process that had never been used or conceived. Jack ultimately decided to go along with the idea of secretly installing her on the ship, even though he knew the government wouldn't have liked that the ship's silicon-based main processor was being replaced with an organic supercomputer whose memory capacity could grow over time.

"What are you thinking about, Jack?" Jennifer said.

Her question brought him out of his memorable daydream, realizing he was being watched. "Oh, I was just thinking about the first time I met you and had you installed on this ship."

Jennifer didn't say anything.

Jacobs realized Jennifer had become quiet and wondered if he may have embarrassed her a bit. From the beginning and when she was first installed on the ship, she was always sincere and her continual human-like emotions caused Jack to daydream of the events a few years later when he received his doctorate in Quantum Microbiology titled, "Quantum Magnetic Effects to Cellular Binding Energies". He knew that doctorate helped him immensely in coming to understand Jennifer's exact lattice cellular/elemental design across the carbon-60 molecular divides and intermeshes. Dr. Gilmore's design was actually an amazing piece of advanced science far ahead of its time, as each carbon-60 molecular intermesh was equivalent to about one terabyte of parallel processing. So, with each of her six organic-laced topological memory boards having two billion carbon-60 molecules each and growing, it would have given her unbelievable computing power on a molecular level.

Jacobs paused with a short deep breath after reminiscing about her design that he had figured out after becoming lost with her in the universe. That would have been about three years, eleven months later in the year 2187, and a time when he looked more closely at her six topological organic memory boards, including her main processor board that incorporated additional carbon-60 cellular materials. He knew after that brief peek into her construction using his advanced handheld electron microscope, a microscope of his design, that he would never look at her cells again, as not only did he feel awkward, but felt she now had the personality of a woman.

Jacobs glanced down at his wristwatch—11:59 p.m. and looked back up to the camera above his console. "Looks like another reverse-order gravity wave coming, Jennifer," he remarked.

"Yes, surely it is," she replied.

Jacobs continued to stare out the curved windows of the planetarium while watching the white streams of light pass by inside their time tunnel. A few moments later, the light suddenly turned red and then back to white. Immediately looking at his watch, it showed a time of 9:40 p.m.

Jack thought about the new space-time shift and glanced down at his console to see how many reverse hundred year cycles were left inside their extended time warp tunnel. He took notice of what was showing and mumbled under his breath, "Looks like there are eight more cycles."

Jacobs turned to one of the cameras with a small sigh and realized they were now less than one Earth solar day away. "Looks like there are around twenty hours and twenty minutes left in our time warp tunnel, Jennifer," he remarked.

Jennifer knew Jack was close. "Actually, there are exactly twenty hours and nineteen minutes," she replied.

Jacobs grinned, realizing she was still keeping track of the time left in their extended time tunnel, along with a multitude of other things on their ship, such as their ship's energy system, its environmental systems, and especially its gravity propulsion system as the gravity element was continually being forced into a nuclear propagation against its own internal vibratory momentum. He sat quietly staring at the waterfall in the planetarium as the water continued to cascade into the pool below, creating a soft rushing sound. It brought back the many memories of his years lost with Jennifer when they visited many different galaxies looking for carbon-based life. But then they were never lucky enough to find an intelligent race that had his level of technology. "Well, at least I never disrupted the technological advancement of their planets," he said to himself, realizing those planets that had a dipole magnetosphere similar to Earth's helped restore the Gaussian energy reserves of their spaceship's energy system over the many years.

He also knew that when entering some of those planet's atmospheres and their ionospheric regions it was tricky to keep his ship from being detected by their radars. Some of the races had primitive systems, while others had advanced tracking and sensing capability. Of course, they only had to worry about radar detection before his phased-matched gravity field cloaking technology was developed and perfected, two years, six months after they were first lost, in what would have been an Earth year of 2186. Cloaking was something that the twenty-second century Earth hadn't figured out or understood.

Jacobs noticed the time on his watch now showed 11:57 p.m. and a year of 2199. Of the eight reverse hundred year cycles of space-time yet to occur outside their time tunnel, he knew one of them was about to happen in less than three minutes. Staring outside the large, curved windows of the planetarium, the white streams of light were again easily visible. They were actually hypnotic to watch because of their pulsations inside the time warp tunnel—almost as if they were varying in intensity. This was another mystery Jacobs could never fully come to understand, but he had always suspected there was a secret light harmonic and wavelength associated with the universe's space-time domain pressures. Now waiting patiently and thinking about that possible secret speed of light harmonic, Jacobs knew that if he could figure out that mystery it would lead to powerful new sciences. Suddenly the streams of light outside the windows turned bright red and then back to white. Jacobs quickly glanced at his watch again and it showed 9:44 p.m. with a year of 2199. Their time warp field was shifted backwards again, yet four more minutes were added to their time, taking them closer to midnight. He looked over at the ship's cosmological time reference back to Earth that Jennifer had just updated and it showed a time of 9:44 p.m., year 799. There was now a fourteen hundred year difference.

Jacobs now sat contently and quietly, while continuing to watch the white streams of light pass by the curvature of their ship. His dreams about Earth kept coming to mind before they were propelled over two hundred eighty million light years out of the Milky Way galaxy and then lost within a large open sea of space. His memories about Earth were stronger because he felt the end of his life was also counting closer to midnight with each hundred year reversal, and was not sure if what they find in the Stormy Way galaxy is solvable. He clearly remembered sixteen years ago when he took the completed first of two prototype deep-space craft without permission from the government. "I hope they're not too mad at me," he said to himself. "I was only going to prove my time warp field propulsion technology. That was the real motivation anyway."

Jacobs continued to think back to that day, knowing again that the only ones who actually knew he was going to take the ship were his parents and Dr. Gilmore. "I would have never guessed how powerful this time warp field technology was going to be," he said again to himself.

"Have a lot on your mind, Jack?" Jennifer calmly asked.

Jacobs came to his senses. "I guess you could say that, Jennifer," he replied softly, realizing she was still watching him. "I was just really looking forward to seeing my family again and explaining to the government why I took their spaceship."

Jennifer began analyzing what Jack had just said, remembering him telling her some of those same thoughts over the course of their last sixteen years together. "I understand," she said.

Jack smiled at her comment while continuing to daydream how he went about taking the ship sixteen years ago. It was an event where not only would the government use force against their expensive prototype spaceship, but couldn't admit to its existence. He knew that once he had it in the air and had overridden all of the secret security lockout commands, some of which he had created, there was nothing the government could do but see what he had planned. They had lots of security ships sitting alongside his ship about 80,000 kilometers from Earth. When the ship finally vanished before their eyes, it had to be a strange sight for them. He also knew one thing they definitely would have detected before he disappeared was the strange energy burst his ship's time warp field would have created for the first time, especially when it was propelled out of control from incorrect time warp field vector summations. After he had vanished without a trace, the secret government surely found paper documentation at his house of what he had secretly incorporated into the ship. They possibly could have also reconstituted some of his research and working time warp field models from his computer's four-thousand terabyte, non-volatile, non-moving parts hard drive unit. For the partition that contained all of his time warp field research, he remembered reformatting it as a precautionary measure before taking the ship. So for them to reconstitute the quantum-tunnel data streams related to the partition that he erased, Jack knew it would have been a challenge. This is because once his computer was turned on and the working voltages used on the main arrays was requested to be entered onto the screen, followed by being entered wrong three times then his algorithms would have started running. It would have changed the main switching array operating voltages with each incorrect entry, including the array voltages for the partition that he had erased. So, it would have taken them years to figure out the correct reference voltages for booting up his computer and to reconstitute the erased partition.

Jacobs felt as though he was backtracking to his current situation and knew the only electronic copy for all of his time warp field research was on a small disc that he took with him prior taking the ship. After taking the ship, there also had to have been unusual circumstances for a lot of people back in 2183, both in the highly secretive lab and for his own family, as none of them would have known what happened to him. Surely, his family inquired many times over the years of his whereabouts, but then the government would have continually gave the excuse of "missing" or "unknown" even when having suspicions that he had secretly developed a highly-advanced gravity propulsion technology and then something had gone wrong after taking the spaceship and testing it.

Jack took a short deep breath, knowing everything that happened back then was now irrelevant, as getting to the galaxy where the anomaly was reversing all space-time of their known universe was his ultimate goal if they were to survive and give him a chance to tell his friends and family what had happened. Suddenly, the white streams of light outside the planetarium's windows turned bright red and then back to white.

Looking at his watch, it showed 9:48 p.m. and Jacobs realized their time had been reset again from midnight, yet pushed forward four minutes closer. "Well," he said under his breath, "you can get some sort of time bearing whenever you continued to watch the time after a red shift in light."

Jacobs knew there was nothing that could be done but patiently wait for them to exit their extended time warp tunnel near the outer reaches of the Stormy Way galaxy. Because of this, he decided to close his eyes again and rest his mind while listening to the soothing sound of the waterfall in the background. It would no doubt help him relax under the darkness of his eyelids. He also knew his mind would still be very active though, thinking, analyzing, going through all of his new time warp field equations and laws, and trying to come up with any possible solution to the many problems they now had in front of them. Their primary problem was the continual loss of time within their time tunnel as time slowly approached midnight in four minute increments.

Jennifer noticed Jack had finally closed his eyes and she sensed his breathing slowing down, knowing he would be going into a level-two sleep within the next thirty minutes. She also began monitoring his heart rate, knowing he wanted to be awake before they came out of their extended time warp tunnel near the Stormy Way galaxy. Pointing a camera at the side windows, she noticed the white streams of light turn red momentarily and then back to white, shifting all space-time of the universe backwards again. Turning her camera back to Jack, she began analyzing his brainwave frequencies and found them already in the alpha-theta range. Jennifer then focused their ship's sensors back on the strange quantum field of the white dwarf star and still did not understand its force-line distributions or its strange methods of propagation. Even for her, she knew it was of great concern for them, as the mass of the galaxy with the white dwarf star was much higher than any other galaxy they had ever visited or discovered. She could not figure out what was causing it. "Maybe it was the white dwarf star's immense density?" she thought.

Every hour, every minute, and every solar Earth second that passed, their ship streamed through its time warp field tunnel at the incredible speed of one hundred light years per second, cutting a path and tunnel within space-time itself. Their time warp field was creating a zero potential space-time tubular tunnel in front of their ship's gravitational field and then, just as quickly, collapsing it from behind with a negative potential energy system, causing immense forward kinetic energy gravitational momentum. It was like stretching out a rubber band, and then from behind, quickly releasing it, or in the case with the space-time domain, squeezing high-frequency vibrating water out of a pressurized tube. Traveling to Alpha Centauri at a distance of three and two-tenths light years from Earth would take only a split second within their ship's time warp field. Jack understood exactly what their time warp field was doing to his ship's gravity propulsion system. It was something that he strangely came to discover and ultimately understand back in the year 2177, less than a month after receiving his first PhD in High Energy Gravitational Mathematics from Cal Tech, at the young age of twenty. The circumstances surrounding how he came to understand the complicated time warp field technology, the required energy source methods for its propagation, and the required ship's hull curvature design would always stand as strange, the reasons why it was secretly revealed to him probably never fully understood. Who would have thought there was a secret resonance cycle that directly corresponded to the gravity element's internal vibration to allow and maintain zero point harmonic gravitational energy? That would always be a very strange revelation to him, and whoever they were did tell him to be very careful with the time warp field technology and its required energy source propagation, as they were extremely dangerous and required certain protocols to be followed. *Maybe whoever they were had secret associations with advanced alien beings?*

In the planetarium, Jack began to arouse and opened his eyes a little. The first thing he noticed was the white streams of light outside the windows and it woke him up from his favorite chair. He lifted up his arms and stretched a little, followed by yawning to gain some of his mental senses. Immediately looking at his wristwatch, it was showing 10:23 p.m. and he didn't know which reverse hundred-year cycle they were on within the time warp tunnel. Now curious, Jacobs looked up to the camera above his console with anticipation. "How many more reverse anomalies before we exit the tunnel, Jennifer?" he asked.

Jennifer knew Jack had rested his mind for six-hours, twelve-minutes. "There are three more cycles," she answered, "and about nine more hours until we exit."

Jack punched a button on the console in front of him and watched as a small door opened, exposing a glass of crystal clear water. He picked the glass up thinking about what Jennifer had said and then took a drink of the pure, highly mineralized water. "Well, I'm going back to the cockpit until then," he firmly stated.

"Okay, Jack."

Jacobs took another sip of his of the cool water and sat for a moment, wondering about the intricacies of the Stormy Way galaxy and what they might find. But he was still not able to recall a thing about it. Drinking down the rest of his water in gulps, he set his glass down and stood up from his chair. Standing for a moment, he finally walked out of the planetarium and now headed toward the cockpit, casually strolling down the hallway. While walking down the hallway, he began to think about the many rooms on their ship that had never been used, and in fact, most of them had never been entered the entire sixteen years he was lost with Jennifer. The lab on the ninth level was definitely used many times, as some of his baseline experiments for technology used on their ship were down in the lab, experiments such as their cloaking technology, new holographic imagery methods, and especially his handheld highly-advanced Positronic Transmission Electron Microscope, or PTEM, as he had called it. Jack knew both his new holographic imagery methods and his highly-advanced microscope that was eight-centimeter long, four-centimeters in diameter would have never been figured out if it weren't for time warp field technology. Who would have thought that the technology would have allowed him to use less than a thousand volts for the incident positronic-electron beam to allow deep penetration into even the higher atomic elements above 109, generating large interaction volumes as a result? Jack additionally knew that this advanced microscope was only because he was able to manipulate the two dissimilar metals inside his Positronic Electron Gun, or PEG, while inside a vacuum, and then focus a beam of both positrons and electrons at speeds that were magnitudes greater than the speed of light, resulting in not only far less required power, but magnification values much higher than what was possible with the electron microscopes of Earth's 22nd century—and without having to worry about any thermionic emission temperatures. But besides all these new advancements of his microscope and holographic imagery, he also had other strange experiments going on in the lab and one of those was using his graviton generator to try splitting the nuclear base of the *extremely heavy* burned-up gravity element that his time warp field created after so many inverse transmutation cycles. It was an element he believed to be 117, possibly 119, but could never be completely certain, even after analyzing it with his advanced microscope, because the element seemed to become reactive and would absorb all of the positrons in the beam emission, even after varying the precise focal point of the beam to the surface of the element at hundreds of times the speed of light. That was why he had to finally classify the element as indeterminable. "That experiment will always stand as strange," Jacobs said to himself, finally walking up to the cockpit entrance. "I wonder how after injecting positrons into its nuclear base it was able to briefly and semi-permanently magnetize an assortment of non-ferrous materials that should have never been magnetized?"

He finally entered the cockpit and headed straight toward his captain's chair thinking about all of those experiments he'd conducted down in his lab dealing with positronic emissions. That was because after he figured out how to strip the positronic charge off the electron, he couldn't at first figure out how to get the positronic-electron incident beam to exist at the speed of light, as it would always end up neutralizing itself. But after manipulating the beam into a faster-than-light emission, the beam propagation worked perfectly. Jack continued over toward his chair thinking about that experiment and his experiments dealing with holographic imagery. What he'd discovered about faster-than-light photon flow within weak transposed magnetic fields was actually amazing in the field of holography, but he still couldn't figure out how to break down living matter, transport it, and then reconstitute it—at least successfully. He knew there just wasn't enough time for him to actually figure out what was going wrong with the matter-transport technology, but was certain he knew where the problem resided. Jack finally sat down with a sudden feeling of contentment and leaned back in his chair. He paused with a short sigh, leaned forward, and then punched a few buttons on his forward center console to see what his ship's sensors were now telling them about the white dwarf star.

What was displayed was something that he had never expected to ever see. A strange image appeared and was now showing a new analysis of the white dwarf's gravity waves as they were being meshed and cross-correlated in a manner clearly violating all known laws of gravity, black hole stars, and any possible perturbation effects they could cause. Even with what he understood about quantum space-time curvatures, the star's gravity did not seem to conform to any of those mass-body laws. From Riemann space-time curvature theories, to Dr. Schwarzschild's model theory of the black hole, including the term "Schwarszchild radius" as it was known back in Earth's 20th century, even reverting back to those underlying theories of understanding, none of them could explain what was happening with the white dwarf star's gravitational waves.

Jack sat quietly, now harboring an unusual feeling. "No wonder you modified the formulas of the time warp tunnel ten thousand light years shorter, Jennifer," he said in wonderment.

Jennifer didn't comment or say a word.

Jacobs sat back in his chair, curious why she wasn't saying anything about the massive white dwarf star that had much too high of a mass density value, yet, it wasn't acting like a neutron or black hole star. Thinking about the way Jennifer was acting, he immediately began fastening his seat belt and shoulder harness while continuing to look at what the display showed for the white dwarf star's gravitational field, knowing what was showing could easily open up their ship's hull like a can opener and tear them apart. "I've never seen anything like that before either," he said to himself. "I wish I knew how to successfully modify the length of our time tunnel in quantum time at light year speed. I would definitely be stopping this ship much further away from the galaxy."

Jennifer continued to quietly monitor Jack's biophysical changes, both throughout his body and within his cerebellum, all as they were related to the new information about the white dwarf star she had already noticed herself. Suddenly the white streams of light outside the cockpit windows turned bright red and then back to white. Jack immediately looked at his wristwatch that showed a time of 10:04 p.m. and knew the Earth's cosmological time outside his time tunnel was now 10:04 p.m., GMT 299 AD. Continuing to sit and gaze over readings from the galaxy and the massive white dwarf star, Jacobs shook his head. "Those storm rifts also have odd readings," he said to himself. "I've never seen anything like that before. They are even stranger than the expanding and contracting gravity waves, almost as if the gravity waves inside the rifts are being shredded apart in different directions….appearing to be worse than any black hole could possibly be or ever imagined…"

Now continuing to wait, time seemed to be getting longer and longer as Jack's concern about the white dwarf star increased. He wasn't sure whether or not the extreme density of the galaxy would immediately exert a pull on his ship after they exited their time warp field tunnel, but had to figure it might, especially if its movement was away from his point of reference. All he could do was hope the galaxy's torsion forces on his ship's hull wouldn't approach any maximum limits. That would immediately put them into a serious situation. His anticipation of them finally exiting the almost fifteen million light year long time warp tunnel was now starting to run even higher. Suddenly, the streams of light outside his cockpit windows turned red and then back to white. Jack again checked his wristwatch and it showed 10:08 p.m. He knew there was now five hours and twenty-three minutes before they exited their time warp tunnel. Continuing to wait patiently for the last hundred-year reversal of space-time, Jacobs had an extremely bad feeling inside about what his ship's sensors were still showing him about the white dwarf star's gravitational field. "Strange," he said to himself, also wondering how they were going to ever go about analyzing the white dwarf star if they successfully escape its gravitational pull. He had no idea in his mind how to modify their time warp field for what was happening with the dwarf star's field of quantum gravity mechanics. It actually appeared to be causing a double-shift of space and time and surely had something to do with the visible red and blue shifts.

Jack began watching outside his windows in anticipation of the coming hundred-year reversal of space-time outside their time warp field tunnel. Now staring at the white streams of light and daydreaming about the dwarf star, he wondered why this particular star was so much different—almost as if it was an aberration to the universe—an aberration to science—an aberration to his understanding. Suddenly, his senses were grabbed after seeing another red shift in light, and knew their time tunnel was shifted backwards once again for what should have been the last time inside the extended tunnel. They would be exiting the time tunnel in one hour and forty-seven minutes.

Their ship's GMT clock Jennifer updated after the last shift of space-time showed a time of 10:12 p.m. and a year 99 AD. Jacobs noticed his ship's new Earth GMT and then glanced at his wristwatch that showed a time of 10:12 p.m., except he knew it was still for a year of 2199 AD—his true plane of existence. There was now a twenty-one hundred year difference between solar time on Earth and the time on his ship, and close to one hour and forty-eight minutes before the next hundred-year reversal. Jack could only sit quietly as the time inside their time warp tunnel approached midnight ever so close. The midnight hour inside their time tunnel, if ever reached, surely meant the end of his life.

7

THE WHITE DWARF STAR

JACK REALIZED THEY SHOULD BE coming out of their extended 14,898,000 light-year long time warp tunnel at any moment, a tunnel that started almost forty-two hours before back in the Milky Way galaxy. "We should be coming out of our time warp tunnel anytime, Jennifer," he remarked, his voice uneasy.

Jennifer immediately noted the change in Jack's voice. "Yes, and I'm starting to sense a slight harmonic distortion between your watch and the ship's gravity field, Jack," she replied.

Jack heard this with additional concern, knowing the extreme density of the dwarf star and the galaxy was causing it, acting like a large well of gravity—a well of energy—a well of unusual activity to the domain of both space and time. He continued watching the white streams of light above his head, daydreaming, wondering, and not knowing for sure what might happen when they finally exited out of their extended time tunnel. Jacobs took a deep breath and then exhaled knowing they were about to exit their time tunnel and encounter the dense gravity field of the white dwarf star and its galaxy.

Suddenly, before his eyes the white streams of light vanished and they finally exited their extended time tunnel. Dark matter space showed all around their spaceship. The Stormy Way galaxy was noticed off in the distance, nearly ten thousand light years away, and looked to be an odd-shaped galaxy. Jacobs began thinking about Earth and its current timeline of history, when all of a sudden he felt their spaceship reversing its course.

He grabbed the armrests of his captain's chair. "What's going on?" he said to himself. "What I'm seeing now and feeling should never be happening."

"Jennifer?" he asked with an unusual surprise. "What's going on?"

Jennifer remained quiet.

Jacobs was caught off guard by her silence and watched the gravity propulsion speed of their ship increase, all while continuing to feel the backwards movement of their spaceship as it traveled further away from the galaxy. Five thousand kilometers per hour, he noticed, 10,000 kilometers, 20,000 kilometers, 40,000 kilometers, 80,000 kilometers, 160,000 kilometers, 320,000 kilometers per hour and climbing!

"Jennifer?" he asked with a resolute concern. "What's going on?"

Jacobs sat in his captain's chair in wonderment, feeling his shoulder harness tightening against his chest, and he began to feel dizzy and lightheaded. Suddenly, outer space turned black around their ship, noticeable directly outside his cockpit windows and inside the dark matter space. He supposed that Jennifer must have applied a time warp field to their spaceship's gravity propulsion drive. White streams of light immediately appeared inside their time warp tunnel, but this time they were traveling away from his ship and his point of view. He no longer felt any acceleration or backwards movement as they traveled farther away from the galaxy. Jacobs regained his full senses and began watching the streams of white light continuing to move away from the front of their ship.

"What the… Jennifer, why did we go into a reverse time warp field tunnel all of a sudden?"

"I have to get us out of the gravitational field of that white dwarf star," she replied. "Its gravitational field was destabilizing our gravity propulsion system and our inertial dampers were starting to fail. I couldn't correct it with gravity propulsion, so I had to reverse our course inside a modified time warp field tunnel."

Jacobs was slightly puzzled over what she had said and continued to watch the white streams of light move away from his point of view, all as their spaceship traveled backwards inside their time warp tunnel. Glancing at his wristwatch, he noticed the time was moving backwards accordingly and appropriately to the gravitational field of their ship. "That makes complete sense," he said to himself, even though he truly didn't believe it was happening or could ever happen, as it would mean that he was continuously aging younger.

Watching in amazement as the time on his wristwatch continued to move backwards and also knowing that an hundred-year reversal of space-time was scheduled to occur, Jacobs stared intensely at the white streams of light above his head that were still moving away from his ship. Suddenly, the streams of light outside the windows turned blue for one second and then back to white.

"What? What happened there?" Jacobs said to himself.

"Jennifer?" he asked with unusual curiosity. "Did our time warp tunnel just shift forward?"

"Yes, it did," she answered. "Another reverse hundred-year gravity distortion from that anomaly just occurred."

Jacobs glanced at his wristwatch—10:07 p.m. He immediately recognized that both his watch and their ship's gravity propulsion system moved four-minutes away from the midnight hour instead of moving closer to midnight by four minutes, as it should have done.

"That is really strange," Jack said to himself, continuing to think about what he just saw and witnessed. He knew his wristwatch would have showed 10:16 p.m. if they would have been traveling inside a normal time warp field tunnel when the last reversal occurred. "The harmonics of that hundred-year anomaly must have pulsated backwards on itself," Jacobs thought to himself, and now wondered if Jennifer *did* know something after all.

Jacobs sat quietly, continuing to watch the white streams of light move away from their ship, knowing they were still moving backwards inside their time warp tunnel. His wristwatch was also still moving backwards and a realization came to his mind. "Hmmm," he mused, "the anomaly generating the space-time reversals probably won't recognize the amount of time we've reversed our course. It didn't recognize the solo minute we spent in the reverse time warp field. So—"

Continuing to watch the white streams of light move away from their ship and his point of view, Jacobs thought again back to Earth's current history and an event came to mind that would forever shape all societies on Earth. "Now that is a strange thought," he said to himself. "So would that mean that the birth of Christ hasn't happened yet?"

Jack noticed the white streams of light vanish before his eyes and it grabbed his senses. Dark matter space immediately became visible outside the cockpit windows and all around their ship. The large helically shaped Stormy Way galaxy was clearly visible in the distance. Jack checked their ship's sensors and for what was being displayed in front of him. It showed that their ship had moved almost forty eight thousand light years farther away from the galaxy. His wristwatch also showed a time of 10:00 p.m. and the year of 2199. He looked back out his cockpit windows again to see the galaxy in the distance. Jack thought it strange that he could physically view the galaxy with his own eyes, but then again they were only 58,000 light years away from a large galaxy that had to be nearly one million light-years in size. The galaxy looked unusual with its helical shape and bright dome showing near its center. But then where the White Dwarf star was believed to be located there was a much brighter dome with white circular streams of light attached to it. There was definitely a tug of war evident inside the galaxy between the black hole star at the galaxy's center versus the massive white dwarf near the galaxy's edge—the two forces seemingly causing the galaxy to flatten out into its current spiral helical shape.

Jack took a short breath. "What's going on, Jennifer?" he asked with a slight jump in his heart.

Jennifer sensed Jack's increased breathing and that his heart had increased. "I repositioned our ship out of the gravitational effects and constraints of that white dwarf star so that we were not pulled into it and destroyed," she answered.

"Why, what happened?" Jack asked.

"Its strange gravitational waves were starting to destabilize our spaceship's gravity element," Jennifer said.

Jack sat quietly thinking about what she had just said to him, not understanding how that was possible for the dwarf star's gravity field to do that. "What do you mean by that?" he asked again in confusion, "How can its gravitational field possibly be stretched that far into space?"

"I don't know, Jack. I'll have to analyze it some more."

"Okay, make it your priority," Jack said.

Jacobs noticed on his forward center display that their ship's gravity propulsion speed was now zero. He inferred that Jennifer must have finally shut off the spaceship's main gravity drive. They now sat completely motionless inside the dark matter between the galaxies in what he supposed were now a cosmological universe that conformed to an Earth solar year of BC 01.

"Jennifer?" he said.

"Yes, Jack."

"How much time did we spend in our reverse time warp field?"

"Eight minutes," she answered.

Jack thought again about the eight minutes his wristwatch had gone backwards, knowing it was not truly correct anymore in relation to the space-time domain and configuration of the cosmos for an exact Earth solar year of BC 01. He knew their actual time was off by eight minutes and that they had truly gone back in time in relation to their own reference. His physical body and Jennifer's organic configuration were also surely eight-minutes younger, but Jack didn't feel he'd lost any memories. "What I want you to do, Jennifer," he finally said, "is to adjust the harmonic cycles of our ship's gravity propulsion system forward eight minutes, so that my harmonic motion wristwatch will also be eight minutes forward."

"Why, Jack?" she asked, concerned.

"Because," he firmly replied. "The anomaly generating the space-time distortions won't recognize the eight minutes we spent inside our reverse time warp field, and I don't want to get mixed up on the true time line of our Earth and its universe."

Jennifer analyzed what Jack had told her, as it did make sense because she knew like before that their cellular and molecular structures had actually physically gone backwards inside the time tunnel while they traveled away from the galaxy. "Okay. I think I understand," she replied, and began adjusting the harmonic cycles of their ship's gravity propulsion system forward eight Earth solar minutes.

Jacobs patiently and calmly waited for her adjustments and noticed the instrument panels and lights inside their spaceship momentarily black out. There was also no gravity, and Jacobs felt weightlessness for a few moments, followed by his body feeling warm inside. The lights in the cockpit suddenly came back on and his body no longer felt warm. "That was strange," he said, and looked at his wristwatch. It now showed a time of 10:09 p.m. and Jack realized his watch had instantly moved eight minutes forward to match the new harmonics of their spaceship's gravity field. He had no idea why his body felt warm all of a sudden, and didn't bother asking Jennifer.

"Well, at least the two times are correct again in relation to each other," he said to himself.

Jacobs put that thought out of his mind and began thinking about the strange gravitational field of the white dwarf star, and especially the anomaly that was surely located on the other side deeper into the galaxy. Why the anomaly would be located on the other side of an extremely dense rotating white dwarf star whose density was beyond what was conceivable, he had no idea. He had to look down at his forward center display again and did not understand the readings their ship's sensors were telling him regarding the galaxy, even after manipulating their gravitational lensing method and moving the Great Circle Displacement tangent line to a new space-time shift. Strangely, his display did seem to indicate that the white dwarf star was shifting the galaxy on one end, even overcoming the effects and forces of the black hole star at the galaxy's center. Jacobs could only shake his head with increased curiosity for Jennifer's observations, knowing the dwarf star's mass could possibly exceed the mass of the entire rest of the galaxy and be causing its helical shape. He finally asked, "Can you figure out the size and mass of the star, Jennifer?"

"Yes, I can," she answered, "already verified. It has a diameter of 71,500 kilometers and has a mass of 2.0891×10^{33} kilograms."

"What?" Jack said surprised. "That dwarf star must have a solid core then! How can its mass ever be that high?"

"It is strange," Jennifer said again. "I don't know how it's possible, either."

Jack sat back in his chair, knowing that according to the Chandrasekhar limit set in 1930, dwarf stars should be no more than 1.44 times the mass of their sun back home, as electron degeneracy and compression should have collapsed it into a black hole singularity, but it clearly was not a black hole. He also knew according to his calculations and what was displayed on his center forward display, that the strange white dwarf star not only exceeded the binding fraction, but it had a mass value that was exactly 729 times greater than the Chandrasekhar limit. Jack knew this strange value of 729 meant something, but could not understand how it was ever possible for the dwarf star's electrons to be packed so tightly. "I wonder how it is ever possible?" he asked himself, "and what does the value 729 have to do with quantum mechanical space? What might it also have to do with the πr^3 hyperbolic time warp field functions? Better yet, what might it have to do with the empirical electropi limit values set forth in the laws of quantum molecular chemistry?"

He continued to think about the strange number and its possible relationship to his spaceship's carbon nanotube computer technology and finally put it out of his mind, especially after seeing on his forward display that the calculated dwarf star's initial size would have had to have been larger than the entire sun's solar system back home, for it ever to compress down to a quantum mechanical size about half the size of the planet Jupiter. That just didn't seem possible, so some underlying principle was going on that didn't make any sense. *Maybe its strange rotation also had something to do with its extreme density?*

Jacobs now knew the dwarf star was even stranger than what he first thought—much stranger than the Black Neutron star they encountered years before. "So how wide is the Stormy Way galaxy by your sensors, Jennifer?" he asked.

"It is approximately one million, one hundred eighty thousand light years in elliptical spherical shape," she replied.

Jack didn't like her answer. "How far away do you believe the time anomaly to be?" he again asked.

She answered, "According to the resultant field strengths taken back in the Milky Way galaxy to our current position, I believe it is on the other side of the Stormy Way galaxy and around six hundred ten thousand light years away. I might add that it is also outside the effects of the dwarf star's gravitational field and its storm rifts."

Jack thought about Jennifer's comment, realizing that was definitely some good news. However, the dwarf star directly in their path was surely a problem for them. After looking down at his display one more time and for what their ship's sensors were telling them about the white dwarf's storm rifts, it was clearly showing the storms destroying all matter and space. "This isn't looking good," he said to himself, but then wondered about the storm's actual characteristics and asked, "Is it possible for us to time warp through the storm rifts?"

"I don't believe so," she answered with concern. "There appears to be highly projectional gravitational time waves inside the rifts and of an unknown order. They would immediately distort our time warp tunnel, collapse it, and then we would be destroyed."

Jack believed that to also be the case. "That makes complete sense," he said to himself, but still did not understand how it was possible to have what would be called highly projectional time waves associated with gravity. This is because it would seem to indicate that a new speed of light compression force was trying to be created. It caused him to become extremely curious about the rifts. "Why or how are there projectional gravitational waves inside the rifts?" he asked.

"I don't know for sure, Jack," Jennifer answered. "It should not be possible by any known laws. Our ship's sensors also show the white dwarf star's gravitational field has been modified."

"What?" Jack said surprised. "How in the world did that happen?"

"I don't know," she answered again. "But the ship's sensors do show that the dwarf star is rotating around its own compressed gravitational field at exactly fifty times per second. That's why there is violent storm rifts associated with the highly projectional gravitational waves."

Jack was amazed to hear this, knowing the dwarf star was accomplishing something that was not normally possible, especially for the amount of mass density it contained. He also knew it was spinning around its circumference and not around its axis like a neutron star would do. That would make the dwarf star's size appear twice as big as its diameter. "So what can you determine about the white dwarf star's gravitational field?" he asked her.

"What I can find out so far, Jack," she replied, "is that its intense magnetic and gravitational field extends the length of the galaxy on the northeastern half down to the southeastern half and is around one million, two hundred thousand light years in length. It also extends out in our direction about forty thousand light years and is about two hundred ninety thousand light years wide in the middle, less toward its northern and southern ends."

Jack was surprised again by her response. "That gravitational field is outside the galaxy," he said to himself. "What is going on here? No gravitational field of any star should be able to extend beyond the boundaries of its own galaxy! Its gravity waves should have been degenerated by the dark matter space…Not only that but the super-massive black hole in the middle of the galaxy should have never allowed it."

Jacobs began pressing a series of buttons on his center forward touch-activated display. After seeing what his ship's sensors were now telling him and thinking about what Jennifer had already told him, he noticed the magnetic dipole field of the star had definitely shifted to its surface, leaving the star with no true spherical axis. The entire mass of the dwarf star was rotating around its magnetic field and was bending the magnetic field in the shape of an arched half circle. He also further realized that the compression forces at the very center of its magnetic dipole field were seemingly immeasurable, creating a continuous stream of immense x-ray expulsions from out of the top and bottom, just like a neutron star, yet, the x-ray energies being emitted were surely trillions upon trillions of times higher than the total energy output of their sun back in the Milky Way. "Maybe that is how it's overcoming the electron degeneracy pressures?" Jacobs thought, "Hmmm…."

He continued thinking about that, knowing anything in the universe that was in a direct path and inline with the x-ray emissions would surely be instantly vaporized, because the emissions would also be cutting a path of curved rotational energy. It would be similar to what a huge large lightning bolt would do when vaporizing and ionizing air molecules in the atmosphere of a planet, he thought, and then creating a force density vacuum afterwards. Jack now wondered how far the immense x-rays might travel through the universe, essentially whether they might travel to the edges and reaches of its own existence, its own formulation of space and time. But then even stranger to him than the x-ray emissions were the storm rifts the dwarf star was generating, and like before, he knew the rifts were destroying all space and matter, possibly creating a large field of anti-matter. That would explain why all objects entering the field would explode and be instantly vaporized, just as Jennifer had told him. This possibility only raised his level of interest, as they had never encountered a natural occurring area of space containing only anti-matter. "So how far do the storm rifts extend, Jennifer?" he asked with even more curiosity.

Jennifer paused, after sensing Jack's immense interest. "They appear to extend up and down directly in front of us, Jack," she replied, "and around two hundred thousand light years, elliptically, in both the northern and southern directions from the dwarf star."

This new information was intriguing to Jacobs and had his mind racing again. "Can we time-warp jump through the gravitational field of the white dwarf star and be okay?"

"Yes, we can," she replied with noticeable concern in her voice. "But we can't come out of the time warp tunnel while inside the white dwarf star's gravitational field, or it would immediately destabilize our gravity propulsion system and we would be destroyed."

Jack clearly recognized the concern in her voice. "I understand, Jennifer," he said.

Jacobs wondered again about the strange white dwarf star that was producing violent storm rifts, had a mass value exceeding known limits, and having an unusual gravitational field stretching both into and out of the galaxy to unbelievable distances. He knew its strange gravity field was somewhat understandable, knowing it was rotating around its compressed gravitational field and having no true axis, but then he could not see how it was ever possible for it to move its own quantum mass in and out of its magnetic field so quickly. It would definitely be creating unusual quantum magnetic vectors, much different than what a neutron star would project.

Jacobs put that information out of his mind, knowing they had to get around the dwarf star's gravitational field and its resultant storm rifts in the most efficient manner in order to save his ship's precious Gaussian energy. "Let's see," he finally said out loud to himself.

"If I were to use two straight time warp field tunnels, the first one would have to be almost three hundred thousand light years straight down from our position just to be able to jump under the storm rifts of the dwarf star. And that would only to be able to line up with the other side of the galaxy and the origin of the anomaly. But then that tunnel would cause my next time warp tunnel to be even longer than the first. It would get me on the other side of the galaxy, but we'd be losing valuable time, not to mention using additional energy reserves of my spaceship's gravity propulsion system for each time warp jump."

Looking at his ship's energy reserves now displayed on his forward center display, he saw a surprising sixty-nine percent efficiency. He knew the unusual reverse time-warp field jump Jennifer had just accomplished was very taxing on their ship's energy reserves. Of course if they hadn't accomplished the reverse time warp field jump, the white dwarf star's gravitational field would have destroyed them.

"I'm going to the planetarium to think about this, Jennifer," Jack said.

"Okay, I understand."

Jack unfastened his seat belt and shoulder harness and immediately stood up from out of his captain's chair. He headed toward the exit and left the cockpit without hesitation. While walking down the hallway and still thinking about the white dwarf star, he had to glance out the windows into outer space. Outer space looked different when inside the dark matter between the galaxies, he knew, and showed a musty black look, but strangely was not entirely pitch black. There were strange etchings of white light, photons, showing inside and throughout the dark matter Jack knew had no place to go or dissipate under the constraints of gravitational forces. This is what he and Jennifer had also determined was happening many years before, at least according to the gravity law compression forces between galaxies they had derived. It was also a very familiar sight, as they did have to jump into the dark matter a few times while galaxy-hopping the last sixteen years. This was because some of the galaxies were farther away than they were willing to jump to at the time, a square median distance they had set of one hundred thirty thousand light years. It was also a distance ratio they determined existed between most galaxies and stellar formations in the universe.

Jack finally arrived at the planetarium entrance and noticed the waterfall right away, as there was a light mist of moisture in the air that was soothing to his senses. He walked inside and took a seat in his favorite chair by the waterfall, wondering how they were ever going to get to the other side of the galaxy and beyond the white dwarf star, avoiding both its gravitational field and its violent anti-matter storm rifts. "Okay," he finally said to himself. "We're nearly sixty thousand light years from the galaxy, the storm rifts from the dwarf star extend up and down elliptically around two hundred thousand light years in both directions, and its gravitational field is two hundred ninety thousand light years wide. That's the horizontal gravity space and vertical storm rift paradox parameters I must overcome." Jack paused while thinking about that, knowing he also needed the star's vertical gravity paradox parameter and continued on in his thoughts, "The star's intense magnetic field is also elliptical, one million two hundred thousand light years tall and the time anomaly is around six hundred ten thousand light years away. How do I ever defeat this white dwarf star's gravitational field and its storm rifts to get to the other side alive?"

Jack continued to ponder the white dwarf star's attributes and its paradox parameters. "Let's see," he said under his breath, "what if I can come up with something that will allow a half circle time warp field tunnel in order to go under the white dwarf star's storm rifts, but then also travel through its gravitational field in the same time warp field tunnel? Hmmm..."

Continuing to think about how to complete a half circle time warp field tunnel both around and under the storm rifts, but through the dwarf star's gravitational field, an answer finally came to his mind. Jack began thinking about three straight end to end time warp field tunnels that would be positioned on the lower half of an imaginary sphere, forming half of a hexagon. He immediately became excited at the prospect of what he had just thought of. "I think I've come up with a way to do it!" he said to himself, with more excitement. "This definitely has never been contemplated, and of course, I'm not even sure the time warp field tunnel will even hold up to the space-time curvature pressures, especially at the ninety degree tangent function."

Looking at his watch, it showed a time of 10:35 p.m. "Well, doesn't matter," he said again. "As I can't waste anymore time. I've got to try and modify the formulas in time before the next hundred-year reversal of space-time."

The waterfall and the water splashing into the pool below was a relaxing sight for Jack, as it caused his heart to palpitate heavily for a few seconds. But then this palpitation was also because he knew that in attempting a curved time warp tunnel, it would possibly cause strange new events to science never envisioned, events leading to the origins of the universe. As he continued watching the waterfall push water in the pool out of its way, the sound was not only very intriguing to his ears, but what he was seeing became intriguing to his thoughts. "Hmmm," he said to himself, "now that's a interesting thought, especially as far as pushing gravity out in a formed curvature path to form a continuous harmonically bridged envelope."

After staring at the waterfall for a few more minutes, Jack's anticipation rose to the prospect of what he had just come up with. He immediately grabbed his notebook again and opened it up to a blank page, believing his time warp field equations had to be modified in a manner to curve their ship's gravity field through space, all while their ship moved inside the time tunnel. It would curve them in a manner that his time warp field would still conform to and take into account the normal curvature of both space and time in relation to the speed of light.

Pausing with a pen in his right hand, he looked back down at his notebook and began writing down the mathematical concepts of his curved time warp field tunnel. "Let's see now," he said to himself, "If I were to take three straight time-warp field tunnels and put them end to end inside a half sphere, then that would make the first leg and my starting position the equator of the sphere. From the equator, the first time tunnel would have to travel down at a sixty degree angle. The second time tunnel from this sixty-degree point on the imaginary sphere's surface would then have to travel directly above the South Pole and continue another thirty degrees past the South Pole to one-hundred and twenty degrees away from my starting position. The third time tunnel would have to start at this one hundred and twenty degree point on the sphere's surface and travel back up to the equator again at another sixty degree angle to exactly one-hundred and eighty degrees away from my starting position." Jack paused in his thoughts and added, "And all that would be just to get around the white dwarf star's gravitational field in a half circle. I definitely can't come out of either of the first two time tunnels or the gravity field of the star would destabilize my ship's gravity propulsion system, leading to us being destroyed."

Jacobs continued his time warp field curvature equations for another thirty minutes more, trying to figure out how to cross the ninety degree tangent limit at the south pole of the sphere within his surface subtension equations. He had to glance at his watch. It showed 11:20 p.m.—forty minutes before they had to take another time warp jump. If his modified equations weren't finished in time, they would have to make another short time warp jump farther away from the galaxy and somewhere deeper into dark matter space. Jacobs suddenly looked up and began staring at the waterfall. "I've got it!" he exclaimed excitedly.

"Jennifer?" he asked with additional excitement.

"Yes, Jack," she replied, noting Jack's extra excitement in his voice.

"I know how to get around the white dwarf star with one time warp jump."

"How?" she asked.

Jack paused for a moment. "I'm going to enter the basic equations into the computer console here in the planetarium as I explain it to you. Okay?"

"Okay," she said. "I'm listening."

Jacobs smiled to her reply, realizing the anticipation in her voice. "Okay, thirty-six thousand light years directly below our position, I want you to mathematically create a three hundred sixty-thousand light-year-diameter imaginary sphere that extends directly into the Stormy Way galaxy toward the anomaly. The white dwarf star will be fairly close to the center of this sphere, but in the northern hemisphere farthest from us."

"Okay," she said.

Jack paused to her interest and he continued on, "The center of the storm rifts will also be fairly close to this same hemisphere. First, we have to apply our time warp field equations to the sphere to create a hundred-light-year-per-second time base for the sphere. After doing this, I want you to start with zero degrees being the equator of this sphere and parallel thirty-six thousand light years directly below our position. At this zero degrees equator position on the sphere's surface, subtend the sphere directly down at sixty degrees where it will be thirty degrees away from the South Pole.

"From this sixty degrees position, I want you to subtend the steradian again to one hundred and twenty degrees from our starting position, a subtended line that will also travel above and directly over the South Pole. From this one hundred and twenty degree point on the sphere's surface, subtend another line back up to the equator that will be one hundred and eighty degrees away. Be sure to use the time warp field arc angles of the four-minute cycle as you subtend each of them. From the harmonics of these time warp field arc angles, accomplish parabolic functions of the South Pole spherical polar coordinates in relation to our equatorial position, at thirty degrees, the South Pole ninety degree position, and then one hundred and fifty degrees."

"I will," she said.

"Good. Make sure the wave functions at the thirty and one hundred and twenty degree positions are moving counterclockwise in relation to the South Pole of the sphere. For the ninety degree South Pole parabolic function, I want you to create a North Pole counterclockwise inverted wave function. Do you understand all of this,

Jennifer?"

Jennifer paused, thinking about the South Pole ninety degree parabolic function Jack wanted her to create in relation to the North Pole, as it was an inverted wave function in order to get by the South Pole ninety degree tangent limit. "Yes, I do," she answered.

"Great," he said and continued on, "Once you have created these new wave functions according to what I've told you, I want you to apply them to our time warp field equations and *circular mesh* the ends of the three time tunnels together so that they become one parabolic function and subtension, matching the radius of the steradian for a full one hundred and eighty degrees of harmonic rotation." Jack paused again and thought about what he had just explained to her. "Are you still with me on this, Jennifer?"

"Yes, I am," she answered again.

"Okay," Jack continued without hesitation. "Taking all of this into account, then everything I've told you should convert into a perfect half-circle time warp field tunnel having a hundred light years per second of travel. It should also allow us to travel around and under the storm rifts of the white dwarf star in one time warp jump, including traveling through the dwarf star's gravitational field to the other side of the galaxy for our next trek toward the anomaly. To make our transition out of the curved time warp field tunnel a little easier, add an additional straight thirty-six thousand light year time warp tunnel at the end of the curved tunnel, which would extend straight upwards to a point in space that matches our exact elevation position where we currently sit. It will be as though we traveled straight over there."

Jennifer quietly analyzed everything Jack had been saying to her and what he entered into the touch screen display on the console. Jacobs sat quietly waiting for her to check his time warp field curvature math and for her to look at the new time warp field equations as they would be applied to the gravity propulsion system of their ship.

"Okay, Jack," she finally said after a few minutes. "I understand. Are you sure our time warp field tunnel can take the additional warp stress?"

"I believe so, but I'm not certain," Jack replied. "We have no choice but to try, Jennifer. We don't have enough time left *not* to try. It will also save additional drains on our ship's energy system by not taking additional time warp jumps, especially with no gravitational fields from any planets with the correct dipole polarities to recharge it."

"I understand," she said again, knowing Jack was right. "I'll start the rest of the new time warp field curvature equations right now."

"Thank you, Jennifer." Jack sat alone in the planetarium and wiped his brow with his right hand, now wondering if they would have a future, especially since the usage of a curved time warp tunnel had never been considered before. He knew all of his new time warp field subtension equations he had just created were quite advanced. They had actually caused his eyebrows to perspire, yet, he knew his mental alertness and faculties were still one-hundred percent intact. Jacobs took a deep breath and exhaled. "This will be an interesting sight to behold," he said to himself.

"Jennifer?"

"Yes, Jack."

"I'm coming back to the cockpit to wait."

"Okay. I'll see you there," she said softly.

Jack smiled at Jennifer's continual sincerity and to her soft voice, even while knowing that what they were about to attempt was extremely dangerous and might never work.

Jennifer sensed Jack's increased excitement as he stood up from out of his chair. Walking out of the planetarium, he stopped in the hallway for a brief moment, thinking about the curved time warp tunnel, wondering if their ship would indeed survive the additional time warp field stresses that would be encountered at the South Pole tangent function. This was especially true, as they were already traveling at the upper limit of space travel, a speed of one hundred light years per second. "I wonder what will happen if we were to exceed the upper limit?" he asked himself.

Finally proceeding on down the hallway and toward the cockpit, Jacobs continued to think about the curved time-warp tunnel, realizing that the arc angles within the subtension should momentarily flip-flop when reaching the ninety-degree tangent point of the half circle. This was especially true because of his new Gaussian-Cartesian mathematical conventions that used an eight-domain spherical space reference within four zero planes, all which now had to be modified in an unconventional method. "Hmmm," he said, "I wonder how that will truly end up affecting our time tunnel and cause it to come under stress."

Jennifer quietly listened to Jacobs talking out loud to himself as he walked down the hallway and approached closer to the cockpit entrance. Finally walking into the cockpit, he immediately headed over to his captain's chair and calmly took a seat. "How are you doing on the modified formulas, Jennifer?" he asked.

"Getting close, Jack," she answered.

Jacobs's anticipation rose even more, knowing they were about to attempt a first, something that had probably never been contemplated by any advanced race having time warp field technology, at least not at the upper limit of space travel. Looking at his watch again it showed a time of 11:40 p.m.

"I'm done with the modified equations, Jack," she calmly said.

Jack raised his eyebrows and was surprised how fast she had calculated the new displacement formulas. "Okay," he replied, "and be sure to apply the formulas exactly one second before midnight."

"Okay," she softly said. "I'll reposition our ship down ninety degrees about twenty seconds beforehand."

"Okay, Jennifer."

Jack thought about what might be visualized inside their curved time warp tunnel as their ship traveled down the straight 36,000 light-year-long tunnel and into the curl, completing the one hundred eighty degrees of rotation. It would surely look the same as a normal curved time-warp field tunnel, but could not be, as the white streams of light would have to be bent against normal space curvature.

The ninety degree tangent point and function would also have to change and modify their ship's time warp field and its gravity field immensely for it to ever be overcome. "That will be interesting," he said to himself.

Jack punched a series of six buttons on his center forward display and began looking over Jennifer's modified time warp field equations. They showed the first turn into the loop at zero-degrees and the equator of the imaginary sphere was when they would enter the curved time warp tunnel. This passage into the curved time warp tunnel would also occur exactly six minutes after traveling down the mathematically created straight time warp tunnel directly below them. When finally inside the curved time warp tunnel and curving around the sphere, the second noticeable change in their time warp field would be at ninety degrees, the sphere's South Pole, and it would occur quicker than normal. Surely, strange events to science would also show itself right before the South Pole ninety-degree point on the sphere, he figured, and also once again before escaping the gravitational forces that would be encountered for the ninety-degree South Pole tangent-line function. The last change in their curved time warp tunnel around the surface of the imaginary sphere, one hundred eighty degrees away, would then occur more slowly. Four minutes after passing the one hundred and eighty degree equator point and traveling out of the curved time tunnel into the last 36,000 light-year-long straight tunnel, another hundred-year reversal should occur, causing no ill effects to them. After this new reversal of space-time, they would be only two minutes away from exiting the straight thirty-six thousand light-year-long time tunnel. Outer space would then be visible again.

"Looks pretty good," Jack said to himself while glancing at his wristwatch. It showed a time of 11:57 p.m., fifty-eight seconds and counting. "I wonder how our time will truly be affected inside this new time warp tunnel?" he asked himself. "If it works as predicted and theoretically possible, there should be a noticeable change of our ship's gravity propulsion system speeding up toward infinity when approaching the sphere's South Pole tangent line function. After passing the ninety-degree mark, my watch and the ship's gravity propulsion system should start to slow down again after traveling away in rotation from the South Pole and continue to slow until the tangent function is finally overcome." He rubbed his eyes. "I hope this ship can withstand the time warp stresses of that event. If it can't, well, we're dead anyway. I can't wait to see how all this works out."

Jack paused while opening his eyes and began staring at one of the cameras. "How about it, Jennifer, are you ready for our curved time warp tunnel?"

No comment from her was forthcoming.

8

THE CURVED TIME WARP
TUNNEL FEAT

JACOBS GLANCED AT THE TIME on his watch—11:59 p.m.,
forty seconds and counting. Jennifer started repositioning their ship
down at a ninety-degree angle in relation to the Stormy Way galaxy, as
they noticed the galaxy changing its position through the cockpit windows. Jack's heartbeat sped up slightly again, knowing they were getting ready to enter the first thirty-six thousand light-year-long time
warp tunnel that also had a mathematically-created, curved time tunnel directly below it.   What was going to actually happen was
unknown, even to Jack Jacobs…master of the improbable calculation.
He only had speculations in his mind of what could happen, and certainly not would happen.

Suddenly, dark matter space turned black and darker around
their spaceship, noticeable through the cockpit windows, as Jennifer

applied the time warp field to their spaceship's gravity propulsion system. Just as quickly, white streams of light began appearing inside their tunnel and passing by the windows toward the back end of their spaceship. It was one Earth second later when the streams of light turned red and then back to white. "There's our hundred-year reversal," Jack said to himself. "Another four minutes closer to midnight. I never dreamed four minutes of my life would be so valuable."

Glancing at his wristwatch again, it showed a time of 10:12 p.m., with an Earth year of 2199. Looking over at the ship's GMT clock that Jennifer had just updated, it showed 10:12 p.m. with an Earth year of 101 BC, the actual time and year of the cosmological universe. Jacobs thought about the two times, realizing there was now a twenty-three hundred year difference. The time on his watch was correct for him and Jennifer for their plane of existence, and the time shown on the atomic clock referenced inside their ship was correct for the rest of the universe. He truly did not and could not know with a complete surety what plane of existence was correct, but suspected that it was probably his ship and everything inside, organic and inorganic.

Glancing out his windows again and watching the white streams of light pass by, Jacobs thought about their new time tunnel that had a one hundred eighty degree half circle time warp field mathematically created on the surface of an imaginary sphere. He knew it would also be using changing curvilinear vectors within the subtension equations in order for their ship to not shoot off the imaginary sphere's surface like a rock skipping across water. This fact made him realize that the streams of light outside the cockpit windows would look straight when inside their time warp tunnel, but in reality he knew they would actually be curved and conforming to their new time warp field subtension laws. "What a strange thought," he said to himself. "To know that light can actually be bent by a curved time warp field tunnel similar in nature to what a black hole star would be doing. That is a most amazing realization."

Jacobs continued to sit quietly contemplating this, knowing he and Jennifer were poised to possibly meet an eternal death from a curved time warp field tunnel that, once they had entered, could not be changed or stopped. It would have to be ridden out to the very end. Glancing at his wristwatch, he noticed by the time showing that the first turn into the half-circle loop should occur at 10:16 p.m. and mumbled under his breath, "The first change in the time warp tunnel that will put us in the loop at the equator should occur about 10:16."

Jennifer remained quiet and listened to everything Jack was saying. She sensed his slightly increased heart rate and tried to understand what was causing it to speed up in relation to his body's negative feedback system via baroreceptors in the arch of his aorta, but she couldn't figure it out. She could now only continue analyzing these unusual electrical signals from his central brainstem to his heart, including the amount of stretch in his arterial walls. She found them not to be normal in relation to Jack's mental calmness, but then their curved time warp tunnel was not normal either.

Jacobs continued watching the white streams of light pass by his cockpit windows and he had to glance at his wristwatch again. It showed a time of 10:15 p.m., fifty seconds and counting. "In ten seconds we're going to make our first turn into the curved time warp tunnel, Jennifer," he said.

"Yes, I know," she replied. "I'm watching it too. I must say that I've enjoyed knowing you, Jack, especially over the last sixteen years, even with the possible end of our future together in a few seconds."

Jack smiled at Jennifer's method of contemplating death. "Yes, you may say that," he replied.

While the white streams of light continued passing by the cockpit windows of their ship, Jacobs noticed the light outside the windows turn red momentarily and then back to white. He realized their ship's time warp field had momentarily shifted space in his direction, similar to what the anomaly was causing to space, but then his spaceship's manipulation was surely infinitesimally small compared to the anomaly's magnitude of space manipulation. "There was our first turn at zero degrees, Jennifer," he commented. "We're now in the loop."

Jennifer remained quiet after hearing this and continued to watch both the curved streams of light and Jack Jacobs. She began analyzing the unusual flow of the white light outside their spaceship, including Jack's bodily functions in relation to his lungs, heart, cerebral activity, and complete cardiovascular system. The electrical impulses from his cognitive brain were somewhat different this time, even from what they had been over the last sixteen years when they were lost. But she knew Jack's synaptic cell junctures were always extremely active, and now found they were more active than ever before. With what they were currently up against, it was somewhat understandable though, as she knew they were now at a point of no return inside the mathematical envelope of their curved time warp tunnel. Even she did not know whether they would survive the curved time warp field tunnel, and especially the South Pole ninety degree tangent line function, a very mysterious point on their curved time tunnel.

Jacobs sat quietly, engulfed in going over the subtension equations in his mind and also watching the curved streams of light. He did notice they were starting to get a little brighter. "Hmmm," he said to himself. "Light must be passing by our ship at a faster rate now. The time warp tunnel held through the first turn at zero degrees."

His watch showed a time of 10:33 p.m. and Jacobs was mildly surprised to be able to notice the seconds counting by at a faster rate. "That was actually unforeseen," he said to himself, "To be able to notice the seconds going by faster. The bioelectrical energy of my body must not be speeding up much though, otherwise, I surely would be dying of old age…"

Jacobs continued to watch intensely as the bright streams of light inside their curved time warp tunnel continued to get brighter and brighter. He knew their spaceship was approaching and coming ever so close to the South Pole ninety-degree tangent function of the half circle curved time warp tunnel. It was also the most important part of the mathematical half circle where the most stress would occur—just beyond ninety degrees. Jack's heart rate sped up slightly again and his breathing increased, realizing this could truly be the end for him and Jennifer.

Jennifer sensed Jack had another heart rate increase and that his breathing changed. She didn't fully understand why it had happened and figured it had to be related to the ninety degree tangent line function of their mathematical sphere. She also knew that at any second they were going to be approaching the ninety degree mark and then on to the other half of their curved time warp tunnel, traveling away from the South Pole. She trained her cameras on both Jack and the curved white streams of light outside the cockpit windows, not fully understanding what was happening now with Jack's bioelectrical bodily functions or their time warp tunnel. The streams of white light were starting to become extremely bright.

Jacobs remained calm though, as he understood what was happening, and stared directly at the camera above his center console. "Notice the white streams of light getting even brighter, Jennifer?" he asked.

"Yes," she replied.

"Well, I believe our ship is starting to exceed the hundred light years per second of travel for our time warp field tunnel, and trying to approach a symptotic mathematical infinity limit."

"That's interesting," she said.

Jack paused, thinking about Jennifer's comment and glanced at the seconds on his wristwatch to notice they were moving forward at even a faster rate—the minutes were counting like seconds. "Hmmm," he mused to himself, "the gravitational field harmonics of the ship's gravity drive must also be speeding up more than before. Strange."

Outside the cockpit windows, some of the white streams of light started turning blue. Jacobs watched as the white streams of light were constantly mixed in with blue streams of light. Strangely, a light harmonic vibration was evident inside their ship. Their ship continued to vibrate and then started to shake. Jack looked around his ship and could not see anything vibrating, yet he could still feel it. "That is also strange," he said to himself, "I can't see anything vibrating inside the ship, so everything must be vibrating within the same resonance cycles."

The blue streams of light quickly disappeared and there was a momentary flash of white solid light for the ninety degree tangent limit. The white streams of light immediately appeared again and were noticed still traveling toward the back of their ship. Suddenly, red streams of light began showing and were now mixed in with the white streams of light. The vibrations suddenly stopped.

Jacobs held his breath for a short moment, knowing their ship had just successfully passed the ninety degree South Pole position on the sphere's imaginary surface, and that their ship's gravitational field was starting to come under maximum time warp tunnel stress from trying to pull away from the maximum limit function he had to null out in his equations. He also knew they were traveling along an asymptotic curvature plane in relation to quantum space and wondered if their ship's hull could take the additional time warp field pressures and overcome the quantum zero limit that was now inverted.

Jennifer sensed Jack wasn't breathing the same as before and she checked the arterial pressure of his heart's left ventricle to find there was a sudden contraction followed by a systolic blood pressure rise of fifteen points. She was again confused by his cardiovascular changes, as she knew his normal blood pressure was 130 over 70. One-hundred and forty-five had never been reached before, except for when he was exercising.

The red streams of light inside the time tunnel became brighter and brighter with intensity as the white streams of light seemingly started to vanish. Jennifer watched both Jack and the red streams of light outside the cockpit windows as he continued to sit calmly in his captain's chair with only an intense stare. He knew there was nothing they could do and that the coming event inside their curved time warp tunnel could also be the end of his life, the end of both his and Jennifer's existence. Suddenly, all of the streams of light showing outside their windows turned completely red. Their spaceship was now being gravitationally pushed under immense stress through the curved time warp tunnel that now had only solid streams of red light. It was also being pulled from behind from the south pole of their mathematically created imaginary time sphere.

"Here we go, Jennifer," Jack still calmly said. "We're coming under maximum time warp tunnel stress. Will our time warp tunnel hold?"

Jennifer didn't fully understand the way Jack was acting and continued to train her cameras on both Jack and the windows, while also watching the red streams of light. Suddenly, the time warp tunnel turned solid red and there was another vibration inside their ship, except this time everything inside their ship vibrated as though it was in slow motion. Jacobs could also see himself starting to vibrate, visible against the glass of his forward displays, and continued to sit calmly in his chair, as nothing could stop the inevitable outcome. Glancing down at his arms, he noticed they were starting to become invisible to his physical eyes and his cognitive mind, yet, everything else on the ship seemed to be fully visible. It was a strange sight to behold, as it seemed to him that only biological matter was being affected. Looking at the time on his wristwatch, the seconds didn't appear to be moving—they weren't counting anymore. It was as if the gravitational field of their ship was about to stop inside the time warp field tunnel and completely stop all time resonances inside his ship: the biological, structural, molecular, nuclear, and even all gravity resonances. This would be something that should not be mathematically possible by any time warp field laws, so it would definitely result in a complete erasure from existence for his ship, himself, and Jennifer. That is what he believed would happen.

Jacobs glanced back outside the cockpit windows to see that their time tunnel was now solid bright red in color. It had a strange glow, as though it was reflecting their ship's outer hull like a mirror. There were no streams of white or red light visible anywhere, just solid bright red.

Jack took a deep breath, wondering if they would survive, and started reflecting back on his life as though it was passing before him. He saw his life as a young boy, skipping kindergarten and first grade, and quickly attending sixth grade by the time he was age seven. There was already much talk about him in the science community, he remembered. Then there was his graduation from high school at age eleven, before finally enrolling into college at age twelve. Jacobs continued to think about his college years as a young teenage boy, remembering all the professors being extremely nice to him while acing his classes, especially in the science fields. He also remembered talking with many of them at sixteen years of age, contemplating and reflecting on the origins of universe, when suddenly, the vibrations stopped and the solid red curved time warp tunnel turned white again, showing only streams of white light. "Whew!" Jack said with relief. "We made it through the most important first half, Jennifer. The time warp tunnel held. Not that I believed we wouldn't, but I was never one hundred percent sure."

Jennifer didn't say anything in response. She had also sensed Jack's relief and how it had changed his body's limbic system. It was a strange analysis of his cellular DNA, as not only did his DNA molecules start to change, but she had also felt and noticed her own cellular material changing, especially the manganese molecules reverting back to their zero ground state. She began analyzing everything that was affected biologically by the ninety-degree mathematical limit, and was strangely intrigued. Now she only quietly analyzed as many of Jack's bioelectrical and molecular changes over this curved time warp tunnel as she could, wondering what she might possibly learn from it and of her own cognitive self-awareness.

Jacobs continued to watch the brightly-lit streams of light pass by the cockpit windows and noticed that they were now starting to dim. "Our ship must be finally slowing down," he said to himself, knowing they were also just slingshot away from the South Pole of their imaginary and mathematically created sphere. He glanced at his wristwatch again and saw that the seconds appeared to be counting by at a faster rate than what they were when they had first entered the curved tunnel, yet, they were also slowing down. Jack thought about that and mumbled under his breath, "The harmonics of my ship's time warp field must also be starting to slow down. Interesting…"

Jacobs continued to watch the streams of light pass by his cockpit windows as they traveled toward the back of his ship, and noticed they were becoming dimmer in intensity. He also knew by the time showing on his wristwatch that the last point in their time warp field tunnel and surface of their imaginary sphere, the one hundred eighty degrees mark, was coming up very soon. Jennifer had never taken her bio-sensors off Jack or stopped analyzing the characteristics of the time tunnel outside the spaceship, as the tunnel changed to blue, to red, and then back to white while they traveled through the tangent. It was a strange sight to behold, even for her.

Suddenly, the white streams of light turned light blue momentarily and then immediately back to white, as they had just entered inside their mathematically created 36,000 light-year long straight time tunnel. Jack realized their ship's time warp field had again shifted normal space, except this time space was briefly pushed away from their ship's gravity field. "We're home free, Jennifer," he said. "We've made it through the last one hundred and eighty degree mark of our imaginary sphere. I believe we're going to make it."

Jennifer remained quiet while continuing to analyze the curved time warp field tunnel, as well as Jack's biophysical body.

Jacobs realized Jennifer was probably analyzing their curved time warp field, including what changes it had caused to his body in relation to his heart, breathing, adrenalin, cerebrum, and a host of other things. He quietly analyzed for himself what he was now witnessing and seeing with the streams of white light, and what he had previously witnessed at the ninety-degree tangent line function. The white streams of light appeared to be of the same intensity as when they had first entered the time warp tunnel on the other side of the white dwarf star.

Jack looked down at his wristwatch and noticed the seconds

were counting by at a normal rate again, just as they would have been with a time tunnel that had not altered the normal curvature of space. He looked up again at the white streams of light and noticed they were still traveling toward the back of their ship, when suddenly they turned red momentarily and then back to white. "There's our other hundred year anomaly, Jennifer," he remarked, and quickly looked at his wristwatch. It showed 10:16 p.m. and still a year of 2199. "We should be exiting our time warp tunnel in about two minutes," he said.

"Yes, Jack, I know," Jennifer finally replied, after being quiet for quite some time. "But we'll actually be exiting the time warp field tunnel in one minute, fifty-five seconds."

Jacobs smiled to Jennifer after realizing she had been keeping track of the time within their very unusual curved time warp field tunnel. How accurately she could have ever accomplished it would be an interesting topic of conversation, if they can solve what is causing the time anomalies. Outer space was finally showing after exiting out of their time warp tunnel and it brought Jack to his senses. He looked directly at one of the cameras. "We're out, Jennifer," he said with a slight grin. "So how did you like that little roller coaster ride?"

"What do you mean, Jack?" she asked with a voice of confusion.

"Go back and check the ship's databanks, Jennifer, and you'll see."

Jennifer cross-checked what Jack had asked her against their ship's historical databanks and she loaded them into her organic memory cells. After a few moments, she finally understood and created a new personality matrix on one of her memory boards. "I understand, Jack," she said with humor in her voice.

Jacobs was surprised with her tone of humor. "Let's find the source of that time anomaly," he immediately said.

"Okay Jack," she calmly replied. "I'll have the location here shortly."

Jennifer repositioned their ship back to the ninety-degree position and direction that it was orientated before their curved time warp field tunnel. Their ship now pointed further into the heart of the galaxy.

Sitting quietly, Jacobs glanced at his wristwatch again and it showed 10:18 p.m. "We don't have as much time as I wished we had," he said to himself, now starting to worry about the amount of time they had left before midnight.

Jennifer immediately sensed the change in Jack's heart rhythms, and knew he was starting to worry. "Are you okay, Jack?" she asked.

"Yes, I am, Jennifer. I'm just becoming concerned on the amount of time we have left, is all."

"I understand. I'll make the checks and find the source of the anomaly as quick as possible."

Jacobs paused and thought about how Jennifer was continuing to monitor his body, even with everything that was now happening. He also wondered if she may have correctly analyzed his heart rhythms, as he had felt some anxiety.

Jennifer continued searching the Stormy Way galaxy in order to vector and pinpoint where the anomaly was propagating its strange distortions of space-time, causing oscillations across the juncture between space and time like a Doppler signal. "I found it, Jack," she said with excitement. "It is located inside a solar system with a large sun."

Jacobs was somewhat surprised that the anomaly's origin was from a solar system with a sun and was now curious if it also had a planetary system. He also wasn't going to ignore the fact that his computer was still responding with excitement in her voice, which to him meant she still had curiosity, and that was a very good thing. But it was time to make what he believed to be their next-to-last leg of their long journey, and Jacobs moved on in his thoughts. "Okay, Jennifer, how many light years away is the sun?" he finally asked.

"Approximately two hundred fifty thousand light years," she answered.

"How long will it take you to calculate the new time warp

field?"

"I should have it in a few minutes," Jennifer answered again, having a pleasant tone in her voice.

"Okay, thank you, Jennifer," Jack said. "Let's go ahead and jump to the outer reaches of the sun's heliospheric bubble so that we can get some accurate time bearings on the ecliptic planes of the planets in the solar system, if there is a planetary system and if they even have an ecliptic. If there is no planetary system, then we'll have to start looking for fixed stars against the rotating plane of the sun instead. This is all required and mandatory for us to get a new time reference of that solar system's arrangement and configuration to its galaxy, so that it can all be referenced back to the Earth's GMT according to our ship's gravitational field. Do you understand everything that I just told you, Jennifer?"

"Yes, I understand," she answered, already knowing there was a planetary system, but then she didn't say anything about it. She also knew Jack wanted them to jump outside the solar system's heliosphere so they could determine more easily the speed of light space-curvature differences outside the bubble versus inside the bubble and the exact orthogonal displacement angles. Jennifer began calculating a time warp field jump to the outer ridges of the sun's magnetic field, the heliopause, and its expansions out into deep space where it met the interstellar medium.

Jacobs sat quietly in his captain's chair with anticipation, looking forward to finding out if the anomaly was located inside a solar system having some type of a planetary arrangement. Was it a time machine or maybe some strange cosmological rift in space-time that would leave him clueless on what to do? Regardless of whichever it was, it was still causing a hundred year loss of time to the entire universe every twenty-four Earth solar hours. In his case though, it was four minutes closer to midnight for every hundred year reversal. He looked down at his ship's energy reserves displayed on the center console in front of him and noticed they were down to sixty-two percent efficiency. Their ship's Gaussian energy reserves would also continue to drop faster with each new time warp field jump. "I must get to a correctly aligned magnetic field dipole planet to recharge my gravity propulsion energy system soon," Jacobs said to himself, and began thinking about the strange anomaly, still not understanding how all space-time, including curved space, could ever change instantaneously.

"The time warp field equations are done, Jack," Jennifer said.

Jacobs came out of his daydream of thinking about what could be causing hundred-year anomalies to the universe and all space-time. He was also becoming increasingly concerned about his ship's dropping and dwindling energy reserves. "Okay, Jennifer," he finally replied. "Go ahead and apply the time warp field at your discretion."

He quietly watched out his cockpit windows and then noticed outer space immediately turned black around their ship. White streams of light showed up just as quickly and they began passing by their ship toward the backend. "Well, we have entered the tunnel again," Jack said to himself, "Soon we'll be finding out what is causing the hundred year anomalies."

Looking at his wristwatch, he noticed it showed 10:25 p.m., and after looking at his forward center display, knew their 250,000 light year long time warp tunnel should only take their spaceship forty-one minutes, forty seconds to reach the solar system. Jacobs thought more about that. "Hmmm," he said to himself. "We should be exiting the time tunnel in less than forty one minutes now. We're almost there."

Quietly watching the white streams of light, he began thinking about the solar system and whether the anomaly would be located down on the surface of a planet with a viable atmosphere. If it were on a planet, would the planet be populated with any intelligent life? Would they even know about the time anomaly? Would the race be more advanced than he? Better yet, what if it was not some strange occurrence down on a planet, but in outer space like a small black hole? Where would it have ever come from in the first place? Was it created by some intelligence, a natural occurring phenomenon of space, or possibly even created by their ship's own time warp field drive from some catastrophic event?

Jacobs continued to sit quietly pondering all those questions and watching the white streams of light from their two hundred and fifty thousand light year long time warp tunnel. While quietly day-dreaming about the solar system they were about to come upon, his thoughts were again on the galaxy they currently occupied. He still couldn't recall discovering the galaxy that was classified as NCG2199A. Why he classified it with the year 2199 and a letter A, he also didn't know? Was it a possible secret message to himself to make him remember something? Surely he and Jennifer had already been to the galaxy and maybe even to the source of what was causing their time dilations. He continued staring at the light outside the cockpit windows and thinking about all those intriguing possibilities.

"Maybe something did happen," Jack said out loud to himself. "Maybe were also revisiting something that was strange to science, strange to the universe, strange even to our ship's time warp field and its manipulation of space and time."

Suddenly outer space appeared before Jack's eyes and his heart-beat sped up. He knew they were now very near the strange time anomaly, regardless of what it turned out to be.

Jacobs reached to his forward center console and began using his ship's OGCD optical lensing and high frequency radio sensors to see what was in front of them. He found there was indeed a planetary configuration rotating around their sun in an ecliptic. It caused him some additional excitement inside, but on the outside he remained calm as ever. "Okay, Jennifer," he finally said. "I want you to check the planets for their time bearings within their solar system, including their ecliptic planes of orbit around their sun. Note the current time harmonic resonance of this ship's gravitational field, with which my watch is also in harmonic motion, and then cross reference them against their planetary orbits."

"Okay, Jack. I'm checking the solar time references of the planets right now."

Jennifer trained their ship's many sensors to the sun and the twelve planets of the solar system, using their OGCD gravitational lensing method. She analyzed their ecliptic planes of rotation, their angular paths, and any perturbations that might be between them. She also checked for any eccentric changes between the sun and any of its planets within its massive magnetic field, a sun also having solar winds near its surface traveling nearly sixteen million kilometers per hour. In addition, she also began looking at the sun to see if it was rotating, its vibratory nature, and how it might be moving through the galaxy. She continued analyzing for fifteen more minutes, obtaining extremely accurate information she knew they had to have.

Jacobs patiently waited, knowing Jennifer would be very thorough in order to get an initial accurate solar time reference for the twelve planets. He began thinking back on everything they had to go through just to make it to the solar system in the Stormy Way galaxy, especially after traveling almost 15,000,000 light years inside a single time warp field tunnel. "What a trip this has become," he said to himself.

Jennifer finally finished her detailed analysis of the solar system and its planetary system. "I'm done, Jack," she said.

"Great!" he replied with a good feeling, and then noted the reference time now being displayed on the computer screen in front of him. "Go ahead and display that new solar time on the clocks of our ship, Jennifer, referencing it to our Earth's GMT."

"Okay," she replied, and updated the time references throughout the cockpit and the ship to agree with the solar system's arrangement.

Jack glanced briefly over at the GMT clock on the left wall. It showed 11:22 p.m., with a year of 201 BC. Looking back at his wristwatch, it also showed a time of 11:22 p.m., but was for the year of 2199. There was exactly a twenty-four hundred year difference and Jacobs knew he was over 2400 years old to the Earth now. "Well," he mumbled to himself, knowing they were already ahead of the problem. "All three of the systems agree and are synchronized now. At least we have a time bearing in this solar system that is tied directly back to Earth's solar system and its time bearings."

Jacobs continued to stare at the GMT reference showing on the wall and it caused him to smile because he realized that the true GMT on Earth was over 15,000,000 light years away and at a distance that was almost inconceivable.

"Jennifer?" he asked.

"Yes, Jack," she answered.

"What can you tell me about this solar system?"

Jennifer retrieved the information from her organic memory and, like before, was surprised to find some of the information already there, seeming to be that of a previous memory. She finally replied, "From everything that I have determined and know, it does indeed contain twelve planets that are all in ecliptic planes of twenty-two degrees, with all but the fifth planet in a tight azmuthal orbital offset of only six degrees. The sun is also four times larger than our sun back home at approximately four million eight-hundred and thirty kilometers in diameter. It appears that whatever is generating the anomalies is located down on the surface of the sixth planet, Jack."

Jacobs raised his eyebrows. "Oh really?" he said with surprise. "Now that's interesting!"

Jennifer continued, "It is also the sixth biggest planet with a diameter of nearly fourteen thousand eight hundred kilometers and has a right ascension of twenty-two degrees."

"That's about the same size as Earth," Jack said to himself.

"It also has two moons," Jennifer said.

"Is that right?" Jack commented, now extremely interested. "Is the planet hospitable for life, Jennifer?"

"Yes, it is," she replied. "The shifts within the spectral lines indicate that it has an atmospheric base of mostly nitrogen and oxygen."

Jack's anticipation started to rise even more after hearing the planet had an Earth-type atmosphere and had to glance at his wristwatch—11:24 p.m. Their ship's energy reserves still showed an efficiency of fifty-one percent. He looked back up to the camera above his center console. "Let's make another time warp jump just outside of the inner magnetic field of the planet, Jennifer, and stay out of its magnetotail and polar cusps. In doing this, I want you to also take us just outside its North Pole polar cusp, yet directly behind the bow shock."

"Okay, Jack," she replied, understanding exactly what he had requested. "I'll have the formulas for our exact position inside the magnetosheath shortly."

Jacobs sat quietly in his chair, knowing Jennifer would take them just outside the forward lobe of the planet's magnetic field. He began daydreaming about what they might find down on the planet's surface. "I wonder if this truly is another time machine?" he asked himself. "Better yet, why would it be down on a viable planet that can sustain life, of all things?"

"I have the formulas done, Jack," Jennifer informed him.

Jacobs was filled anticipation after hearing this. "Okay, Jennifer. Apply the time warp field at your discretion."

Jennifer hesitated for only a short moment and then applied the time warp field to their spaceship's gravity propulsion system. It immediately turned black all around their spaceship, as white streams of light appeared and started passing by the windows—their bright pulsations traveling toward the back of their ship. Jacobs knew the streams of light wouldn't last long. Suddenly, the white light vanished and a brilliant blue atmosphere now showed on the planet in front of them. "What a pretty sight," Jack said to himself, and immediately looked at his wristwatch—year 2199, May 17, and a time of 11:26 p.m.

"Jennifer?" he asked.

"Yes, Jack."

"What is the exact atmospheric composition for the planet?"

"Let me check, Jack," Jennifer replied, and began analyzing the planet in further detail, optically, passively with microwave energy, and analytically, by combining the variables of known elemental line frequencies in direct relation to the atmospheric temperature of the planet, the strength of the planet's magnetic field, as well as the known nanometer spectral wavelengths, all four variables used in an analysis known as Polarized Radiative Spectral Transfer Assimilation, or PRSTA. Jennifer finally finished her analysis. "The planet's atmosphere is fifty-eight percent nitrogen, thirty-nine percent oxygen, and three percent trace gases," she answered.

Jack was amazed in what she had said. "So it is very hospitable for life?" he asked.

"It would seem so, yes."

He began wondering what the other three percent gases might be since Earth had close to a 98 percent oxygen and nitrogen atmospheric level back in 2183. "What is the other three percent?" Jack asked.

Jennifer already knew the answer. "They are argon, carbon dioxide, helium, hydrogen, krypton, methane, neon, nitrous oxide, and xenon," she replied.

Those gases were also present in Earth atmosphere, Jacobs knew, but this planet did not seem to have carbon monoxide. So for what she had told him it did make sense to have a high oxygen level and no hydrocarbon fossil fuel emissions. He began checking the planet with his ship's multi-phased array, transverse topological sensors to find no ELF, VLF, HF, VHF, UHF, or EHF radio waves from terrestrial life. Nor were there any frequency emissions between those ranges that would indicate intelligence, only static energy from various thunderstorms and winds blowing down on its surface. His ship's sensors also locked in on the natural Schumann resonances for the planet's magnetic spherical body and Jack noticed the resonances were four percent lower than Earth's known frequencies. He began checking the planet for its magnetic field type knowing that the Schumann values verified the planet was slightly larger than Earth and he also noticed the planet did have a North-South magnetic dipole field very similar to Earth. At least it would quickly recharge their ship's Gaussian energy system once they were beneath its ionospheric layers. Jack paused, knowing the planet's dipole field was very good luck, but then he knew something strange could still be going on down on its surface in relation to the anomaly. He looked up again directly to the camera above his center console, still wondering if there might be non-carbon based life on the planet that they couldn't detect and finally asked, "Can you determine if the planet will actually support life such as myself, and are there any beings, intelligent or otherwise, that you can detect?"

Jennifer again already knew the answer, as their ship's silicon-based computer had already computed the probabilities. "All indications are that the planet has no intelligent life forms whatsoever," she replied. "And yes, it is extremely habitable for humans."

This last statement did not make complete sense and it had Jacobs now thoroughly confused. "So is there any evidence, any evidence at all, of a race ever having lived on the planet?" he again asked.

"No evidence at all," she calmly replied.

"Hmmm," he said to himself. "If that's the case, they must have first populated the planet many thousands of years ago and the anomaly ended up wiping out their complete existence."

Jack regained his senses with anticipation of finally finding out the reason they had to trek across the universe. "Let's go find the source of the time anomaly, Jennifer," he told her.

"Okay, Jack," Jennifer immediately replied, and now with additional curiosity in her voice.

Jacobs heard the way Jennifer had replied and smiled about it, as he knew with no doubt that she too was looking forward to finding out what was causing the space-time reversals to the entire universe every twenty-four Earth hours.

Jennifer began completely analyzing the planet's magnetic field in relation to the Schumann resonances and the strange gravitational wakes the anomaly seemed to be causing to the juncture between space and time, referencing them all to the planet's sun and its magnetic heliospheric bubble. She finally picked up the slight residual harmonic vibration across the juncture of the sun's bubble to interstellar space, and then referenced that vibration back again to the planet's magnetosphere. "Okay, Jack," she finally said. "Using our position as zero longitude, the anomaly is located down on the surface of the planet at latitude forty-degrees, thirty-five minutes north, and a longitude of sixty-degrees, twenty-five minutes west."

Jack was amazed. "Okay, take us to it," he said.

Jacobs watched outside his cockpit windows as Jennifer applied polarized magnetic south gravity propulsion energy to their spaceship and it quickly approached the outer boundaries of the planet's ionosphere. "Jennifer," he calmly said. "Activate our magnetic ionic stream at the front edge of our ship. We wouldn't want the atmosphere to heat it up too much."

"Okay, Jack, I understand," she said, and activated a magnetic ion field on the front edge of their ship as it began descending into the ionosphere at nineteen thousand kilometers per hour. Jack noticed slight turbulence from thin air as their ship entered the mesosphere of the planet. Suddenly, white flames appeared outside his cockpit windows. The flames turned red and then blue, as they began entering the upper boundary of the atmospheric layer and colliding head-on with the planet's billions of oxygen molecules. Jack continued to watch the red, white, and blue hot flames pass by his cockpit windows and looked down at his center console display, realizing the flames seemed brighter than what showed for other planets they had visited. He also took notice of what their ship's spectrophotometric sensors were telling them about the planet's ozone layer and then looked back up to the camera. "This planet has a thick ozone layer, huh, Jennifer?"

"Yes, it does," she replied.

Jacobs continued watching the multi-colored flames pass by his cockpit windows that now had a touch of purple and green mixed in with them. He began wondering again what they might find down on the planet's surface, when all of a sudden the flames of fire stopped and the planet's surface was showing to be 115 kilometers away. Jennifer shut off the magnetic ionic field and Jacobs looked down again at his forward center console to see they were now dropping at two kilometers per second, so Jennifer had slowed their ship down to

7200 kilometers per hour. He then reached forward to his left console and touched a few buttons, activating his holographic imagery menu. Dozens of images showed on his forward display and Jacobs selected the three images that seemed to be of most significance. Suddenly, three spherical in shape color holographic images appeared above each of his forward consoles.

What was now showing in the images only caused his anticipation to rise. He looked down to his forward center instrument panel to see their ship was now at an altitude of 22,000 meters and continuing to drop. Jack looked up again at holographic image to his left and noticed there were quite a number of trees and plants across the foothills of the mountainside where they were traveling. It was truly a magnificent sight to see the new planet for the first time. "What a pretty looking planet," he said to himself, and noticed the types of trees showing in the image did not appear to be trees found on Earth. Continuing to stare at this holograph, he also noticed there was a heavy forest. Looking over at the holographic image to his right, it showed one of the planet's magnificent blue oceans that seemed to stretch for hundreds of miles. "This planet must have about a seventy percent water surface, much like Earth," he said again to himself.

Jacobs noticed it was still daylight down on the surface where they were heading and checked his forward center display for when the sun would be setting at that point on the planet. After touching three buttons on his display, it showed that the sunset would occur at 9:15 p.m. Since Jennifer already knew the current time of day on the surface of the planet where they were traveling, she displayed that time on Jack's forward console. It showed the solar time on the planet to be 5:59 p.m. Jack then glanced at his wristwatch—11:32 p.m.

He knew there was now a direct time comparison to the planet below versus his wristwatch, including a correlation back to Earth's solar time back. "Hmmm," he said to himself, thinking about the similarity. "At least we'll have some daylight to look at whatever we're going to find down there."

Jack looked back up to the three magnificent-looking holographic images that were now only showing the mountainside, all while Jennifer continued dropping their spaceship. She then slowed their ship down and guided it toward the surface at eight-hundred kilometers per hour. Their ship's altitude showed three hundred eighty meters, as moving holographic images of the planet and its mountainside, its trees, and its vegetation continued to show in front of Jack. One of the images in the center holograph immediately caught Jacobs's attention, as it was taken from the onboard optical telescope pointed to the area in the forest where the anomaly was believed to be located.

A round white colored building in the shape of a geodesic dome and appearing to be made of ceramic, or plastic, stood in the foothills of the heavy forest by itself.

9

THE STRANGE BUILDING

THEIR SPACECRAFT FINALLY TOUCHED DOWN thirty meters from the strange dome-shaped building. Jacobs sat quietly in his captain's chair thirty-seven meters above the planet's surface, and looked around the countryside to see many tall magnificent trees— some of the treetops reached the height of his cockpit. He realized the trees did look very much like spruce and pine evergreens, except their bark appeared to be bluish-red in color. Looking upward, he noticed there was a partly cloudy sky with quite a lot of altocumulus clouds, noticeable by their many progressive parallel bands. He finally looked back down at the dome that was partially buried in the ground and immediately gained his scientific mental senses, contemplating its shape and placement on the planet. The building was off-white in color like a perfect dome made of ceramic, and its very top twenty-two meters below his vantage point. All Jacobs could do was to continue studying the geodesic dome with mathematical curiosity, as the pentagonal and hexagonal geometric shapes were clearly visible on the twenty-one meter diameter sphere structure.   Something seemed strange and different with their configurations. He finally caught his breath to the optical illusion of the dome and mumbled out loud, "In the first place, with no life on the planet, why is there a building here at all?"

"I'm not sure, Jack," Jennifer replied, hesitantly. "There does appear to be a force field around it though."

Jack raised his eyebrows in surprise. "A what?" he said, "Oh really? So what kind of force field type is it?"

"I'm not certain."

This surprising answer from Jennifer made Jack feel uneasy. "Well, what do our ship's sensors show?" he immediately asked.

Jennifer was quiet for a moment. "It appears to be some type of gravity well," she replied.

This information was also surprising to Jack, as even though he understood the gravity technologies that would encompass gravity force fields, at no time had they ever encountered any type of gravity well other than a black hole star. His interest was immediately increased. "In which directions are the gravity force lines traveling?" Jack asked again.

Jennifer again already knew the answer. "They are traveling down at the very center of the dome," she replied, concern filling her voice.

Jack realized her intonation and could understand it, as it was a gravity well that they were dealing with and probably of a first order. "I understand what you're getting at, Jennifer," he said. "If I were to walk into the well, I know I would never return."

"Yes, Jack, I figured you knew that."

"Do you have any suggestions Jennifer?" Jack asked without hesitation.

"I don't know what to do, Jack."

Jacobs sat back in his chair after hearing this. He didn't have a clue what to do next either. As he sat thinking about how they were going to go about finding out what was inside the dome, an unusual thought popped into his head, as though it was from a deeply hidden memory. "Jennifer?" he asked.

"Yes, Jack."

"A thought…What if we were to apply a time warp field around our ship without movement in space, so that we were to stay right where we are presently inside this planet's magnetic field?"

Jack sat quietly, waiting for Jennifer to respond to what he had said, wondering if she understood what he wanted to do with their ship's time warp field in creating an altered dimension of time and space.

"Yes, Jack," she finally replied. "I think it's a possibility, other factors unforeseen…."

"I thought you would say that," Jacobs said with a smile. "Do you understand how to apply the time warp field against our stationary spaceship so that it propagates out two times the speed of light into a ninety-one meter diameter sphere?"

"Yes, I do."

"Great!" Jack said again. "Go ahead and start the calculations for that exact stationary time warp field that should also encompass the dome. In the meantime, I'm going down to the planetarium for about ten minutes to relax my mind a bit and to think about everything that is going on with both the gravity well force field and the strange dome it seems to be protecting."

"Okay, Jack," she said, sincerely. "I'll let you know when I'm done with the calculations."

"Thank you, Jennifer," Jack remarked with a slight grin.

"You're welcome."

Jacobs could only grin again while getting up from out of his captain's seat, because he knew that by attempting a stationary time warp field around their ship, they would be delving into a strange new science. It was a field of science that could possibly create a new dimension of both time and space, altering the normal planes of time. He finally walked up to the hallway entrance thinking about that exact thing, wondering if their stationary time warp field would truly be effective against the gravity well force field. Maybe the stationary time warp field would only partially nullify the gravity well, or maybe not at all?

Jacobs finally walked out of the cockpit and headed down the hallway toward the planetarium, still thinking about the gravity well force field that was surrounding the strange dome-shaped building, knowing like before that they had never experienced a well force field, at least that he could remember. Black holes seemed to be the closest thing to them, but then they never attempted to even approach close to a black hole star.

Finally walking up to the planetarium entrance, Jack stopped and he began staring through the hallway windows down to the planet's surface. He again noticed the planet's lush plant life and its many trees. What he saw only reminded him of the George Washington Forest back home, but soon the foliage and heavy forest on the planet was quickly overshadowed by the gravity well force field. He finally turned back around to the planetarium and walked inside to notice its twelve-foot waterfall cascading into the pool below. Next to the pool of water, he saw his planetarium's perennial plants and had to admire them, as he knew they were from many generations of plants over the last sixteen years. But then again, how many generations really were his planetarium's plants and foliage if he and Jennifer were caught in some strange time loop or rift in time? Would the many generations of his plants be exactly the same for each loop, or would they be slightly altered within their own DNA patterns?

Jacobs knew he'd probably never know the answers and continued toward his favorite chair while listening to the sound of the water flowing across the rocks. It was a sound to which he had developed a special liking and it made him feel good inside. Finally taking a seat near the waterfall, Jacobs glanced at his wristwatch and began thinking about the dome that was protected by a gravity well force field.

"Why in the world is there a force field?" he asked himself, continuing to stare at the waterfall and its running water. He began daydreaming about what his next step should be whenever they were to finally look inside the geodesic dome. Hopefully the dome wasn't booby-trapped or had defensive fail-safe measures, but then Jennifer would have surely detected those with their ship's sensors. Jack regained his thoughts while staring at the mountainside through the planetarium's side windows and thought to himself, "Assuming inside the dome there is a device that is causing our time anomalies, I wonder how advanced it might be? Would it be fixed, rotating, or imaginary? What if it wasn't even a structural piece of machinery at all, but organic in nature? The anomaly could be the dome itself...."

Jacobs came out of his daydream and had to glance at his wristwatch—11:46 p.m. He knew they'd have to make another time warp field jump away from the planet into outer space and then come back to inspect the dome. His interest was immediately increased for that future event. "I can't wait to see the dome up close," he mumbled to himself, but then wondered again whether the anomaly causing their problems might be the dome itself. Hopefully it wasn't, otherwise, they might have to attempt a stationary time warp field sphere around the dome at midnight. But then that would create problems, Jack figured, and began wondering if maybe they'd tried it once before. This is because by what he could envision, his stationary time warp field sphere would become the new boundaries of the universe for the dome and its strange propagation. So it would most likely either destroy their ship or send them into a different dimension of space and time, possibly even further into their past. "We're not going to try that," he mumbled to himself, "At least not if we don't have to."

The thought of their time warp field sphere caused Jack to think more about his time warp field technology and all of the new equations as a direct result of the previously unknown twenty-four minute cycle. This caused him to also think about stationary time warp field technology and all of its possible new uses, especially if it were to be used in conjunction with his phased-matched cloaking technology. "Interesting!" he said to himself. "That would definitely create a very unusual cloaking field and possibly a whole new space-time dimensional base."

Jacobs continued to think about everything that was going on in such a short period of time. Glancing down at his wristwatch again, it showed 11:47 p.m. and figured he'd better get back to the cockpit. Finally standing up from out of his chair, he departed the planetarium and slowly walked down the hallway toward the cockpit. On the way, he glanced out the windows again and down to the planet's surface, interested in what he now saw. He focused his attention in detail to its many trees and vegetation and found himself looking forward to seeing them up close. There were rolling hills off to the northwest filled with a series of waterfalls. The planet's waterfalls only reminded him again of the Crabtree Falls in Virginia. Jacobs continued to think about what he was now seeing, knowing the planet could very well be a virgin planet, one new in evolving, especially if there was not any life beyond the plant kingdom, at least any that he or Jennifer could detect.

He also noticed the sun still shining down on the planet's surface from out of the western horizon and finally walked up to the cockpit entrance. Walking into the cockpit and over to his captain's chair, Jacobs immediately sat back down wondering how Jennifer was doing on the stationary time warp field sphere calculations. "How you doing, Jennifer?" he asked.

"I'm doing fine, Jack. I'm almost done with the stationary time warp field calculations for our exact magnetic field line location on this planet's surface."

Jack nodded quietly to her statement, as he knew the field line polarity strengths of the planet's magnetic field would definitely have to be taken into account in relation to a very large aperture of their ship's Spherical Interactive Dome. "Great!" he said. "Let's go up to an altitude of fifteen-hundred meters for our next time warp jump, and only after you've completed the stationary time warp field equations.

But then let's also not let the coming reversal of space-time catch up with us."

"Okay. I understand," Jennifer said.

Jacobs, while sitting there, again wondered about what might be inside the geodesic dome building, if anything, once they've successfully deactivated its gravity well force field with a stationary time warp field sphere.

"Jack!" Jennifer said with excitement in her voice. "I have the stationary time warp field calculations done."

Jacobs was surprised that she had figured them so fast and knew she was now a time warp field expert of the highest order, understanding as much about the technology as he did. "Okay, Jennifer," he finally replied. "Let's take our next time warp jump a little over one million three hundred thousand kilometers out into space, and make it four seconds in duration starting at 11:59 p.m. and 58 seconds. This four second time jump should put us right over the edge of the speed of light's velocity envelope for this solar system."

Jennifer knew Jack was correct. "Okay, Jack, will do," she said again.

Jack watched as their spaceship quickly lifted off the planet's surface and they rose straight up into the air at an eighty-degree angle of incline. A few seconds later their ship reached an altitude of fifteen hundred meters and then stopped in a stationary pattern. It now hovered in place in a geosynchronous type orbit above the Earth's surface. Jacobs looked down at his center forward display and noticed Jennifer had already applied a highly-accurate stationary gravity field pattern to their ship in direct relation to the planet's rotation. He then looked back up to the camera above his center console and took a deep breath, knowing their ship was now locked into a orbit in relation to the planet's magnetic field. Jacobs slowly exhaled, wondering whether or not they should have left the planet's atmosphere and its magnetic field. "Do you have our four-second time warp field calculation ready to go at 11:59 p.m. and fifty-eight seconds, Jennifer?" he calmly asked.

"I'll have it here shortly," she replied, and quickly finished the computations for a four-second time warp field tunnel that exceeded the speed of light's own compression velocity. "I'm done, Jack," she said.

Her voice brought Jack out of his daydream. He looked to the camera above his forward center console. "Okay, Jennifer, thank you," he replied. "This new time jump is important and the only way we'll ever inspect that building is by jumping out into outer space and then coming back."

"I understand," she said in an extremely kind voice. "And you're welcome as always, Jack."

Jacobs noticed Jennifer's extreme sincerity to him and it calmed his spirit. He now sat quietly, waiting for the midnight hour, pondering, thinking, wondering again and again about the gravity-well force field and what might be inside the dome. Maybe it was something they should not be inspecting? Maybe they had also inspected it once before? But then Jack knew it really didn't matter, because whatever it turned out to be was causing severe consequences to not only him, but to the entire space-time universe as he and Jennifer once knew it, changing anything and everything.

Glancing at his wristwatch one more time, it showed 11:59 p.m. forty seconds and counting—twenty seconds before another space-time reversal was about to occur. Continuing to stare at his watch, he wondered if being so close to the origin and source of the anomaly would make a difference to their ship's time warp field. "Probably not," he said to himself, and then noticed there were now only four seconds before midnight. Two seconds later, it turned pitch black around their spaceship as Jennifer applied a one-million three-hundred thousand kilometer time warp field tunnel to their spaceship. White streams of light immediately showed inside their time tunnel and traveled toward the back of their ship. Two seconds later the white streams of light turned bright red and a second later, back to white. Deep space suddenly showed.

"That was quick," Jack said to himself, and noticed his wrist-watch showed a time of 10:20 p.m., and a year of 2199. "Another four minutes lost," he said to himself. "We don't have much time."

"Okay, Jennifer," he said out loud. "Let's accomplish a one second time warp jump back to where we just came from."

"Okay, Jack."

Jennifer repositioned their ship one hundred eighty degrees back toward the planet and the planet appeared magnificently silhouetted against the heavens, a deep dark blue atmospheric color filling its sphere. The outside ridges of the invisible ionospheric layers were now noticeable, their many spheres surrounding the blue planet like soap bubbles against the colors of the rainbow. Jacobs was amazed at what he saw and knew Jennifer had to pause to this fabulous view before she finally applied a one-million three-hundred thousand kilometer, one-second time warp field equation to their spaceship's gravity propulsion system. Space turned black around their ship and a quick flash of white light for one second glared, and the planet's atmosphere suddenly showed. "That was quick," Jack said to himself. "At least there were no red streams of light in that one second time jump."

"Let's get back down to the dome, Jennifer," he said with urgency.

"Okay," she replied, and applied polarized magnetic south gravity propulsion to their spaceship. Their ship immediately took off and began dropping back down toward the dome building. On the way, Jennifer checked the planet in right ascension and for its sidereal orbital reference to the other eleven planets. She then compared the locations of the twelve planets, relative to their sun, and then referenced them to their previous time warp jump. A few moments later, she updated the clocks on their ship in relation to Earth's GMT.

Jacobs glanced over to see the GMT reference to Earth was now 301 BC, with a time 10:20 p.m. 25 seconds and counting. A few seconds later their spaceship softly touched down again at the exact location on the surface as the last time, thirty meters from the dome. Jennifer checked the building and found the gravity well force field was still active. "Jack," she said, "the force field is still in place."

"Okay, Jennifer. Go ahead and apply the time warp field

sphere to our stationary spaceship."

"Okay." Jennifer applied a ninety-one meter spherical polar time warp field at two times the speed of light to their spaceship's gravity propulsion system, all as their ship sat motionless on the planet's surface thirty meters from the dome. The stationary time warp field projected out from the very center of their ship's spherical interactive dome, up into a mushroom pattern, and then filled in the two poles directly above and below their spaceship.

Jennifer checked the gravity well force field surrounding the dome and knew it was now encompassed by their ship's time warp field sphere. "Jack," she exclaimed, "the force field is nullified....Gone!"

Jack took a deep breath after hearing this. "Okay, Jennifer," he said, mentally prepared to look at the dome.

He looked down at his center forward display and noted the atmospheric conditions of the planet. It showed a mild temperature of 68 degrees Fahrenheit and a barometric pressure of 1015.25 millibars. It was beautiful outside his ship on the mountainside, Jack knew, with no rain in the forecast—only partly cloudy skies. He also saw that they had two hours, fourteen Earth minutes left before the sun would set in the western horizon. Jacobs stood up and picked up his black leather utility belt just to the left of his chair. He also grabbed his special sensors and his electron particle accelerator pistol, and then stuck them inside his utility belt. After strapping the black leather belt firmly around his waist, he cinched it tight. Over farther to the left of his captain's chair, he picked up a shoulder strap with a small high-definition color camera and multi-directional-array microphone capable of canceling out audible frequencies to hear a pin drop over a hundred meters away. This small camera and microphone unit was firmly positioned onto his left shoulder. Walking to the back of the cockpit and behind his captain's seat to a wall cabinet, he grabbed two gravity generators and headed over toward the hallway. Jack finally left the cockpit and down the hallway toward the elevator. On the way, he began staring through the hallway windows again and noticed the many trees down on the surface of the planet and off to their north. Over to his northeast, it appeared that there must have been a large forest fire, most likely from lightning, as thousands of acres of burned trees covered the landscape. Jacobs also noticed about a kilometer away there was a large waterway, evident by the many rows of adjacent trees that had not burned. He knew the remnants of a forest fire and all of the charred wood was not showing the last time they were on the planet, which to the planet would have been a hundred years into its future. So the many trees and plants would have had a century and many generations to grown back since the last time he visited. "What a strange thought," Jacobs said to himself. "To know I was just on the planet and had witnessed all of those new trees and shrubs."

Walking by the planetarium, Jack didn't stop or glance inside this time and headed straight for his small personnel elevator. The door was noticed already open, so after entering inside, he reached down to the control panel and selected the tenth and bottom level of his ship. The door closed behind him. The elevator began quickly dropping, and Jacobs had to wonder again what might be inside the dome that had to be protected by a gravity well force field. Suddenly the elevator stopped and the door opened again.

Jacobs immediately noticed the sun shining brightly through the outer door to their ship that Jennifer had already opened, as if a solar flare had just occurred in the planet's atmosphere. That was a strange thought in itself, but then Jennifer would have told him if the radiation levels had become dangerous. "Maybe it was also their stationary time warp field interacting with both the dome and the planet?" Jack thought, and continued out of the elevator. He knew it was somewhat strange how the solar time on the planet was directly correlated to the time they had spent inside their time tunnel.

Jacobs headed straight to the open doorway, walked down the ramp, and finally onto the surface of the planet. Having both his feet firmly planted on the surface for the first time, he had to take a deep breath of fresh air. Exhaling, he noticed the atmospheric air quality seemed almost equivalent to Earth's environment, yet, there was no doubt in his mind that it had a much cleaner and fresher smell in the air, most likely due to the thirty-nine percent oxygen level and no hydrocarbon pollution emissions. Looking around the vicinity of his ship, he saw many colorful plants and flowers, varying in the colors of red, blue, green, and white. There were also trees near his ship and around the dome that had survived the fire. They looked very similar to evergreens, except their bark was a magnificent bluish-red in color and had vertical yellow streaks. The green and blue needle-leaves of the coniferous, evergreen-looking trees were shaped much differently than evergreens on Earth, as their spines looked somewhat inverted. Looking up into the sky, he noticed its deep dark blue background with many high level cirrus clouds that appeared to be moving toward the east and northeast. Jacobs regained his visual senses to his surroundings and he could now hear, thinking it strange there were no animals, birds, or insects evident in sight. Neither were there the echoing sounds of any of them as he would have expected. This lack of all physical life beyond the taxonomic plant kingdom was something that Jennifer had also failed to detect. Jacobs found it additionally strange to be able to only hear the bristling sound of the wind in the background as it echoed and blew throughout all of the plants and trees.

All of this thinking, postulating, and wondering about the planet caused Jacobs to finally turn to his right, and he immediately noticed the large dome now in full view. While standing there a little while longer, he began wondering again what might be hidden inside the geodesic dome. "What could be inside a dome that had to be protected by a force field?" he asked himself.

Jack finally began his inevitable walk toward the building, carrying his three kilogram in weight antigravity generators. Strapped to his right hip was his electron particle accelerator pistol, and on his other hip were special tools and a gravitational force-line sensor for looking at whatever mystery might be inside. On his left shoulder were the small color camera and multi-directional-array microphone so Jennifer could watch and listen to everything that happened along the way. She had full control over the camera to zoom, rotate, and pan in any direction she so wished.

Jacobs looked at his wristwatch again while approaching closer to the dome and felt a light easterly wind at his back. The time was now 10:46 p.m. He knew that he had less than an hour to get inside the dome, see what it was, find out any characteristics, if any, provided the anomaly wasn't the dome itself, and then return back to the ship for another time warp field jump before midnight. He took short deep breath thinking about that and then exhaled. "I don't have a lot of time until we have to time warp jump again," he said to Jennifer. "I better not take too much time here."

Jennifer remained quiet.

Approaching closer to the dome-shaped building, he noticed that like before that the dome was twenty-one meters in diameter with close to six meters of it buried in the ground. It looked familiar to the geodesic dome antennas on Earth, except for the unorthodox geometric shapes. "This dome setup," he said to himself, "seems to be shaped as possibly some sort of huge high frequency impulse antenna."

Walking up next to the dome, Jacobs began to look around. "No door anywhere?" he said to himself. "Jennifer?" he asked.

"Yes, Jack."

"Can your sensors locate the door on this geodesic dome?"

"Yes, I believe so," she replied. "Go seven and one-half meters farther around to your left. The outline of the door should be visible."

Jack walked on around the dome in a northeasterly direction and soon noticed what appeared to be an outline of a large door, eight meters tall by two and one-half meters wide. "I wonder how I'm going to get inside this dome," he said. "Do you have any suggestions, Jennifer?"

"I'm analyzing the door configuration now, Jack."

"Okay."

Jennifer began computing and analyzing the gravity force line vectors of the door lock that were strangely not being deactivated by their ship's stationary time warp field, all while Jack stood patiently waiting. Glancing at his watch again, it showed 10:59 p.m. and Jack knew each second that now passed became even more precious to him. "I may have to make one more time warp jump before I can really look this thing over good," he said to himself. "But let's hope not."

Jennifer finally finished her gravitational field analysis of the door lock on the dome structure and determined it was a gravity actuated lock. "There is a gravity control mechanism inside the dome and eight-meters above the door," she told Jack. "You should be able to deactivate it with one of your gravity generators."

"Yes, that's what I figured," Jack replied, yet he also did not understand the gravity lock's immunity to their ship's stationary time warp field sphere. "I'll do it right now," he said.

Setting one of his gravity generators down on the ground six meters from the door, Jacobs angled it up at the top of the door. Removing the gravity force line sensor from his belt, he pointed it down at his gravity generator to check the harmonic alignment of his generator to the gravity lock. He made a slight elevation adjustment to his gravity generator of twenty-five degrees and finally got the fields of his generator and the door lock to match in close alignment. A few moments later, the two gravitational fields were perfectly aligned in harmonic resonance.

"I'm going to go ahead and apply a reverse gravity field to my generator, Jennifer," he said with anticipation.

"Okay, Jack. I'll monitor any changes in the gravity field from here."

Jack actuated his gravity generator, and a beam of inverted gravitational energy was projected through the outer surface of the dome, directly at the gravity lock. There was a sudden light hum after his generator deactivated the door lock and took control of its function. "What is that, Jennifer?" he asked.

"I don't know, Jack."

The hum stopped and a few seconds later the door to the dome started opening at the bottom and continued to rise up inside the dome structure. Jacobs stood quietly as the eight-meter door finally opened all the way to the top and then stopped. He stood motionless in front of the open doorway, staring into what looked to be a brightly lit interior. "I'm entering now," he told Jennifer.

"Okay, Jack."

Jacobs walked inside, but then stopped in his tracks after seeing a strange cylindrical object standing upright in the very center of the dome—and nothing else.

"Do you see this object, Jennifer?" Jack said.

"Indeed so," she said.

"The object must be almost six meters tall," he said to Jennifer. "Do you see what I'm seeing?"

"Yes, I do," she replied again and with uneasiness in her voice.

Jacobs sensed Jennifer's change in tone and walked up next to the object and stopped. Coils were attached from top to bottom and seemed to go all the way around the cylinder like rings. The cylinder was silver and gray in color and had skewed vertical and horizontal gold streaks intersecting each other to form engraved diamond designs into the tubular cylindrical material. The coils were separated from each other by nearly a half meter and were light silver in color, eight centimeters wide by sixteen centimeters deep. They all touched the cylinder. Up higher on the cylinder about midway and between two of the coils, he noticed strange markings that looked to be possibly an alien language. The cylinder's size, its many details, and its diameter were intriguing. "The object is about two meters in diameter, Jennifer," he said, hoping for a statement of great insight from her. Nothing was forthcoming.

Jack continued looking over the strange object and he pulled out his gravitational force-line sensor again, hoping to learn something from the device. After turning on his sensor, he pointed it up at the cylindrical device and took a gravitational signature reading. His sensor strangely beeped to his surprise. "What the... did you pick up the change in the gravity wave signature, Jennifer?" he asked in amazement.

"Yes, I did, Jack. I don't like it."

"Do you know what just happened?"

"No, I don't," she replied with a sense of urgency.

Jack glanced at his watch—11:38 p.m. "I'm coming back to the ship in a hurry, Jennifer," he said, and in an uneasy tone. "We're going to have to make another time warp jump and come back."

"I understand, Jack, and the reasons for it."

Jacobs started toward the doorway of the dome and looked up to see the gravity lock mechanism at the top of the door. Pulling out his electron particle accelerator pistol that was twenty-five centimeters long and shaped similar to the pistols of Earth's 21st century, except for its beveled barrel, he adjusted it for low power and then pointed it up at the gravity lock. After pulling the trigger with his right index finger, there was a high-pitched whine from faster-than-light electron energy penetrating the surface of the metallic-looking lock and "POW!" Jacobs then stuck his particle accelerator pistol back in his holster and pulled out his field sensor again. He pointed it up at the rectangular-shaped gravity lock that now had a two-centimeter hole blown in the side of it and looked down at the sensor readings—no gravity field registered anymore on the door lock. "That took care of that," he remarked. "I'm coming back to the ship, Jennifer. The door is deactivated for all time."

Jack then stopped at the doorway again and noticed a strange looking console over by the northwest wall, something he hadn't noticed before as though it had been previously invisible. There was strange writing on the front of it that appeared to be written in some sort of alien hieroglyphic language much different than Earth's Egyptian hieroglyphics, or any Earth glyphs for that matter. Some of the symbols appeared to have five and six-pointed non-uniform stars mixed in with some of the strange symbols, as though the points on the stars had meaning.

Jacobs passed from thinking about what the console could possibly say, or better yet, what it had to do with the strange alien device. This console and its design captured his imagination. He finally looked up at the eight-meter tall door that curved up into the top section of the dome as though it was flexible, perfectly matching the dome's curved inner wall. The door looked to be around one centimeter thick and had tracks on each side of it. Now he didn't know if destroying the gravity lock and then removing his gravity generator on the ground outside would suddenly cause the door to fall back down under the forces of the planet's gravity. Jack pulled his pistol back out of his holster for the second time and pointed it up at the very middle of the east door track. Making sure the accelerator pistol was still set on low power he finally pulled the trigger again, but just briefly. There was another sudden whine and then POW! The track blew apart in a small section of few centimeters, as did a portion of the door. Jack knew the door was now jammed and would definitely not be falling down after removing his generator. So, he continued on through the doorway of the dome and straight toward his gravity generator. "I'm picking up my gravity generator right now, Jennifer," he said. "I'll be back in less than a minute."

"Okay, Jack."

Jack finally picked up his gravity generator and headed quickly back in the direction of his spaceship. "Why was there a hum from that device?" he asked himself. "And why was there a change in the device's gravity signature? What might that console be used for anyway?"

Jack approached closer to his ship where the door was still down and finally walked up the ramp and back into the ship. The door started to close behind him as he headed toward the elevator. Upon entering, he immediately punched the button for the cockpit and top floor of his ship. The door began to close behind him. "How are you doing, Jennifer?" he asked.

"Pretty good, Jack," she answered.

The elevator door closed and the elevator quickly rose toward the top floor. A few moments later, the door opened and Jacobs walked out into the hallway and straight toward the cockpit. On the way, he thought about the strange cylindrical alien device in the dome, tying to understand its design, but he could not. He continued by the planetarium without looking inside and on toward the cockpit still thinking about the mysterious alien device. Finally walking into the cockpit, he set his gravity generators down and took the camera with microphone off his shoulder. He removed his belt with the sensors and electron particle pistol. "Why in the world is an impulse antenna surrounding what could be a reverberating time machine?" he asked himself, while sitting down in the captain's chair.

He sat only for a short moment while thinking about all those possibilities. "Jennifer," he finally said. "Let's take our ship back up to an altitude of fifteen-hundred meters and to the exact magnetic field location as our last time warp jump. Make a four second time warp jump two seconds before midnight again, one million three hundred thousand kilometers away to the exact area of space as the last time."

"Okay, Jack," she replied, and shut off the stationary time warp field sphere around their ship. Their ship's sensors immediately detected the gravity well force field becoming active again around the dome. She activated the gravity propulsion system and their ship quickly rose off the ground and straight up into the air at an eighty degree angle of incline away from the planet's surface. The geodesic dome quickly got smaller down below, as their ship rose to an altitude of fifteen-hundred meters and then stopped. Looking at the time, Jacobs noticed it was now 11:51 p.m. "We're cutting this one close," he said to himself.

Jennifer finished the highly-accurate stationary gravity field pattern above the planet again that was exactly like the time before. She was also prepared to use the same exact four-second time warp field jump. "Okay, Jack, we're at the proper altitude and coordinates as the last time," she said.

"Okay, Jennifer, thank you. Is the time warp field formulas also ready?"

"Yes, they are," she answered.

Jack now sat content, quietly waiting for the midnight hour and thinking about the alien cylindrical device. He still could not understand its method of design, nor the control functions to it. There were no electrical cables to it, so it had to be using some type of radio wave transmission technology, possibly even a gravity force line distribution transmission system. He glanced down at his wristwatch again and it showed 11:59 p.m., fifty-six seconds and counting, two seconds before their next time warp field jump.

Two seconds later, he noticed the atmosphere turn black around their ship, as Jennifer applied the time warp field and white streams of light, visible through the cockpit windows, started passing by their ship toward the backend. Two seconds later, the white streams of light started turning red, but then glowed extremely bright red. They turned back to white right afterwards and deep space was again visible. "What? What happened just then?" Jack said somewhat confused.

"Jennifer, do you know why the red streams of light were more brightly lit this time?"

Jennifer wasn't certain herself and could only speculate. "Space-time must have moved the opposite direction at a faster rate, Jack," she says.

"That makes sense for a red shift," Jack said to himself..."Hmmm."

He wondered what might have caused it and looked directly at the camera above his forward center console. "Okay, Jennifer, let's time warp back to that planet and find out about the alien device."

"Okay, Jack."

Jennifer rotated their ship one hundred eighty degrees and the planet was again visible against the heavens and its sun. She quickly applied a one million three hundred thousand kilometer one second time warp field to the gravity field of their ship. Jack noticed space turn black again around their ship and white steams of light momentarily appear inside their time tunnel, traveling toward the back of the ship. One second later, the atmosphere of the planet was showing.

"Take us back to the dome, Jennifer," he firmly said, "and to the exact magnetic field force line distribution location on the planet's surface that we were before."

"Okay, Jack." Jennifer applied gravity propulsion and their ship took off again, dropping quickly in altitude.

Jack's watch showed 10:24 p.m., thirty seconds and counting. "This is going to be close this time," he said out loud to himself.

Immediately looking over at their cockpit's reference GMT, Jack noticed the clock was still off. "Can you update the GMT reference to Earth on the ship again, Jennifer?" he asked.

"Okay, Jack, I'll do it right now."

As they descended back down toward the dome, Jacobs suddenly relaxed back in his captain's chair, now wondering why Jennifer hadn't updated their ship's clocks. Their altitude showed 304 meters and dropping. The dome started to come into view and the GMT referenced back to Earth was finally displayed on the wall of the cockpit. Jack noticed this new time with extreme surprise. "What the heck," he exclaimed in confusion. "The cosmological time of the universe changed a thousand years this time!"

"Jennifer?" he asked with concern.

"Yes, Jack."

"Is that the new correct time for the universe in relation to Earth?"

"Yes, it is," she replied, calmly. "That is what the ecliptic positions of the planets and this planet in right ascension show in relation to the last time we were at this planet."

Jack stared at his watch, which showed a time of 10:25 p.m., and a year of 2199. Glancing over at the ship's GMT reference back to Earth, he had to shake his head, as the display now showed a time of 10:25 p.m., except it was for the Earth year of 1301 BC.

Jacobs sat quietly, staring off with a distant blank look. "So now the alien device is propagating reverse thousand-year cycles to all space-time? That can't be good."

10

THE UNUSUAL DEVICE

JACOBS LOOKED OUT HIS COCKPIT window to see the day-light hours again and knew it was close to the same time of day as the last time they were on the planet. He watched as the geodesic dome finally came into his full visual view and they softly touched down. "Are we positioned exactly the same as before in relation to the dome, Jennifer?" he asked with concern.

"Yes, we are, Jack....Verified."

"Good. Go ahead and apply the stationary time warp field around our ship once again, and exactly the same as before."

"Okay."

Jennifer applied the stationary time warp field sphere around their ship and checked for the gravity well force field that was protect-ing the dome. "The force field is nullified again, Jack," she commented.

"Okay, thank you, Jennifer."

Jack grabbed his black leather belt with the sensors and pistol. Putting on the belt, he strapped it tightly around his waist and cinched it tight. He then picked up the small shoulder-mounted strap with the camera and microphone and mounted them back on his left shoulder. The size of the alien cylindrical device came to mind. "I'm taking extra gravity generators with me this time, Jennifer," he said.

"Why, Jack?" she asked, confused.

"I may need to bring that time machine—or whatever it is— back to our ship."

Jennifer was quiet. Jack noticed that his computer wasn't saying anything about his last statement and could understand why.

Picking up the two generators that were used before, he walked over to his equipment cabinet, opened the cabinet door, and grabbed two extra generators plus their control panel. The small three centimeters long, two centimeters thick control panel was latched onto his belt. "Are you still with me, Jennifer?" he asked.

"Yes, I am, Jack."

"Good."

Carrying his four gravity generators now, Jack headed straight to the hallway for his trip back to the dome. Walking out of the cockpit and into the hallway, he slowly continued down the hallway thinking about the alien device and suddenly took a deep sigh, as he did not know what would happen when removing the alien device from the dome. Continuing on by the planetarium without a look inside, he glanced the other direction down to the planet's surface and saw the same type of evergreen-looking trees all around his ship and the geodesic dome. Looking upwards in the sky, he noticed it was a partly cloudy, showing both low and mid-level clouds to the west with a possible rain storm directly to their north. A lightning bolt suddenly struck the mountain near the ship and it quickly grabbed Jacobs's attention. But he knew the thunder could not be heard inside his ship as the sound waves and their associated atmospheric vibrations would not reverberate through the ship's encompassing gravity field. This was especially true while inside a time warp field sphere.

He finally arrived at the elevator to find the door open and entered inside. The door closed behind him and he selected the bottom floor without a moment's hesitation. The elevator quickly dropped again, nine levels, down to the bottom of their ship and the elevator door opened back up. Jack, like before, noticed the sun shining brightly on the planet's surface, visible through the outer door to their ship Jennifer had already once again opened.

With no time to waste, he walked out of the elevator and straight to the outer open door, exited the ship, and then slowly down the ramp to the surface of the planet again for the second time. Standing for a brief moment, he noticed vegetation in the vicinity of their spaceship that was over a meter high and had beautiful pink and orange flowers. It was a type of vegetation that also didn't appear to be found on Earth, but did have thick one-meter long green leaves similar to aloe vera plants. He didn't notice them the last time, so maybe the plants had died out in the last thousand years. With his stronger than steel rubberized space boots, Jack began walking straight through the thick vegetation and plants toward the dome with no hesitation in his mind whatsoever. His heartbeat had sped up and Jennifer immediately sensed Jack's increased pulse with their spaceship's molecular sensors. "Are you okay, Jack?" she asked.

"Yes, Jennifer."

Jacobs continued toward the dome and glanced at his watch. It showed 10:44 p.m. "I can't waste any time," he said to himself.

Up ahead and around toward the northeast side of the dome, the door to the dome was still open, just like he had left it a thousand years earlier. Evidently the gravity well force field encompassing the dome must have caused the dome to be completely immune to its own reversal of space-time. Otherwise, the door to the dome would have surely been locked again as though they had never visited it. That was a strange thought in itself. Jack finally walked up to the brightly lit open doorway and stopped in the doorway with a small rise in anticipation. The alien machine was noticed still standing upright and exactly in the middle of the dome. "I'm probably going to have to lay it on its side," he said to himself.

He walked through the doorway and up to the alien device, followed by setting his four gravity generators down on the floor next to what he was now figuring was a time machine of some kind. Picking up his first generator, he walked over and set it down on the floor near the entrance to the dome and angled it up at the top of the alien device. Walking back over to the alien device, he picked up two more generators and carried them over to the west wall of the dome. He placed one of the generators down on the floor and angled it up toward the center of the device. Jack then walked all the way over to the east wall with the other generator and placed it down on the floor, also angling it up at the center of the device. He walked back over to the last generator near the device, picked it up, and carried it over to the south wall. This generator was positioned on the floor near the south wall and then angled at the bottom of the alien device. Jack looked at the time on his watch again. It showed 11:10 p.m., and knew his gravity generators were now in place. "I can't waste much time," he said.

Jennifer closely watched what Jack was doing.

Jacobs unhooked the strap on his belt that was holding the control box for his generators and now held it in his left hand. After turning it on, he set up the proper four-vector parameters for the generators and then touched a button. This immediately actuated the control box and the four generators applied proportional power in an attempt to tilt the alien device down in the direction of the door. A humming sound filled the air again and then abruptly stopped. "I don't like that sound," he said to himself, while continuing to increase the antigravity fields of his gravity generators in a balanced flow of energy. The generator over at the west wall was projecting a twisting clockwise force to the center of the device, while the generator near the east wall was projecting a twisting counterclockwise force to the device. The generator at the doorway was trying to lift the device up and push it to the south, while the far south generator was also trying to lift it up, but at the same time push it toward the doorway. It was less than a minute later when the alien device finally lifted up in the air about two-meters off the floor of the dome and then started to slowly tilt toward the doorway. Jack slowed down the gravity force fields of his generators so that the alien device didn't tilt too fast. After five patient, long grueling minutes, the device was finally horizontal inside the dome and propelling the planet's gravity half a meter off the floor of the dome. He slowly and methodically repositioned each of the four gravity generators directly under the alien device, and then applied antigravity force to the gravity generators so that they too were also suspended off the floor of the dome. They were now located within a half meter of the alien device. "Okay, Jennifer," he said with strange excitement, "I have the alien device down and ready to bring to our ship."

"Is that a good idea, Jack?"

"We have no choice, Jennifer," he replied. "I don't know how to go about counteracting the space-time reversals it's generating or in some other way fix it. We have to take it into deep space where I can look at it more closely."

"I understand," she said, calmly.

Jack noticed his watch now showed 11:33 p.m. "I must hurry," he said to Jennifer, and walked out of the doorway of the dome still holding the control box for the four gravity generators. Applying non-polarized magnetic south antigravity force energy to his generators, the alien device began slowly moving out of the dome and through the doorway. Applying additional energy to his anti-gravity generators located under the device's right side, the device tilted and then turned back in the direction of his ship. Jack now began slowly walking beside the alien device. He could tell by what was displayed on the control box that the device was stressing his generators and thought that the device must be extremely heavy. At least they didn't have far to go. Up ahead, he could see the door to his ship was still open and again glanced at the time on his wristwatch. "Eleven thirty-eight p.m.," he said. "I think I'm going to make it."

Approaching closer to the ramp up into his ship, Jack noticed the vegetation with the colorful pink and orange flowers were being bent over by the alien time machine. The vegetation also appeared to have ripened seed pods that were dark brown in color and shaped like teardrops. The pods were nearly six-centimeters long and a temptation to Jack, since they were not on the planet the last time. He reached down, broke off one of the seed pods, and stuck it in his small side pouch, because he knew it could be an extinct plant. Thinking no more about that, he continued on toward the ramp with the suspended device and after arriving at the bottom of the ramp, slowly walked and guided the alien device up the ramp. After getting the large device all the way inside the ship, Jennifer wasted no time closing the door behind Jack. She immediately started training all of her cameras and their ship's sensors on the strange looking device.

Jacobs thought about the size of the possible time machine and wanted to look at it as soon as possible. After applying additional non-polarized antigravity force to his generators, he turned the alien device to his left and guided it directly toward the freight elevator. The door to the freight elevator opened a few moments later and his gravity generators guided the device all the way inside. Jacobs also entered inside and then quietly stood as the door behind him closed. Reaching over, he immediately selected the top floor and cockpit of his ship, knowing he'd never taken anything as large as the alien machine to the top floor. Standing patiently with a distant look, his thoughts about the alien device being inside their spaceship's gravitational field was something he already knew might have consequences. Suddenly, the freight elevator door opened and it brought Jack out of his strange daydream. He walked on out into the hallway, still holding his control box, and applied additional forward antigravity force energy to his generators. The alien device was finally guided out of the elevator and into the hallway. Jacobs slowly walked ahead of the large device toward the cockpit, knowing the device took up quite a lot of the hallway, but still cleared the three-meter tall ceiling.

On the way, Jennifer continued to train their ship's internal sensors on the device, instinctively despising it, but analyzing it nonetheless, unable to figure out its internal construction. None of their ship's sensors could penetrate the device's hull, whether they were of the extremely high frequency band or down in the extremely low-frequency subsonic-energy range. It was as though the alien device was made of some strange material unknown to Earth's 22nd century sciences—unknown even to Jack Jacobs and Jennifer.

Jack sighed deeply as he noticed the cockpit entrance just up ahead. He knew he wouldn't be walking by the planetarium this time, as the freight elevator was closer to the cockpit than the personnel elevator. After finally arriving at the cockpit entrance he stopped in the hallway and stood as the alien device moved all the way into the cockpit, still floating up in the air and on top of the gravity fields of his four anti-gravity generators.

He walked into the cockpit himself and followed the alien device along until finally stopping it six-meters to the left of his captain's chair. Jacobs sighed deeply again and began worrying about how much time he had left before the midnight hour. He then slowly turned off the antigravity energy fields to the four generators. The strange-looking time machine started to drop and then softly set down on the floor. He applied a small residual gravity field to his four generators to hold the alien device in place. Standing there for only a short moment longer, Jacobs headed straight over to his captain's chair and sat down with another deep sigh. Another quick glance over at the strange-looking time machine made him begin to wonder even more about the possible consequences of his actions. But he knew that, like before, there was no other choice but to do what he had just done.

"Okay, Jennifer," he said with urgency, "take us into deep space."

Jennifer sensed Jack's change in attitude, but she also knew the urgency. "Okay, Jack," she replied, and shut off the stationary time warp field around their ship. After activating their ship's gravity propulsion system, they rose up into the air and accelerated to ninety-six hundred kilometers per hour within only a few seconds. Their speed quickly increased to over 64,000 kilometers per hour at an incline of seventy-five degrees away from the planet's surface. Less than five seconds later, they plunged through the ozone layer and into the upper atmosphere. Jacobs calmly watched, as there was much turbulence while traveling through the mesosphere at a high rate of speed. Suddenly, the turbulence stopped as they quickly flew through the ionosphere and farther out into deep space at now over one million kilometers per hour. Jack looked back through one his side windows and noticed the planet getting smaller very quickly.

"Okay, Jennifer," he said. "Stop the ship."

Jennifer complied and the ship began to quickly slow until it had finally stopped.

Jacobs paused while looking at his ship's onboard time again. It showed 11:44 p.m. He continued to sit in silence thinking about the alien machine now aboard their ship and inside its gravity field. Quietly glancing at his wristwatch again, he saw the minute change and it now showed 11:45 p.m. "Jennifer?" he finally asked.

"Yes, Jack," she replied in a curious tone, trying to figure out what he was up to.

He took a deep breath and exhaled. "Let's make a one hundred million light year time warp jump the exact opposite direction from where we came out of the Milky Way....just head somewhere out in space."

"Why, Jack?" she asked with a confused voice.

"I'm not for certain," he replied, doubt filling his voice.

Jennifer sensed a slight change in Jack's heartbeat and his respiratory breathing and knew he was not telling her everything. "Okay, Jack," she replied anyway. "I'll start the calculations."

Jennifer began the calculations for an extremely long time warp field tunnel, referencing the end of their tunnel against the Stormy Way galaxy, catalogued as NGC 2199A, the irregular galaxy known as the Small Magellanic Cloud, catalogued as NGC 292, and a whirlpool spiral galaxy close to the same size as the Milky Way, cat-

alogued as NGC 14565. The starting point of their new time warp
tunnel was referenced against the Milky Way galaxy, classified as NGC
0001, because she knew it was considered to be the center of the universe for Earth. These four references were used because Jennifer did-
n't know what other references would be accurate enough for a one
hundred-million light year time warp tunnel out into deep space
where they'd never been.

While she continued calculating their new time warp field tunnel, Jack sat quiet in his chair still thinking about the alien machine
that he had just brought aboard their spaceship. He thought back to
the second harmonic cycle of four minutes versus the harmonic of the
twenty-four-minute cycle, and suddenly realized that the four-minute
cycle only applied when the alien device was outside their time warp
tunnel. Now it was inside their spaceship's gravity propulsion system
and, therefore, ultimately, inside their time warp field tunnel. He had
to shake his head while continuing to ponder the harmonic cycles,
because he knew with the device now on his ship that it would be
propagating from the inside out and could not possibly react the same
to his ship's own time warp field.

"Jack," Jennifer calmly said. "I've got the time warp field calculations done."

"Okay, Jennifer. Thank you."

Jacobs continued to think about the twenty-four minute harmonic cycle and took another deep sigh. Finally pulling the camera
and microphone off his left shoulder, he didn't like what he was starting to see in his head—the alien device being inside and encompassed
by his own spaceship's gravity field. Setting the shoulder mounted
camera and microphone down over to the right side of his captain's
chair, he glanced at his watch one more time. It showed 11:53 p.m.,
thirty seconds and counting. Another strange thought came into his
mind as though it was a message to himself from his past, or maybe it
was from his future.

"Jennifer?" he suddenly said.

"Yes, Jack."

"Let's activate the time warp field at exactly 11:55 p.m., five minutes before the scheduled time anomaly."

"Why, Jack?"

"I'll tell you later."

Jennifer analyzed this request and didn't understand what would motivate such a command that clearly violated everything that had happened before at the midnight hour. "Okay, Jack," she finally replied. "The formula will be ready."

Jacobs's watch now showed 11:54 p.m., fifty seconds and counting. As soon as the time on his wristwatch reached 11:55 p.m. sharp, he looked outside the cockpit windows to notice it had turned black again around their spaceship. White streams of light immediately appeared outside the cockpit windows and began passing by their ship toward the backend. He knew Jennifer had applied the time warp field to their spaceship just as he had asked. They had also just entered their one-hundred million light year long time warp field tunnel and all Jack could do now was to wait, but he still continued to intensely watch as the seconds ticked by and approached the time of 11:56 p.m. Jennifer also noticed this about Jack with unusual curiosity, even herself seemingly envisioning something strange was about to occur.

Their time now showed 11:55 p.m., fifty-eight seconds and counting, as they continued to travel at one hundred light years per second inside their time tunnel. It was a few seconds later when a blue haze started to show inside their time tunnel, mixed in with the white streams of light. Jacobs quickly looked at his wristwatch and it showed a year, date, and time of 2199, May 17, exactly 11:56 p.m. "Hmmm, that's what I thought," he said to himself. "Finally...."

Jennifer trained their ship's sensors and her cameras the best she could to the blue haze now showing inside their time warp tunnel and didn't understand why it was happening.

Their ship continued traveling at well over one hundred light years per second now within the time warp tunnel. What actual speed their ship was traveling, Jacobs did not know for sure and could only speculate. The blue haze inside their time warp field tunnel started to darken. The time on his watch was also moving at a faster rate, just like it had done while they were inside the curved time warp tunnel and approaching the South Pole tangent line function, an event when he noticed the minutes counting by like seconds. But this time they were not in a curved time warp field tunnel, but inside a straight tunnel. "So what does that mean?" Jack asked himself. "Are we now bending space and time?"

As Jack continued quietly staring and watching the streams of white light mixing in with the blue haze, suddenly all of the white streams of light outside the windows started turning light blue. The streams of light passing by outside the cockpit windows were now steady blue in color, not a single white stream of light among them. "Hmmm, interesting," Jack said again to himself. "That's what I also figured would happen. My time warp tunnel is now being continually pushed forward in time at who knows how fast." He had to glance at his watch one more time to see the minutes now counting by in tenths of a second, even faster than what was showing in the curved time warp tunnel.

Jacobs continued to watch in amazement to this realization, feeling no vibrations, yet wondering if their ship's time warp field would end up correcting the inverse time field of the strange-looking device taken from the dome. Traveling at well over one hundred light years per second now, he knew that their time jump inside the time warp field tunnel should last a little under two hundred seventy-eight hours, or around eleven and a half Earth days. So, all they could do was wait, at least for a short while longer.

"Jack?" Jennifer asked.

"Yes, Jennifer," Jacobs said.

"Why did the alien device activate four minutes early this time?" she asked, curiosity filling in her voice.

Jack paused to her question and could understand her curiosity. "Because," he answered. "It is now inside our spaceship's gravity field and ultimately inside the time tunnel of our time warp field, Jennifer. The four-minute harmonic cycles are now activating in reverse order, as our ship's time warp field tunnel is now being pushed forward in time to compensate."

"That's interesting," she commented.

Jack smiled at her remark. "Yes, it is," he replied. "Really the only explanation...."

Jack continued to watch the steady blue streams of light pass by his cockpit windows, when they suddenly turned white again. Immediately looking at his watch, it showed a time of twelve midnight. This was something he hadn't seen in quite some time. Jacobs took another deep breath, having suspicions they had not entirely solved their problem. Jennifer had sensed Jack's reaction to seeing midnight, and even though she didn't understand it, she also didn't say anything about it. She did notice his heartbeat had sped up a few extra beats a minute and it made her even more curious about what might be now going on.

Jacobs continued to watch the steady streams of white light pass by their ship and looked at his watch again. It showed year 2199, May 18, 12:03 a.m., fifty seconds and counting forward at a normal rate. All he could do was continue intently watching his wristwatch as time approached 12:04 a.m.

At exactly 12:04 a.m., the white streams of light started to change blue again. Jacobs thought, "Oh, no, that's what I was afraid of!"

Jennifer also noticed the blue streams of light. "Jack," she said with a confused voice. "Why is the time warp tunnel turning blue again?"

Jack didn't say anything and just stared outside his windows as the blue streams of light turned progressively darker. Their time warp field tunnel was now solid blue in color. Looking down at his wristwatch, it didn't register any time. He began to hear a hum in their time warp field. "What? That's impossible!" he said.

Immediately the blue light vanished and it became pitch black outside their spaceship. Jacobs just sat motionless, trying to think of an explanation.

"Jack!" Jennifer asked, thinking about the best way to pose the question. "Where are we?"

"I don't know." There was silence in the cockpit.

Jennifer was surprised in Jack's answer and couldn't determine anything from their ship's sensors.

Jacobs checked his instruments to the outside world and nothing was registering. Everything was zero. There was no gravity, no light, no plasma radiation—even neutrinos were showing as non-existent. There was also no black body radiation whatsoever! It was as though nothing was out there. Checking the energy reserves of their ship, they still registered an efficiency of eighty-four percent, but strangely showed a high power load. The gravity propulsion system showed to be fully functional.

"Jennifer?" he asked.

"Yes, Jack."

"Is our time warp field still operable?"

"I don't know. I cannot determine that, Jack," she said in a mild tone.

"That's okay, Jennifer." Jack turned to his left and looked over at the strange device that he had brought aboard their ship. It was all black. "What the... The device is burned out?" he asked himself.

"Can you tell me what has happened to the onboard alien machine, Jennifer?"

"What I can determine, Jack," she replied, "is inconclusive at best. The device was a doomsday time machine. Our time warp field within the time tunnel exceeded its reverse time function capability, rendering it useless."

Jacobs was strangely intrigued. "That's interesting to think about," he remarked with a distant look, continuing to think about what she had just told him. He wondered for what purpose an alien race may have created the device. Was it to be used as an offensive or defensive weapon, or maybe even somehow related to the white dwarf star's strange storm rifts that were generating anti-matter space? Thinking no more about that he began staring down at his instrument panels that were lit only by a few emergency lights in the cockpit, and wondered why the outside space pressure was so high that it would cause such an unusual power drain on their ship's Gaussian energy system. It was almost as if the blackness of space was trying to crush their ship and collapse its gravity field in the process. It was a good thing the shape of their ship and its encompassing gravity field was optimized to take maximum pressure loads, and an even better thing that their gravity propulsion system was still showing functional. "Can you rotate our ship one hundred eighty degrees, Jennifer?" he finally asked.

"Yes, I can, Jack, but I'll have to use the ship's gravity force vectors to calculate the rotation."

"I understand," he said calmly. "Go ahead and do it."

Jack sat in his captain's chair staring out through the cockpit windows that were still pitch black. "Are we rotating, Jennifer?"

"Yes, we are."

"That is so strange," he said to himself, "To not be able to reference movement to anything."

"Our ship has finished rotating one hundred eighty degrees, Jack," she informed him.

"Okay, Jennifer. I've got to go down to the planetarium to think about what has just happened to us."

"Okay, I understand," she replied, accepting that he needed some time alone.

Jack stood up from out of his captain's chair, and after grabbing his notebook, started toward the doorway to the hallway, but then stopped. "Oh, Jennifer?" he asked while turning around.

"Yes, Jack."

"Continue monitoring the black matter space around our spaceship for anything, anything at all."

Jennifer's organic memory cells registered surprise to hear the new term *black matter space*. "Okay, Jack," she replied, and started analyzing Jack's "black matter" terminology.

Jacobs stood for a short moment longer, knowing they were now in a very strange and possibly worse situation than ever before.

"Do you have any idea how much time may have passed for us?" he calmly asked.

"I cannot make such a determination," she replied. "There is nothing to reference it to. Even our ship's gravity field is not in resonance with anything."

Jacobs heard the words and knew exactly what Jennifer was telling him. "Makes sense," he said to himself, and walked out of the cockpit toward the planetarium, carrying the notebook with his new time warp field equations.

"I'll need about six hours to myself, Jennifer," he remarked.

"Okay, Jack," she calmly replied.

Jack smiled a little, realizing Jennifer did not know what had happened to them either. Continuing toward the planetarium and down the hallway, Jacobs noticed the emergency lights in the hallway were also activated, yet outside the windows there was total darkness. It was like outside their spaceship nothing existed, just blackness and uncertainty. It just didn't make any sense to him.

Finally arriving at the planetarium, Jacobs noted the artificial sunlight had also been activated for their plants and trees. "I'm glad that doesn't take much of our ship's energy reserves," he said out loud, and then walked into the planetarium toward his favorite chair. Jack then sat down next to the waterfall and began listening to the soothing sound of the water running across the rocks, wondering what could have possibly just happened to them.

11

THE SURPRISE DISCOVERY

"LET'S SEE NOW," he said out loud to himself, while staring down at his notebook. "We had a reverse time-field doomsday time machine, a twenty-four minute harmonic cycle that was converted down to its second harmonic of four minutes, and a positive forward time field of my ship's time warp field. What a combination! Using the reverse time machine within my time warp tunnel and having a one hundred million light-year line element vector, things get very interesting."

Jacobs began to think very hard about what had happened and opened up his notebook. He first took a one-million-to-one light year time factor ratio into account, accomplishing gravity harmonic formulas in relation to a reverse four-minute cycle that got re-inverted and then squared. At least it seemed that way to him. He began slowly filling up pages of his notebook with new squared inversion formulas that were calculating across the zero-point denumerator functions, and began to realize that completely new gravity harmonic formulas were being created that he'd never envisioned. They were formulas that would seemingly alter the gravity element into even heavier elements, similar to what he was already doing with his inverse transmutations for basic time warp field propulsion. But he couldn't see any uses of the new elements using time warp field methodologies and put those possibilities out of his mind. He quickly went back to his notebook and began using the new gravity formulas back into his time warp field equations, all as they would be applied to a speed of light reference in normal space. After filling up a few more pages, he raised his eyebrows and began staring at the new figures. "My God!" he said with a little shock. "I'm going to have to exponentially factor!"

Jacobs pulled his chair over to the console in the planetarium with a sudden feeling of déjà vu and began entering his latest equations into the touch-activated keyboard, knowing Jennifer would see his exponential equations that were now using new positive zero offset functions. Upon entering a hundredth power exponential factor of this new offset into his five-state multi-dimensional equations, all as it would be applied to the new time warp field laws, he began patiently waiting with much anticipation of what Jennifer may determine. Looking over at his old 21st century Mahoakany pendulum-driven wall clock, his surprises continued as the time showing did not make any sense....The hour and minute hands appeared to be running *backwards* of all things.

Continuing to wait for a reply back from his computer, he started to get antsy wondering why it was taking her so long. Glancing down at his wristwatch he had been ignoring, it showed a year of 0001 and a time of 4:45 a.m., twenty-five seconds and counting forward. "What the heck. My time has started over from zero!"

Looking down at his display again, he noticed Jennifer had finally come back with the answer to his new equations. He had to take a double look at what the screen was showing him. "It is incalculable," he said, out loud to himself. "We are at infinity—"

Jacobs sat back in his chair and thought about what was just determined. "How do I fix that?" he said to himself, not fully understanding how it was possible or could have ever happened.

He began to think again, realizing infinity meant nothingness, a void in space and time, a void of all matter and energies. But then he also knew everything had to have an answer to any previous event or action, and his ship was the previous action. He finally regained his scientific mental senses. "Let me see," he said to himself. "I have a reverse function doomsday time machine, a four-minute cycle which got re-inverted and then squared, and a positive function of my ship's time warp field. What does this all do?"

He continued to think about what could have happened. "How can this be?" he asked himself in wonderment. "There must have been a four-minute time cycle generated by my ship's own time warp field that squared the original function somehow. Why else would that alien machine have burned out? I know my ship's time warp field drive is much more powerful. Hmmm…"

Jack sat for a little while longer, thinking about why the alien time machine may have burned out. "Could it be that two time machines occupied the same space at the same time?"

Jack immediately turned the page in his notebook and began calculations for two time machines occupying the same area of space at the same time, activating at the same time, with one more powerful than the other. "The answer must be here," he said again to himself. "There had to be some sort of quake in space-time itself."

Jack continued to calculate new zero-offset integral formulas that were related to two opposing time machines activating at the same time with one inside the other, one more powerful than the other, and all happening within the same area of space. It had to have opened up a hole in space-time itself, he figured. By factoring his ship's time warp field and its harmonic cycles into the alien time machine's squared inversion formulas, additional new complex modulus formulas were created that were, heretofore, never envisioned and unthinkable. They were very strange formulas and not making any sense for any useable theories of science, time warp field laws, or any augmentations of the modulus complexes. The strange formulas he thought might lead to a field of science not able to be called science anymore, possibly what initially created the universe, created time, created space, created matter, and even created all energy. Jacobs felt lightheaded all of a sudden and then closed his eyes while trying to solve these new modulus equations that were seemingly unsolvable. He finally had to put the equations out of his mind and no longer felt lightheaded, as they were much too complicated. He then opened his eyes again while listening to the sound of the running water. This time, for some strange reason, the sound vibrations from the water flowing over the many rocks clearly caught Jack's attention.

Quietly, he began listening to the gentle sound being generated by the flow of the water over the rocks; its many harmonic vibrations, its ripples of wave mechanics continually flowing through the open air and space of the planetarium. A strange look of intuition suddenly appeared on his face and he immediately looked up at the running water, thinking about what he now heard, seeming to be a familiar sound. He then looked over again at his mechanical pendulum-driven wall clock that was still running backwards. "That's it!" he said excitedly. "That's why there was a hum in our time warp tunnel!"

"Jennifer!"

"Yes, Jack," she replied, noting a difference in Jack's attitude. "You sound like you've come up with something. Am I right?"

"Yes, and I'm coming back to the cockpit. We're getting out of here!"

Jennifer was surprised by Jack's new attitude, as she didn't have any idea how to get out of the black matter space their ship currently occupied. She trained her cameras on Jack as he walked quickly out of the planetarium and headed back down the hallway toward the cockpit. There was a half smile showing on his face. Jack had heard the camera zoom in on him, so he smiled to Jennifer while continuing on toward the cockpit with an extremely relaxed and warm spirit to the realization of figuring out what had happened to them. Finally walking back into the cockpit, he looked over and noticed the burned out alien time machine. "Won't ever have to worry about that doomsday device again," he commented, and then sat down in his captain's chair.

Jacobs relaxed back in his chair. "Okay, Jennifer," he finally said.

"Yes, Jack," she replied with partial excitement.

Jack realized his computer was responding with excitement in her voice, and knew she was waiting for him to tell her what he had found or determined. He paused for a short breath and then looked down at his wristwatch which showed a time of 0001, 7:30 a.m., fifty-four seconds and still counting forward. He looked back up to the camera above his forward center console.

"You've picked up on our time starting over at zero, haven't you, Jennifer?" he asked with a smile.

"Yes, I have, Jack, and I'm confused about it."

"Well, we've traveled to the end of time and now sit at infinity," Jack said, pausing a moment. "We have started a new existence of time," he added.

Jennifer began to think and analyze what Jack had just said to her. "Jack," she says, "that makes complete sense."

Jack smiled again and thought about Jennifer's response. He then thought about how they were going to return back to a normal existence. "Okay, Jennifer," he finally said. "Here's how we are going to get back home."

"Okay Jack, I'm listening," she excitedly answered.

"Since we know we have our ship orientated to the exact opposite direction that we came, we need to apply an inverse time warp field to our ship. Following me on that, Jennifer?"

Jennifer thought about what Jack had just said. "But we will go further forward in time," she exclaimed.

"Further forward in time in relation to what, Jennifer?"

Jennifer began analyzing what Jack had just told her. "I don't understand, Jack," she said.

"Jennifer," Jack said, "our time has started over. We can't go back to zero from where we came from or we would cease to exist. Do you understand?"

Jennifer paused. "I believe I do," she answered.

"Good. Because we have to travel backwards with our ship's gravity field, yet forward in time within our time warp tunnel. That's the only way we can ever exist again in normal space-time, Jennifer." Jack paused. "Look at it like rewinding our gravity field clock, so we can start ticking again," he said with a little humor.

Jennifer gave a soft computer laugh.

Jack raised his eyebrows in surprise. His computer had never laughed before.

"Jack," she said. "You are a wonderful man."

Jacobs sat back in his chair, not knowing what to say because of the way his computer was now talking to him. He changed his thoughts to getting out of the black matter space of existence, an existence with seemingly no substance and no time. The only existence was their ship and everything inside.

"Okay, Jennifer," he instructed. "Apply a one hundred million, inverse light-year time warp field equation to our ship's gravity propulsion system. Use the exact opposite equation that you used for our last time warp jump."

"Okay, Jack. I'll have it here shortly."

Jacobs had feelings of anticipation to finally making it home to the right time frame in the universe, but wondered if their ship might be stuck in eternity. Had the black matter space of existence captured their ship, or were they in a strange time loop of infinite possibilities, a loop with only one possible outcome?

Jennifer finally finished her calculations. "Okay, Jack," she said. "I'm ready."

Jack's heart sped up while coming out of his daydream. "Okay, Jennifer. Apply the time warp field," he said.

Jennifer applied the inverse time warp field to their ship's gravity propulsion system and nothing seemed to happen. It was still pitch black outside their spaceship and cockpit windows. Jack immediately looked at his wristwatch and it showed January 01, 0001, exactly 8:10 a.m. He knew the time showing on his wristwatch was directly correlating to the amount of time their ship's gravity propulsion system had been inside the black matter space. "Hmmm, interesting," he said to himself, realizing they must have entered the new time warp field tunnel at 8:10 a.m.

Jack continued to sit calmly as nothing appeared to be happening outside their spaceship, even though he suspected differently. It remained completely black outside the cockpit windows.

Jennifer was now confused. "Are we moving within the time warp tunnel?" she asked.

"I believe so," Jack replied. "Our ship was so far into eternity that light didn't exist."

"Jack," she remarked. "What insight you have."

Jack smiled a little and continued to intensely watch out the windows, strangely knowing what was going to happen next, but not from where it would be generated. Calmly glancing down at his wristwatch, it showed 8:13 a.m., fifty seconds and counting and he looked up to one of the cameras. "Jennifer?"

"Yes, Jack."

"Train your cameras to the windows and get ready to watch the birth of light," he said.

Jennifer trained all of her cameras in the cockpit to the cockpit windows, surprised at his request. Jack also intensely watched his wristwatch to see it was now 8:13 a.m., fifty-nine seconds and quickly looked up through the cockpit windows.

Suddenly, a small single stream of white light appeared away from their point of view and spaceship and moved down the time tunnel straight at them. It quickly passed by their ship in a steady stream and toward the back of their ship. This surprised Jacobs, as he was expecting white streams of light to have suddenly appeared all around their spaceship like a normal time warp field tunnel. Suddenly, another white stream of light appeared away from their cockpit windows and moved down the time tunnel straight toward them. It also began quickly passing by their ship in a steady stream toward the back of their ship. Then there was another. Before long many other streams of white light appeared away from their point of view and traveled toward the back of their ship. Jacobs glanced at his watch again and had an idea what was now happening with the creation of light, yet, was also relieved that the white streams of light were now appearing all around their spaceship. Their new time warp field tunnel showing outside the cockpit windows looked just like a normal time warp field tunnel, except Jacobs knew the streams of light were moving in the same direction as their spaceship—backwards. He sat calmly waiting, watching as the white streams of light continued to pass by their ship, wondering again from what source the light was being generated since light did not exist previously. Was it from a highly-advanced intelligence greater than what he could imagine, or maybe even a part of their being, their sustenance, their spiritual energy? Why would there first be a single stream of light, then two, and then three before light could be called light?

Jacobs continued to wonder about that and thought back to the first book of the Bible, first chapter. He then put on his religious and theological thinking cap for a moment, trying to understand what meaning it might have, but found he could not come up with an answer. Finally glancing down at his wristwatch, he saw the time was still counting forward at a normal rate and approaching what he believed to be the start of a new reality for Jennifer and him. His watch finally showed exactly 8:18 a.m. and he looked up to the camera above his center console. "We are now moving forward in time," he remarked, "in the reverse manner from which we came."

"What do you mean by that?" Jennifer asked, sounding confused.

"I think we'll end up where we initially time jumped from, Jennifer."

"I think I understand, Jack."

Jack continued to sit quietly watching the streams of light pass by their ship at a speed he knew was well over one hundred light years per second, all as though they were traveling forward inside their time tunnel. Yet he knew their ship was actually still traveling backwards inside the time tunnel and being continually overtaken by the speed of light that was being generated from an unknown source. "This is so strange to think about," he said to himself, "to have light passing us by as we're moving backwards in our ship. So how fast does that really mean our ship is then traveling? Maybe our ship is not moving at all and it is the black matter space outside the ship that is moving? How else could light be continually overtaking our ship?"

Jacobs regained his thoughts while continuing to watch the light pass by their spaceship, relieved once again to see the white streams of light completely encasing their ship inside the time tunnel, isolating them from the black matter space of existence that was void of everything—void of existence, void of matter, void of all energy. The only existence as he now viewed it was his inverse time warp field tunnel and their time travel backwards for what, hopefully, would be a new existence from where they first came—a universe with an Earth year of 2199.

Jacobs continued to sit quietly with relief, mixed with antici-pation, to finally getting to the end of their inverse time warp field tunnel that he believed to be one hundred million light years long in duration—a tunnel that was being strangely modified in a time warp field projection. He knew whatever current modifications it was going through should be exactly opposite of the previous time warp tunnel that got them into their predicament to begin with. Jack looked at his watch and it now showed 8:41 a.m., forty-five seconds and counting. Almost twenty-four minutes had passed since their ship was encased in the white streams of light traveling the same backwards direction as their spaceship. "Here comes the twenty-four minute cycle, Jennifer," he said, excited.

Jennifer, after hearing this, also began watching the white streams of light as they continued passing by their cockpit windows toward the back of their ship, especially as their time approached 8:42 a.m., just as Jack had told her.

His wristwatch finally counted to 8:42 a.m., and just as suddenly, the white streams of light turned solid white with intense brightness. Jacobs immediately closed his eyes surprised, while fumbling to pick up his sun goggles. He finally found them and after putting them on, the intense brightness was like that of a thousand suns, even with the automatic photo tinting of the cockpit windows. Again, he had no idea what was now happening or showing outside their ship, unless what he was seeing was simulating something similar to a Big Bang, a creation, a unification of all forces into one physical existence. Watching, not knowing what to expect and only suspecting, his heartbeat sped up a bit to that possibility. Now keeping track of the time in his head, he finally lifted his arm and wristwatch up close to his goggles and took a quick squinting peek behind the shadow of his arm. The time showing was 8:45 a.m., fifty seconds and counting.

He set his arm back down and firmly repositioned the goggles back over his eyes. White glimmers of light continued reflecting and shining off his goggles as he sat patiently, all the while wondering if their new existence would soon begin like he thought it might, back in the original Earth year of 2199 and their true plane of existence. Jacobs finally turned to one of the cameras and then back to the intense brightness outside the cockpit windows. "Eight forty-six a.m. is the moment of truth, Jenny," he said with a slight grin.

"Is that our four-minute cycle on top of the twenty-four minute cycle?" she asked.

"Yes, it is."

They both continued to stare intensely out the windows, with Jennifer using ultraviolet light filters on her cameras. The cockpit got completely quiet at that moment, as Jacobs held his breath, not knowing what would happen, wondering if they might be flattened into oblivion or be successfully pushed back into a physical reality through a hole from eternity—a hole back into a true existence for Jennifer and him.

Suddenly, there was a light vibration felt inside their ship followed by a very loud and strange hum. The vibration and hum abruptly stopped and the bright light vanished. Outer space and the energy from a sun became immediately visible.

"We made it!" Jacobs exclaimed excitedly, his heartbeat finally starting to slow down.

Taking off his goggles, the planet where he first took the doomsday time machine aboard his spaceship was showing in the far distance. The Earth-sized planet was still surrounded by a magnificent blue atmosphere, silhouetted against the bright rays of its sun. Looking over at the alien time machine, it was still all black in color. "Whew!" he said with a sigh and looked at his wristwatch, which showed no time.

"Jennifer?"

"Yes, Jack."

"Do you remember the cosmological time reference of the planets in their ecliptic planes of orbit to their sun, including the planet from where we took the alien time machine?"

"Yes."

"How about as they all compare and relate to Earth for its GMT?" he asked again.

"Yes, I do," she answered.

"Great! Figure out if there are any reference time differences prior to our time warp jump, and let me know if our time reference back to Earth and its solar system is correct at 2199, May 17, 11:55 p.m."

"Okay, Jack. Hold on—"

Jack sat back relaxed in his captain's chair, waiting to hear from Jennifer and to find out if they were in the correct time frame in the universe. The planet looked the same from a distance and his forward center display was showing it still had an atmospheric base of 58 percent nitrogen, 39 percent oxygen. His ship's sensors were also telling him that it had the same geomagnetic dipole field, except measuring 0.73 gauss at its equator, only a two percent drop from what it was before taking the alien time machine off its surface.

"Jack, I have the new time!" she said, sounding confused.

Jack was surprised by her reaction. "Well, what is it?" he asked with an unusual, strange feeling inside.

"Our time in reference to Earth is…is May 17, 11:55 p.m., 2299!"

"What?"

"I'm certain that's correct, Jack. Yes, I'm sure of it," she said.

"So then what happened to a hundred years?"

"I don't know Jack," she replied.

Jacobs looked back out through his cockpit windows again at the planet in the distance and was thoroughly confused by what had happened to them. They were a hundred years into their future. He also noticed the automatic photo-tinting of his ship's cockpit windows were still darkened, as though the strange intense energy burst they had encountered coming back from eternity may have etched them dark and caused them permanent damage. Looking back at his wristwatch, it was now showing a time of 12:09 A. M., January 01, and the year 0001. "What the heck! Our time has started over again!"

"Jennifer?" he asked.

"Yes, Jack."

"Why did our time start over again?"

Jennifer wasn't certain herself, but knew from her previous analysis that their ship's gravity field was reacting strangely with the magnetic fields of both the planet and its large sun. "Our ship's gravity propulsion system appears not to be in resonance with anything," she answered.

Jacobs thought he understood what she had said, because he knew their ship and everything inside didn't belong in the new universe. He also knew that for them to remain in the new universe, they would have to make another harmonic adjustment of their ship's gravity propulsion system two-thousand, two-hundred and ninety-nine years, nearly four and one-half months forward to the day of May 18th. He additionally knew that if they were to make this large harmonic adjustment out in outer space and not down on the surface of the planet, their ship's gravity propulsion system would probably permanently die, rendering the ship useless. "Let's head back to the planet, Jennifer," he said, "and back to the area of the mountains where the dome building was last known to be standing."

"Okay, Jack."

Jennifer rotated and repositioned their ship toward the planet and applied gravity propulsion. Their ship quickly took off in the direction of the planet at 132,000 kilometers per hour. On the way, Jacobs punched a series of buttons on his center forward display that showed the planet's magnetosphere and became curious if its magnetic field may have flip-flopped since the last time they were on the planet. He could not tell from what his display was showing, but did notice their ship had already entered into the outer reaches of the planet's magnetic field and its ionosphere. Jennifer quickly slowed their ship down to 32,000 kilometers per second and activated a magneticion field on the front edge of their ship. Suddenly, red, white, and blue flames appeared outside the cockpit windows as they entered the mesosphere. It was a familiar sight, so Jacobs continued to sit calmly as their ship's hull began interacting again with the planet's upper atmosphere at over 8 kilometers per second. Yet, he also found himself filled with anticipation of whether the dome building was still down on the surface of the planet. The flames abruptly stopped as their ship continued through the thick ozone layer and toward the surface.

He reached forward and touched a series of buttons on his forward center console. Three holographic images immediately appeared in front of him. To his left was a half-meter in diameter spherical image and to his right were two flat-shaped, yet highly-detailed images. He began looking at the three different holographic images taken from the surface of the planet and mountainside where they were headed. There were still lots of trees and shrubbery, but he did not know if there were any intelligent alien beings now living on the planet. "Jennifer?" he asked.

"Yes, Jack."

"Have you detected any intelligent terrestrial life on the planet?"

"Not that I can determine, Jack," she answered. "But I am picking up low-frequency sounds emanating off the surfaces of its many oceans."

Jack was surprised. "Oh really?" he said. "What's causing them?"

"According to our ship's databanks, they closely match those of the large Blue Whales back home."

"Interesting," Jack said out loud. "So the planet has marine life now?"

"It appears so," Jennifer said.

"Are you detecting the presence of any animals or insects?"

"None at all," Jennifer answered.

Jacobs thought about this new information and continued to stare at his three holographic images. One of the images now showed the mountainside where the dome building was last known to be standing. The dome building came into his view and was now visible among the heavy forest of trees. Jack knew there was a chance of something strange still going on with their time in the new universe versus the time on the planet. "Let's land exactly thirty meters from the dome the same as we did before, Jennifer," he said.

"Okay, Jack."

Jacobs watched outside his windows as they continued to descend. Their altitude was now five-hundred meters and continuing to drop as Jennifer slowed their ship down to one-hundred and sixty kilometers per hour. She slowed their ship even more as they approached the mountainside, and a few moments later, they softly touched down exactly thirty meters from the dome building. Jack immediately reached forward and touched a button on his forward center console to see whether the dome was still protected by a gravity well force field. He found that it was. "Jennifer?"

"Yes, Jack."

"Before we create a time warp field sphere around our ship, I want you to go ahead and adjust the harmonics of our ship's gravity propulsion system forward two-thousand, two-hundred, ninety-nine years, four and one-half months to the Earth day of May 18th, taking into account the amount of time we've been inside this new universe."

"Okay," she replied, "are you sure our ship's gravity element won't burn up in the process?"

Jack was unsure. "No, I'm not certain," he answered. "But if we don't, I'm sure our ship's energy system will not charge properly and may even quit working altogether."

"I understand," Jennifer said, and began comparing the solar time on the planet to the amount of time they'd spent inside the new universe. She made absolutely sure her harmonic adjustments were going to be exactly correct and then began adjusting the harmonics of their ship's Gaussian energy system in direct relation to the ship's gravity element.

Jack watched as his instrument panels went blank again, just as it had before, as well as all of the lights in his cockpit. All he could see now was the slight etching of the sun's sunlight into his cockpit as it shined from out of the western horizon. He had to hold his breath, wondering if his ship's gravity element would burn up or not and survive the massive harmonic adjustment. If it were to burn up, it would definitely create a usual problem, leaving them with only limited gravity propulsion from their backup system and no ability to create a time warp field. They would also not be able to create a time warp field sphere and ever see what was still inside the dome or inspect the strange console. Jacobs exhaled and calmly relaxed back in his chair to find his body was starting to get warm again, just like it had done when Jennifer adjusted the harmonics of their gravity propulsion system forward eight minutes when near the White Dwarf star.

Suddenly his body got even warmer to the point where he felt like he might start sweating, and then just as quickly he noticed the lights on his three forward instrument panels light back up and the lights throughout the entire cockpit come back on. His body no longer felt warm and he felt strangely invigorated. Jacobs glanced down at the time showing on his forward center instrument panel and it showed 12:45 a.m., May 18th, and for a year of 2299. He could only take another deep breath, realizing their ship's gravity element survived the massive harmonic adjustment, not to mention whatever had just happened to his body.

Jack finally turned to one of the cameras, now knowing their ship's gravity-based time was synchronized with Earth's solar time that was a hundred years into his future. He knew even his body had possibly gone through the same adjustment, possibly of a hundred years. Why else would it have heated up? The skin texture showing on his hands and arms hadn't changed. He looked back up to the camera above his center console.

"Jennifer?" he asked.

"Yes, Jack," she replied.

"Do your have any idea why my body felt warm again?"

"Only speculation, Jack," she said again. "The flux energy patterns of your body seemed to have changed a little, as though they also synchronized to the new universe."

Jacobs raised his eyebrows. "Oh really?" he commented, and now wondered how that was ever possible. "Did my DNA molecules change any?"

"Not that I can tell, Jack," she replied.

Jacobs knew he'd probably never figure out what really happened to his body and began wondering about the dome-shaped building that was still protected by the gravity well force field. He suddenly looked out through his forward cockpit windows to see the white-colored geodesic dome building in full view and directly below his vantage point. He then looked back to the camera above his forward center console. "Go ahead and apply the time warp field sphere around our ship again, Jennifer."

"Okay, Jack, will do."

Jennifer applied the time warp field sphere around their ship and then checked the gravity well force field around the dome. "Jack!" she said, excited again. "The force-field is nullified!"

Jack new from her excitement that she was also curious of what was still inside the dome. "Okay, Jennifer, thank you. Let's get ready to go back to the dome."

12

A STRANGE NEW BEGINNING

"**O**KAY, JACK," Jennifer said. "I'm ready."

Jacobs took a short pause and had to glance out his darkened cockpit windows again and down to the planet's surface. Like before, he noticed the many evergreen-looking trees with tall grass and shrubbery growing up near their thick large trunks. When he looked over in the eastern horizon he could see one of the planet's two moons showing in the shape of a magnificent light blue sphere close to twenty-degrees above the horizon. Jack continued to stare at the moon with curiosity and turned to one of the cameras. "Jennifer?"

"Yes, Jack," she answered, curious of his question.

Jack paused for a short moment. "What is the orbital pattern of the two moons in relation to each other?"

Jennifer already knew the answer. "They are one-hundred and

seventy-nine degrees apart," she answered, "with an orbital offset and perturbation of two point seven degrees."

Jacobs was surprised, "Oh really?" he said. "Are they also about the same size?"

"Yes, they are."

"So they're sort of acting like gimbals to the planet then huh?" Jack asked again.

"It would seem so," she said again. "They are also rotating around the planet on the same spherical plane."

Jacobs knew that information made sense or else they'd be in elliptical orbits. Looking over toward his right and to his shoulder-mounted camera, he figured they might as well finally find out if the dome had changed since traveling to eternity and back. He reached over and grabbed the shoulder-mounted camera and microphone and fitted them back on his left shoulder. After strapping it tight, he finally stood up and started toward the cockpit exit, but then stopped. "Jennifer," he said.

"Yes, Jack."

"Do the ship's sensors show the door to the dome still open?"

"Yes, they do," she said. "According to the planet's magnetospheric field-line polarity strengths, there is a drop of 1.8 picogauss on the northeastern side of the dome, starting at the planet's surface and extending up eight meters."

Jacobs knew that was good news, but he still did not know for sure what they might find inside the dome. After reaching down and feeling the handle of his particle accelerator pistol, he headed out of the cockpit and down the hallway. His anticipation rose as he walked down the lighted hallway of his ship, even though the windows in the hallway seemed to have been also slightly damaged by the intense brightness encountered right before they entered into their new universe. They were photo-etched damaged, Jacobs thought, but then he could still see all of the coniferous-looking trees down on the planet's surface and all around his ship. It was as though the windows had finally lightened some. To the north he could see what looked to be the same waterway he had seen before, as there were many trees lining both of its banks. The river seemed much wider than before, noticeable by the amount of separation between the trees along each side of the waterway. As he approached closer to the elevator, the waterfall over in the northwest was again in view, just like he'd seen before, and it caused him to stop. He couldn't help but observe the final plunge of the water as it fell into the pool at the bottom, knowing it had to be at least a hundred meter drop.

"I can't wait to visit that," he mumbled to himself, and walked on by his planetarium toward the open doorway of the elevator. After finally entering inside, he turned around and selected the bottom floor of his ship. The door closed and the elevator quickly dropped, nine levels, and the elevator door opened up again. Jacobs immediately noticed the sun shining through the outer door to their ship that Jennifer had already opened. He headed out of the elevator and toward the open door, but then stopped again. "Is there anything different about the planet's atmosphere than before, Jennifer?" he asked.

"No, nothing at all," she replied.

Jacobs took a small pause and then walked on down the ramp to the planet's surface. Finally stepping onto the planet's surface for the third time, he planted both of his feet firmly and had to take another deep breath of fresh air. He found it invigorating, as the purity of the atmosphere and its thirty-nine percent oxygen level was clearly evident. Looking around the forest, he became cognizant of the evergreen-looking trees again, as their green and blue colored needle-leaves were inverted and opposite to the shapes of the evergreen trees on Earth. But even more evident with the coniferous trees was their magnificent bluish-red bark and many vertical yellow streaks traveling all the way down to the base of their trunks. Mixed in with the coniferous-looking trees he also saw another type of tree he had not seen before, and they looked very similar to the large oak trees back on Earth. Yet their leaves were much bigger—at least forty centimeters long. "Do you see what I see, Jennifer?" Jack asked.

"Yes, I do," she answered. "It is magnificent-looking."

Jacobs quietly acknowledged Jennifer's comment, knowing she was also reacting to the visual beauty of the planet. He finally turned his head to the left and slowly followed the tree line until his attention was caught by the display of very unusual and pretty plants. They looked to be strange cactus plants of some type, nearly one meter tall, having sharp green blades for leaves and yellow flowers in the shape of carnations on the end of long brown stems. The thought was there for him that the many new plants and tree species on the planet could contain new medicinal properties not found or could possibly be known about on Earth. He couldn't wait to check out that possibility and for what new elements might be found in the planet's tectonic plates. Would it contain more than seven major plates, as was the case for the number of plates found in the Earth's lithosphere? He also began wondering if the planet's crust or its mantle plates might contain the extremely-rare stable isotope of the naturally occurring gravity element.

Jacobs finally caught his breath from thinking about the large planet that he and Jennifer were now on, realizing they were the only intelligent life on its surface that could make decisions affecting its entire taxonomic system of plants and trees, including what appeared to be its marine life. That thought suddenly caused him a mental rush of adrenalin and he knew the rush was something that he had never experienced. He finally turned back toward the dome and noticed it now fully displayed to his visual senses. Taking a small pause, he finally began walking toward the dome and thinking about the 23rd century Earth, not knowing whether he was part of its history or not. *Maybe there was already a 23rd century Jack Jacobs and he was now a double?*

"What a strange thought," Jack said to himself, as he approached closer to the dome. "That would definitely create a very unusual problem for me," he mumbled under his breath.

Finally walking up to the geodesic dome, he couldn't help but stare at it, mesmerized at the optical illusion the geometric figures were showing him. He knew the designs and shapes used to form the spherical structure had never been taught in any school or course during his education. The highly unorthodox combinations of the hexagons and pentagons on the sphere were especially intriguing, and he couldn't wait to mathematically analyze their configurations and try figuring them out. But then the gravity well force field surrounding the dome would have to be shut down before the shapes could be examined in more detail.

Jacobs saw the open doorway to the dome up ahead and on his right. Finally walking up to the doorway, he glanced inside to see it still brightly lit and was mildly surprised to see no cylindrically shaped alien time machine—even after already suspected there would not be one. He walked inside the dome and to the very middle, now looking around at the walls and up to the ceiling of the spherical structure. The brightness inside the dome was confusing to him, as there were no incandescent lighting sources visible anywhere. "I wonder how it's being lit then," Jacobs said to himself.

"Jennifer?" he asked.

"Yes, Jack."

"Do you have any idea how this dome is being lit?"

"No, I don't," she answered. "According to the ship's sensors, there is a strange energy source generating it from inside the dome."

Jack's interest perked up. "Where from?" he asked again.

"I don't know," she said.

Jacobs was surprised hearing this. "Why can't you determine where?"

"I believe it's because of our time warp field sphere, Jack," she answered. "The sphere has changed the gravity base around the dome, and as a result the source driving the photon generation cannot be pinpointed."

Jack understood what she had told him, knowing they were going to have to figure out how to deactivate the gravity well force field, in order to learn more about the advanced technologies the dome seemed to possess. He turned around to his right and northwest wall to see that the same console with the alien hieroglyphic language still there. After walking directly up to the brown-colored, two meter wide by three meter long console, he stood quietly and saw that it had a strange assortment of rectangular-shaped buttons and controls. There also seemed to be a large display nearly one meter in size, but everything on the console was blank—as though a master switch was off. Behind the console there was also a single large black high-back cushioned chair with soft armrests. Seeing all of this only caused Jacobs to wonder even more why an advanced race would create a time machine capable of reversing time and space of the entire universe. It just didn't make any sense to him how they could have ever had the level of technology to accomplish such a feat of that magnitude. Jacobs shook his head and he asked himself, "How could a small twenty-one meter geodesic dome have ever generated such massive gravity waves to reverse the entire universe?"

He continued to think about that possibility and the strange White Dwarf star quickly came to his mind as the only possible answer. "It had to be related to the dwarf star," he said again to himself, "especially since it was affecting a very large area of space. Its storm rifts were also creating anti-matter space, possibly even a rupture of the space-time fabric."

Jack had to figure the dome was related to the white dwarf star, somehow. He also knew they would eventually go back to the dwarf star to check out what properties it still might have and see if it was still rotating around the circumference of its own magnetic field. This was especially after they may have destroyed the device that could have been related to it. He additionally knew with their new stationary time warp field technology they would now be able to both approach and travel inside the dwarf star's intense magnetic field without encountering any problems with their ship's gravity element trying to destabilize. That prospect increased Jacobs's anticipation. Finally looking toward the open doorway of the dome and to the mountainside, he noticed it had started becoming dark. The sun was less than thirty minutes away from setting in the western horizon and he glanced at his wristwatch—2:46 a.m.

"Jennifer?" he said again.

"Yes, Jack," she replied, softly.

Jacobs paused to her soft voice. "How many Earth solar hours are there in one day on this planet?"

"Thirty-two hours," she answered.

Jack thought about that, realizing that would be very strange to have thirty-two hours in a day. But then with the planet having an almost identical gravity force as Earth, the adjustments to his body and his mental acuities might not be so bad. He took a deep breath and exhaled with a strange thought about the planet and for his own future, including Jennifer's future. Here they were, the only intelligent beings, as he viewed it, on a large virgin planet that was close to the same size as the Earth. It had no pollution, no wars, no hate, no crime, no poverty, and no greed. It was actually a dream come true for anyone who wanted to live in a perfect society, yet for Jack Jacobs, he still had strange misgivings inside about the 23rd century Earth and whether its history was actually a part of his history or not. His ship could easily travel there and find out, but then what if there was already another Jack Jacobs on Earth? Would he be risking a time paradox of proportions that could easily destroy both him and the entire universe? Maybe that is what had actually started their time dilation to begin with? If that is the case, were they still in a time loop, even after already coming back from eternity? "That is a strange thought," Jack said to himself, pausing with a short deep breath. "Maybe we should never go back to Earth and find out?"

Jacobs now wasn't sure what he wanted to do in his future, especially with him being stuck inside a new universe that was a hundred years into his own future. He was the same as a hundred and forty-two Earth years old to the universe, yet only forty-two biological years of age. It was strange to think about and he had to glance outside the doorway of the dome again to see it was now dark in the foothills of the mountains. And like before, he found it very strange to not be able to hear any insects buzzing or frogs chirping in the background—only a light bristling of wind throughout the many trees.

"Jack," Jennifer said. "Are you okay?"

Jacobs came to his senses in response to Jennifer's question, as he had been daydreaming for quite some time. He also noticed his heartbeat had slowed way down due to his extremely relaxed state of mind. That was the reason she would have asked him the question. "Yes, Jennifer, I'm okay."

"So why did your heartbeat slow down from sixty to fifty-four beats a minute?"

Jack smiled over her question. "Oh, I don't know, maybe I was just extremely relaxed thinking about this large planet that we now own."

Jennifer was quiet for a moment, but then all of a sudden she began laughing with a laugh that was audible on his shoulder-mounted speaker. "I understand, Jack," she said with noticeable humor.

Jacobs suddenly felt content inside to Jennifer's human-like emotions, knowing she would continue to grow and develop her unique female personality across the carbon-60 intermeshes of her circuit boards. It was something that he found himself looking forward to seeing happen. Jack then walked back to the doorway of the dome and stopped again to see the darkness of the mountainside, lit only by one of the planet's two moons. "I'm heading back to the ship, Jennifer," he said.

"Okay, Jack, I'll have a spotlight light up a path to the ship."

"Okay," Jack said again, and walked out of the brightness of the dome and into the darkness of the mountainside. He immediately noticed the moon shining in the east, thirty-degrees above the horizon. Thinking no more about it, he started back toward the ship and began noticing lots of small glowing objects on the ground near the dome and around their ship. This was a surprising sight for him, when suddenly, spotlights from their ship came on and the strange glowing objects disappeared. Jacobs got excited at the prospect of what he thought he had just seen. "Jennifer?"

"Yes, Jack."

"Go ahead and turn the lights from the ship back off."

"Why Jack?"

"Turn them off and you'll see," Jack said again.

Jennifer was surprised to hear this, but then she had never seen the glowing objects. "Okay, Jack, will do."

Jennifer turned off the spotlights from their ship and darkness filled the mountainside again. Showing in the foothills of the mountains were again many bluish-green objects three to five centimeter in diameter, glowing as if they had photonic or luminescent properties, like that of a firefly on Earth. Jack noticed the objects again, but he did not know what they could possibly be. "Do you see what I'm seeing, Jennifer?"

"Yes, I do now," she replied.

"What do you think they are?" he asked her again.

"I don't know, Jack. But the ship's sensors do read that they are non-radioactive."

"Is that right?" Jack said. "What material are they made of?"

"I can't say for sure," she answered. "They could be of a metallic/crystalline base structure, but also seem to have organic flux energies that exist only inside an altered gravity base greater than the speed of light."

"Now that's interesting!" Jack said out loud. "This planet sure is filled with lots of unusual things."

"Yes, it is," Jennifer said, also wondering more about the objects. No matter how hard she used the ship's sensors to analyze their internal molecular construction, she was finding the data to be incomplete and extremely inaccurate. It was as though their bearings and locations on the mountainside were erratic and moving around.

Jacobs continued toward the ship and thought no more about the strange glowing objects, even as strange as they looked, but then noticed they seemed to be moving—almost as if they were following him. But then their movements seemed like mirages and were actually unrecognizable against the surface of the mountain. Up in the distance Jack could see the door to their ship still open, visible by the brightly lit opening above the ramp, and continued through the thick vegetation while it rubbed up against his pants legs.

Finally arriving at his ship, he slowly walked up the ramp and back into the ship, headed toward his elevator still thinking about the glowing objects, especially what Jennifer told him about them having organic flux energies. "Maybe they're insects of some type?" Jacobs thought, "Insects that only exist while inside an altered gravitational time base."

The elevator door opened, and after walking inside, he turned around to see the outer door to their ship had already been closed by Jennifer. Suddenly, the door to the elevator closed and Jacobs stood with strange anticipation while looking down at the control panel. After selecting the top floor of his ship, he began waiting patiently as the elevator quickly rose toward the cockpit. A few moments later, the elevator stopped and the door opened again. Jacobs walked out of the elevator and into the hallway back toward the cockpit. He glanced out through the hallway windows and down to the surface of the planet where the objects were glowing and could again see they were scattered in the vicinity of his ship and around the dome, but seemed to be nowhere else on the mountain. 'Strange," he said to himself. "Jennifer?" he asked.

"Yes, Jack."

"Have you shut off the time warp field sphere?"

"Yes, I have."

Jack had to look down at the glowing objects again. Sure enough, he thought they were still glowing, but strangely their intensity did not seem quite as high. He knew right away that their time warp field technology must have been reacting with the glowing objects, which could only mean they probably had strange magnetic flux properties, just as Jennifer had told him. Their glows were also seemingly continuing to fade as though they had been charged up by their ship's time warp field sphere. Jacobs was finding himself looking forward to analyzing their strange molecular-organic construction in much more detail, but knew he would have to do it while inside a time warp field sphere. If they were insects or living organic material he'd also have to be extra careful.

He finally walked back into the cockpit and noticed the large alien time machine still black in color. He didn't notice any burns on the floor near the device, so the alien machine must not have burned under the constraints of a heat variable. Jacobs continued over toward his captain's chair, knowing that clearly violated all of the laws of Thermodynamics as he understood them. This was also because the alien device had to be composed of some element in the universe, and to turn black would have normally required extremely intense heat. He finally sat down and relaxed all the way back in his chair, thinking about many things and took a deep breath. Finally reaching into his side pouch, he removed the ripened seed pod taken from the planet prior to them traveling to eternity and back. He then laid the brown teardrop-shaped pod on top of his forward center console and began staring at the pod, curious what the plant's molecular structure would reveal to him once he grew a few. They'd definitely be one-thousand year old plants, he knew, but in reality not much older than what he was since they also traveled to eternity. Jacobs now wondered what the bright orange and red colorful flowers of the plant might mean and whether they had any medicinal properties. He suddenly noticed Jennifer had repositioned the camera above his center forward console directly at him. "Well, Jennifer, what do you think?"

"What do you mean?" she replied.

Jack pulled the shoulder mounted camera and microphone unit off his left shoulder and set it over to the right side of his chair. He looked back up to the camera. "About his planet?" he asked again.

"It is a large and beautiful planet," she said again.

"Yes, it is," Jack said.

He took a small breath while reaching forward to his center console and dimmed all of the lights in the cockpit to one-twelfth lumens. Jack then stared up at the many stars now shining brightly in the night sky, when suddenly—a shooting star darted across the western horizon. He knew Jennifer had to have also seen the star and calmly looked back down at the camera above his center console. Taking a deep breath, he stood up from his captain's chair and thought about the large planet they now occupied. The geodesic dome building came to his mind, and after reaching down and picking up the shoulder-mounted camera microphone unit, he strapped it back on his left shoulder. Reaching down and feeling the handle of his particle pistol, Jack then walked toward the back of the cockpit.

Jennifer became curious now what Jack had on his mind.

Jacobs continued through the darkened cockpit and arrived at the equipment cabinet behind his captain's chair. After opening both doors, he grabbed a ten-centimeter in diameter, twenty-five centimeter long tube and then closed the doors. He turned toward the brightly lit hallway and took off walking again, carrying his five kilogram plastic case with an inflatable chair inside—shaped similar to the beanbags of Earth's 21st century. Jack walked around the end of the burned out alien device and into the hallway. While continuing down the hallway, he began thinking again about the planet they were now on, wondering whether any advanced race had charted it in the last hundred years, or in reality, since the beginning of time and their new, raw universe. This was especially true since the planet was water-bearing and could sustain carbon-based life. If it had been charted, then he would have thought there'd be some research teams left on the planet, but then nothing indicated that there were any.

Jack then glanced down through the hallway windows to the darkened mountainside and never saw any of the strange glowing objects he'd seen earlier. That made sense because they didn't have a stationary time warp field sphere activated around their ship. This caused him to start thinking about the gravity well force field around the geodesic dome and knew his ship's active gravity field was creating a small neutralizing, dispersive wave front to the dome's force field, but then he never knew how far the dangerous fields of the gravity well were projected. "Jennifer?" he said.

"Yes, Jack," she replied.

Jack paused. "How far does the dome's force field extend toward our ship?"

"Not too far, Jack," she answered. "Nearly thirty-meters in all directions from the sphere's outer surfaces."

Jacobs thought about that and knew his ship's outer door was nearly fifty meters away from the edge of the gravity well force field. He continued by the entrance of his ship's planetarium and focused in on the sound of the waterfall for a short moment, but then continued on toward his elevator thinking no more about the vibrant rustling sound. Jack knew Jennifer was also kind of quiet again.

"Jack," she finally said. "What are you going to do now?"

Jack paused with a small smile. "Oh, I just thought it would be nice memory for us to spend the first night on this planet outside our ship and on the mountainside."

Jennifer remained quiet and because of what Jack told her, immediately activated their ship's main sensors and its circular phased-array antennas for any extraterrestrial objects or spaceships that might enter into the planet's atmosphere. She then focused a polarized beam of high-frequency, compressed bandwidth energy into a conical pattern up into the atmosphere directly above their ship and began measuring the amount of signal dissipation across the layers of the ionosphere in relation to nearly one-million square meters of atmospheric space. It was a HF signal beam type that would also not skip or hop off the ionosphere, only cause large conically-shaped primary incident angles and signals directly back into the planet's atmosphere.

Jacobs continued down the hallway and never knew Jennifer had projected a HF signal directly into the ionosphere using one of their radio compression radar technologies called Space Plane Ionospheric Reflective Emission, or SPIRE. It was a radar compression technology discovered in Earth's 21st century and used a combination of HF frequencies within an unpolarized base carrier receiver frequency so that it would react directly with the oxygen molecules in the atmosphere. This method allowed a reflective energy signal to be realized in a phase disruption in both the thermospheric and mesospheric layers of the planet, relative to the planes of the ionosphere and stratospheric regions. He finally arrived at the elevator and the door quickly opened.

Continuing inside, he turned around as the door closed behind him, and stood quietly while looking up to the camera in the elevator. He then looked back down at the wall console and selected the bottom floor of the ship. Jennifer remained quiet as the elevator dropped nine levels to the bottom of their ship and stopped again. The elevator door opened.

Jacobs stood for a short moment and saw that the outer door to their ship was still closed and walked out of the elevator. "Jennifer," he said. "Go ahead and open the outer door to our ship."

He noticed the outer door to their ship didn't immediately open as he had asked. "Jack," Jennifer finally said. "Wouldn't it be better that we first check out this planet during the daylight hours?"

Jack slowly continued toward the closed door, considering Jennifer's concern. "Why?" he replied. "We know there is no life on this planet other than the marine life in its many waters." Jack paused with a humorous face. "Besides, I know you'll be monitoring this planet's atmosphere and its mountainside for any surprises or creepy crawlers that we may have missed."

Jennifer felt humor within her organic memory circuits and giggled audibly over the small microphone-speaker unit on Jack's left shoulder. She opened the outer door to their spaceship as Jack walked up to the exit. He now stood quiet as the door dropped all the way down to the planet's surface and then looked back to a camera inside the ship. "You realize, Jennifer, that there could very well be another Jack Jacobs back on the 23rd century Earth."

Jennifer paused to this surprising suggestion. "Yes, Jack, you're right," she said.

Jacobs walked through the exit and started down the ramp to see it wasn't completely dark on the mountainside, due to the one of the planet's two moons shining out of the night sky. "Well," he said again. "Since that is a possibility, this planet might have to become our home." He then walked down to the planet's surface.

Jennifer continued her silence.

Jack noticed this and walked a short ways farther from the ship and out of the bright light of his spaceship's open doorway. He now stood in darkness of the mountainside, lit only by moonlight. "So what do you think about that?" he asked her.

Jennifer was still quiet and activated the infrared function on Jack's shoulder mounted camera. "Yes, I agree," she finally said. "But what if there isn't another Jack Jacobs?"

"Maybe we can't take the chance of that paradox," Jack said again.

Jennifer paused. "I understand what you're saying, Jack," she commented.

Jack took a small deep breath. "Great!" he said. "After sunrise I look forward to seeing more of this planet and what marine life it might contain in its many waters."

"And so do I, Jack," she replied.

Jacobs reached down and set the small cylindrical tube down on the ground. He pushed a small button on the side of the tube and then stood back up, knowing the tube's biological energy proximity sensor had activated. Pssshh! he heard a few seconds later, as a sudden rush of high-pressure carbon dioxide broke the tube in half at its slip joint. The chair quickly expanded into a full-size beanbag shape one meter in diameter and one-meter high. Jack turned around and noticed that the dome building seemed to have a slight luminescent glow, but he figured it was probably related to the moonlight. Finally bending his knees, he fell backwards into the chair and immediately felt its soft cushioning effect up against his body. Now sitting and extremely relaxed with a sense of wisdom, he let out a small sigh and contemplated their current situation. He wondered what secrets the new universe might have awaiting them. Jack looked up at the many stars shining brightly in the night sky and glanced down at the camera on his left shoulder. "Well, it's decided then," he said. "This beautiful planet is now our new home. Let's get settled in for the night and watch the stars."

APPENDIX

ACRONYMS and ABBREVIATIONS

AD	Stands for "Anno Domini" and is Medieval Latin for *in the year of the Lord.* (This etymology was created in 1530 AD)
AWACS	Airborne Warning and Control System
BC	Before Christ
DNA	Deoxyribonucleic Acid
EHF	Extremely High Frequency
ELF	Extremely Low Frequency
EPM	Electrical Pathways Matrix
GMT	Greenwich Mean Time
HF	High Frequency
Mpa	Megapascal
NASA	National Aeronautics and Space Administration
NCG	New General Catalog
NORAD	North American Aerospace Defense

OGCD	Orthogonal Great Circle Displacement
PRSTA	Polarized Radiative Spectral Transfer Assimilation
PEG	Positronic Electron Gun
REM	Rapid Eye Movement
PTA	Planetary Taxonomic Agency
PTEM	Positronic Transmission Electron Microscope
SID	Spherical Interactive Dome
SPIRE	Space Plane Ionospheric Reflective Emission
UFO	Unidentified Flying Object
UHF	Ultra High Frequency
VHF	Very High Frequency
VLF	Very Low Frequency

GLOSSARY

While most of the definitions listed in this section are known to Earth's sciences, a few are not, and shown only as they apply within the realm of this book. Some of the definitions have been expanded upon from the perspective of an advanced science called *Time Warp Field*, and they are nothing more than my perspectives. I hope you can enjoy them as much as I had creating them.

The Author

Arc angles:
Arc angles are angles referenced within a circle or on a celestial sphere in relation to two coordinate points and a center point of reference. In the advanced-science, *time warp field*, the two points of reference are directly related and referenced to a future unrealized speed of light time movement base within a celestial time sphere.

Black Body Radiation:
A term for the amount of radiated energy from an object or body. As temperatures get higher, the wavelengths of radiated energy get shorter. In physics, a black body absorbs all light, so a perfect black body will never allow light to be reflected or absorbed.

Blue Shift:
This is a cosmological term identifying a light-emitting object, or gravitational field that is moving toward your visual point of reference. A blue shift in light becomes visible to the observer because of the contraction of the visible light spectrum to its shorter wavelength end, blue.

Binding Fraction:

This is a value used in determining the amount of electron degeneracy for the gravity field of a referenced star (Dwarf star or Neutron star), as its gravity field is compressed into a quantum state and then releases its energy in direct relation to the binding energy of its elemental nucleons (protons or neutrons) found at its core.

Bow Shock: (Between the Earth and the Sun)

An area of space where the sun's supersonic solar winds, after having followed its own magnetic field lines, first interact with the Earth's dipole magnetic field to form a bow around the Earth. This bow shock slows the solar winds down immensely to subsonic speeds, compresses them, and then deflects them around the Earth to form what is called a magnetosheath.

Carbon-60 molecule:

Carbon-60 stands for a carbon molecule that has been joined together with 60 carbon atoms. Its surface configuration is that of hexagons and pentagons, very similar to a soccer ball design. Since the structure of Carbon-60 is that of a soccer ball, the carbon atoms are located on the points where the hexagons meet. There becomes a bond along each edge as a direct result. Another term that has been used to describe it is the *Buckyball* that was named after Richard Buckminster Fuller, who patented the Geodesic dome in 1954.

Carbon Nanotube:

Carbon Nanotubes are hollow elongated *buckyball* structures that have been rolled into a tube that is nanometers in diameter and use Carbon-60 surface topology design methodologies.

Cesium Atom:

Cesium (symbol Cs) is a soft silvery-gold metal that becomes liquid near room temperature. It is the most electropositive of all alkali chemical metals known today and its stable isotope, Cs-133, is used in atomic clocks.

Chandrasekhar limit:

This limit is named after the astrophysicist Subrahmanyan Chandrasekhar, born October 10, 1910, in Lahore. The town of Lahore, today, is part of Pakistan. He formulated this limit in 1930 using the principles of quantum physics and Albert Einstein's special theory of relativity. It is a limit in which he took into account, the electron degeneracy pressures during quantum mechanical states, or in other words, a point where the electron shell energy levels are compressed to their maximum states before a neutron star or black hole would conceivably form.

Déjà vu:

Déjà vu is a French term and it means "already seen". It is also defined as a sudden familiarity with a current or present event that should not be familiar. It is this sudden familiarity that makes it seem as though it had already happened once before.

Doppler:

This is a term also known as the *Doppler Effect*. It is a change in direction or position for the source of a wave, relative to a stationary observer, or vice-versa, and it will change in frequency according to its directional movement. In sound, as the moving sound waves approach a stationary observer, the frequency emissions of the source will increase. As the source moves away, the frequency emissions will decrease.

Eccentric:

This is a small deviation in the elliptical or circular orbital patterns of the sun, planet, or planets, due to gravity perturbation effects of other bodies or planets.

Ecliptic Plane:

This is the orbital reference plane of our planets in this solar system in reference to their sun, as they rotate around it. It is also the orbital reference plane of any planet or planetary system in any solar system that have fixed or semi-fixed orbits around their own sun.

Electron Degeneracy:
A term used when electrons are compressed into a very small volume
of space, forcing the energy levels of all elements at the core of the
body being compressed to completely fill up all electron energy shells
into quantum states.

Electropi Value:
This is a quantum molecular limit in relation to an element's electron
quantity, its shell energy level, and the value π.

Epithelial:
This is a term in relation to a cell structure or cell tissue lining that is
covering all bodily surfaces, both internal and external.

Four-minute cycle:
This is the second harmonic of the twenty-four minute cycle, which
increases the harmonic resonance beat frequency of the gravity-field
cycle per second in relation to the amount of space and space-curvature taken into account.

Gaussian:
The word Gaussian was created 1905 and stems from the word
"Gauss" that was created in 1882 in honor of Johann Carl Friedrich
Gauss (1777-1855). The definition of one-Gauss is one centimeter-
gram-second (CGS) of *magnetic flux density*, or a three domain,
length-mass-time function of magnetic flux.

Gaussian Energy System:
Taken from the term Gauss and related directly to magnetic flux density. The term to take notice of in the *three-domain Gauss unit* of
length-mass-time is the *second*, or the CGS time domain function. A
Gaussian energy system deals directly with magnetic flux units of *harmonic time distribution*, all referenced against the speed of light *length*
domain, while inside any and all gravitational fields.

Geosynchronous orbit:
This is an orbit taken on by a satellite, spaceship, or space station, which is approximately 35,900 kilometers above the Earth's equator, and would take twenty-four hours to make one complete orbit around the Earth. In other words, it matches the orbital period of Earth for one sidereal rotation of the Earth on its axis, thereby allowing the satellite to stay continually over one position of the Earth's surface along the equator.

Gimbal:
A gimbal by definition can have two or three rings mounted on axes that are at right angles to each other, so that its center rotor can remain suspended in a horizontal plane between them regardless of the position or motion of the mount for the gimbal rings. Gimbals are also referred to as gyroscopes and in spacecraft they use three gyroscopes inside a black box called an Internal Navigation Unit.

Great Circle:
A term used for a circle on a sphere and having the same diameter as the sphere. The equator, or the zero degree latitudinal line of the Earth, would be a *great circle.*

Greenwich Mean Time:
This is also known as GMT for the standard time and in reference to Greenwich, England. All times on Earth are in relation to Greenwich, England, since it is also zero longitude on Earth.

Heliopause:
This is a term used for the outer reaches of our sun's solar winds and where they are slowed by the stellar medium surrounding its magnetic field. It is also where the heliosphere of the sun ends.

Heliosphere:
This is a term used for the total volume of our sun's magnetic field and its energy output in the form of solar winds, similar to a huge bubble inside a stellar medium. It is essentially everything that makes up the sun's construction of all energy output along its magnetic lines of force.

Hertz:
This is a term used for the measurement of frequency and means "cycles per second".

Hexaflexagonal:
This is a term derived from *flexagonal*, and uses equilateral triangles to form tri-pole symmetry structures that can be folded (flexed) to reveal hidden surfaces (faces). In a hexaflexagonal structure, the triangles form loops that are divided into twelve right triangles and can flex into non-hexagonal shapes. Each surface can then pivot or flex like a hinge into many different configurations and show many different faces. Thus comes the term flexagonal. The first flexagon was discovered in 1939 at Princeton University by Arthur H. Stone.

Hyperbolic:
Hyperbolic is taken from the term *hyperbola*, and means a conic section of some type having length, depth, and width, all accordingly to the hyperbolic function. In geometric functions, it is an intersection between a cone and a plane, with the plane cutting through both halves of the cone.

Ionosphere:
This is the area of the Earth's atmosphere, or any planet, where oxygen is ionized by solar radiation against the planet's magnetosphere. There are four known ionospheric layers. It is in this ionospheric region where molecular ionization of O_2 oxygen occurs and is split apart into single oxygen (O) atoms. When one of these single atoms combines

with another non-ionized (O_2) molecule, it forms the extremely important element, ozone, an oxygen molecule having three atoms (O_3). Note: The O_3 gas is highly corrosive and poisonous to breath. Most cellular carbon-based life must breathe or intake the odorless, tasteless, oxygen molecules, (O_2), to survive.

Latitude:

This is in reference to latitudinal (horizontal) imaginary lines running around the Earth parallel to the equator and up to the North and South poles. The equator of the Earth is the dividing line for the northern and southern hemispheres. Above the equator and toward the North Pole is north latitude and south of the equator toward the South Pole is south latitude with the equator being zero latitude.

For a geographical latitudinal perspective on the Earth's globe, the Bahaman Islands are located along a 24-degree north latitude line. Anchorage, Alaska, is along a 61-degree north latitude line. Buenos Aires, Argentina, on the lower South American Continent, is along a 34-degree south latitude line.

Lignin:

This is the second most abundant organic material on Earth after cellulose. It is a chemical compound and component directly related to the cell structure and strength of a tree or plant. Lignin also aids in the tree or plant's vascular functions and its resistance to disease and insects.

Longitudinal:

This is a reference to the (vertical) longitudinal imaginary lines running between the North and South Poles of the Earth. Greenwich, England would be zero longitude as a zero starting point of reference on the Earth, dividing the Earth up into two hemispheres. Standing facing the north, to the right would be east longitude and to the left would be west longitude. The zero point, vertical line going through Greenwich, England is also known as the prime meridian.

Magnetic Flux:
A term used for the measurement of magnetism in relation to the strength of the magnetic field being compared. Mathematically and in known space, it is the magnetic field (average product) times the perpendicular surface area it is penetrating, or in a symmetrical spherical propagation field of open space, it would be the strength of the magnetic field divided by the area of the sphere, creating an inversely proportional field of magnetic energy.

Magnetosheath:
This is in reference to an area of space inside the Earth's magnetic field that is located directly behind the *bow shock*, about 10 Earth radii away, but located in front of the magnetopause. On this sunward side of Earth, the *magnetosheath* is also an area where charged particles are in a transitionary state as they collide with the forward magnetic lobe of the Earth. With the help of the solar winds that constantly emanate from the sun, the magnetosheath helps form the *magnetotail* field lines.

Magnetosphere:
The magnetosphere is the designation for the area of space surrounding the Earth and its dipole magnetic field. On the sunward side, it starts with the bow wave and directly behind the bow wave are the boundary areas called the *magnetosheath* and the *magnetopause*.
On the night-side of the Earth, the magnetosphere ends with a *magnetotail* that can extend beyond 300,000 kilometers. Inside this *magnetotail* are both open and closed field lines, all formed according to the sun's solar winds that are continually expanding and contracting the length of the *magnetotail*.

Megapascals:
Pascal (symbol Pa) is the term used for pressure and is defined as one Newton per square meter. Standard atmospheric pressure on Earth is equivalent to 101,325 Pa. *Megapascal* designates one million pascals. A diamond forms at 10,000 Megapascals.

Mesosphere:
There are three layers of atmosphere above the Earth's surface. The upper layer is the thermosphere, the middle layer is the mesosphere, and the lower layer is the stratosphere. On the planet Earth, the mesosphere layer is located between 50 to 80 kilometers. It is also in this layer where meteorites and objects entering the atmosphere will collide with the many billions of oxygen molecules and create a fireball of intense heat in the sky.

Millibars:
The millibar (symbol mb) is also a term used for a unit of pressure. One *millibar* is equal to 100 *pascals*. For average air pressure at sea level on Earth, one *millibar* is equal (averaged) to 29.92 inches of mercury (one atmosphere), or the amount of air density and pressure required to lift water, approximately 33.9 feet (10.3 meters).

Nanometer:
One nanometer is 1.0×10^{-9} meters.

Neutrinos:
Neutrinos are fundamental particles that make up the construction of electrons and protons in all elements. They also have direct associations to the *resultant* neutron mass states created between negative charge electrons and positive charge protons to maintain elements in their elemental configuration, accordingly, and to all outside influences of their environment. There are three neutrinos that are known to exist, the electron neutrino, the muon neutrino, and the tau neutrino.

Orthogonal:
This term stems from the Greek word, *ortho*, that means *right*, and the word, *gonia*, meaning *angle*. In mathematics, orthogonal means a perpendicular line or lines that are at right angles to each other. In quan-

tum space-curvature geometry, it can also mean a point of reference against a known stellar background that has orthogonal symmetry in relation to space curvature (quantum space).

Parabolic:

This is a mathematical shape and function of the parabola in relation to the *circumcenter* and midpoint *vertex* of a subtended line on a sphere. In a *subtension* formulation referenced against a sphere, the *circumcenter* would be the very center of the sphere in a triangulation of the two subtended points, and where they come together on the other side of the sphere, each angle across the sphere from the two points of the subtended line, the same, thereby allowing for perfect parabolic balance. The *midpoint vertex* point would be the point at the very center of the subtended line and in direct relation to the sphere's circumcenter.

Perturbations:

A term for gravitation effects between planets or another gravity body, which minutely changes their elliptical orbits as they rotate around their sun.

Picosecond:

This term is for one-trillionth of a second, or 1×10^{-12} of a second.

Polar angles:

These are angles that are measured from the top or bottom of a sphere, or celestial sphere, in relation to your location within the celestial sphere itself.

Polar Cusp:

Polar cusps are sections of outer space inside the Earth's magnetosphere and above the magnetic north and south poles, that separate the sunward (flattened) magnetic lobe, from the night side (flared) magnetic lobe of the Earth, creating magnetic-field-line zero paths. It is these zero paths of the polar cusps that also allow plasma energy (energized particles) to flow directly down into lower altitudes of the Earth's ionosphere. During periods of magnetic activity and if an imbalance of the energized particles in the polar cusps occurs, then some of the particles escape into the Earth's atmosphere and interact with its nitrogen and oxygen molecules, creating what we call the *aurora*. The aurora is also known as the *Northern and Southern lights*. It is through the *polar cusps* and their pathways comes the creation of these magnificent auroras.

Polytetrafluoroethylene:
This is a thermoplastic resin also known as PTFE, or by its trade name, Teflon. Polytetrafluoroethylene is a compound consisting of a chain of carbon atoms with two fluorine atoms attached to each carbon atom. After fluorine becomes bound inside the polytetrafluoroethylene molecular structure with the carbon, the fluorine atoms then become repulsive to all other external materials and their molecules, including other external fluorine atoms. As a result, Teflon has one of the highest non-friction surfaces known to Earth's 21st century sciences.

Rapid Eye Movement:
This is also known as REM. Rapid eye movement occurs when you dream, and when dreaming, your eyes will dart around back and forth under your eyelids as though you're watching a movie. This is a natural occurrence every human being experiences.

Red Shift:
This is a cosmological term identifying a light emitting object, or gravitational field that is moving away from your visual point of reference. A red shift in light becomes visible to the observer because of the expansion of the light spectrum to its longer wavelength end, red.

Schumann Resonance:

This is a set of permanent standing wave ELF frequencies in the atmosphere of a planet that is determined by the size of the planet, the size and strength of its magnetic field in relation to the ionosphere, and the speed of light while inside a magnetic field or medium such as the sun's heliosphere, for instance. Resonating waves will then exist between the surface of a planet and its ionosphere due to magnetic activity such as lightning. For the planet Earth, the lowest and strongest resonance was measured and found to be around 7.8 hertz. The Schumann resonances on Earth occur at 14, 20, 26, 33, 39, and 45 hertz, with 45 being the weakest resonance. These natural resonances were mathematically predicted in 1952 by German physicist Winfried Otto Schumann (1888-1974). He helped detect it in 1954. Hence comes the term *Schumann Resonance* that was named after his discovery.

Schwarszchild radius:

This term was named after Karl Schwarszchild (1873-1916). It is a radius of space-time curvature directly associated with gravitational mass bodies. Schwarszchild found this value in 1916. It is also a gravitational radius value that is determined by use of the speed of light constant, the known gravitational constant, and the mass of the star or body in reference.

Steradian:

This term is used for a solid angle (three-dimensional angle) in direct relation to a subtended line on the surface of a sphere. The total surface area of a sphere is measured in 4π steradians, or 4π squared radians. The total surface of a sphere also subtends an angle of 4π steradians at its center. One quarter of the total surface area of the sphere would be 1π steradian. The circumference of a sphere would be 2π steradians.

Subatomic:
Subatomic is used in the term *subatomic particles* and is the main field of study in particle physics. Subatomic particles are the particles smaller than the atom and make up the electromotive-force-composition of the atom. The subatomic particles of ordinary atoms are the neutrons, the electrons, and the protons.

Subtend:
This is a line or *line element* that crosses a sphere at two points of space on the sphere's surface that is not at a maximum length or equal to the sphere's diameter.

Subtension:
This is a mathematical formula or formulas of two or more combined subtended lines on a sphere, which have spherical polar radian angle harmonic cycles in relation to the sphere's diameter. The harmonic cycles also include angular position in time movement on the sphere and in direct relation to the referenced subtended angles versus the sphere's total surface.

Taxonomic:
This is a term derived from taxonomy. Taxonomy in biology means, but is not limited, to the class, genus, order and family for the plant and animal kingdom. Essentially, it is for any living organism that can interbreed within its own species, including humans.

Theorem:
From the Late Latin word *theorema* created in 1551. It means a proposition, a mathematical formula, or mathematical statement demonstrable as part of a general theory.

Time Displacement Vector:
This is a function of the *vector displacement* and the amount of *true* time displaced between two points of space, using the speed of light as the base standard for normal time of 300,000 kilometers per Earth second of travel.

Time Plane Vectors:

Time plane vectors are vectors of space determined within an imaginary plane of time called a *time plane*, a time plane that is continually moving forward in a positive force movement of 300,000 kilometers per second for each cosmological Earth second, all as measured within our sun's heliospheric magnetic field.

Time Warp Field:

Time Warp Field is a technology that modifies space into a *harmonic time plane* to be used in either space-travel to push (propel) a spaceship's gravity propulsion system inside a zero-point-domain space-time field, using positive-force kinetic energy to bridge two coordinate points in outer space, or to separate the electron's "positronic" quantum component from an elements binding energy to cause a controlled oscillatory harmonic action—such as the beam used in a Positronic Transmission Electron Microscope.

Troposphere:

This is an area of a planet's atmosphere where all weather occurs and extends upward from the surface of Earth, or any other planet with Earth-type atmospheres, to a certain altitude according to the planet's size and strength of its magnetic field. For the Earth, the troposphere extends up from the surface nearly 18 kilometers most everywhere around the globe, except at the north and south poles where its altitude decreases to less than 10 kilometers. The troposphere is where nearly 80 percent of the Earth's total atmospheric air mass resides.

Twenty-four minute cycle:

This is a gravity-field *time harmonic* measured in cycles per second of actual time movement-motion inside a referenced elliptical circle or sphere of space, all while in gravity-propulsion resonance.

Vector Displacement:

Vectors are a magnitude of directional force and in time warp field, *vector displacement* it is the movement of an object's mass and kinetic energy resonances from one position in space-time to another position in space-time according to the distance between the two positions being compared to a new space-curvature base.

White Dwarf Star:

This is a star that has exhausted all of its nuclear fuel and its gravity has collapsed back upon itself, crushing all electrons into their maximum energy configurations. The star then becomes degenerate and survives only by the laws of quantum mechanics, thereby stopping its total collapse into a *singularity* called a black hole.